EDITIONS *and* IMPRESSIONS

Also by
Nicholas A. Basbanes

Every Book Its Reader

A Splendor of Letters

Among the Gently Mad

Patience & Fortitude

A Gentle Madness

EDITIONS *and* IMPRESSIONS

TWENTY YEARS ON THE BOOK BEAT

BY *Nicholas A. Basbanes*

FINE BOOKS PRESS 2007
a division of Fine Books & Collections *magazine*

Fɪɴᴇ Bᴏᴏᴋs Pʀᴇss
4905 Pine Cone Drive, #2
Durham, North Carolina 27707

Book design and typesetting
by Roni Mocán and Jessica Lagunas.

ISBN 978-0-9799491-0-4
Library of Congress Control Number 2007936754

First printing

www.finebookspress.com
www.finebooksmagazine.com

For Connie, as always. Happy Birthday.

CONTENTS

PLACES

INTRODUCTION

Although I have spent my entire adulthood writing professionally, it is fair to say that life took on a new meaning for me on August 22, 1995, the day I became a published author. I was fifty-two years old when *A Gentle Madness: Bibliophiles, Bibliomanes, and the Eternal Passion for Books* appeared between hard covers, and the exhilaration I felt the morning the first copy arrived at my front door by express mail remains indescribably sweet to this day. Not long after that unforgettable moment had passed, I was working on *Patience and Fortitude*, a companion volume that was issued in 2001. Three other books about books appeared in quick succession, with two more now in progress: a centennial history of the renowned Yale University Press, scheduled for release in 2008, and a history of paper and papermaking for Alfred A. Knopf, expected to follow in 2009.

I am grateful that there has been a readership to justify this stream of work, and with the column I write six times a year for *Fine Books & Collections* magazine, I am pleased also that I am able to stay active in the world of journalism that I love so dearly. Being an author of books is unquestionably my day job, but producing copy for newspapers and magazines has been part of my makeup for more than forty years and has helped shape the way I go about my work, as the profiles and essays selected for this collection should make abundantly clear.

Years before I had interviewed my first author, book collector, or rare-book librarian, I covered every imaginable kind of story as a newspaper reporter. I wrote about a catastrophic rooming-house fire in the inner city that claimed nine lives; a double murder in the suburbs; a train derailment near a downtown expressway that, for hours, left several tanker cars filled with propane gas in jeopardy of exploding; and the rough-and-tumble blood sport that is Massachusetts politics. Whenever the city editor gave me an assignment, I did it, and I did it on deadline.

Beyond the breaking news stories were the investigative pieces that grew to be my specialty. In the aftermath of Watergate, every newspaper wanted a Bob Woodward and Carl Bernstein–style investigative unit, and I was fortunate enough to be assigned to a team that covered central Massachusetts for the *Evening Gazette.* We went beyond the who, what, when, and where to the *why* of a story. Traditional reportorial skills were mandatory, but we also examined, assessed, interpreted, and even expressed a point of view, all supported by the facts we uncovered. Sometimes there were palpable results. A series I wrote about an arson investigation in Worcester led to high-level changes in the police department; another brought about sweeping policy shifts in the state's Department of Youth Services. More than two decades before such crimes became national news, I wrote an exposé about the abuse of children by a priest who headed a halfway house. A three-month probe into irregularities in the Worcester County Treasurer's Office that I worked on won the top prize for general reporting in New England in 1974, beating out the perennial champion in the category, the *Boston Globe.* And there was my favorite news story of them all, a real cherchez la femme caper. Three years after a prominent local lawyer and former school committeeman had cleverly faked his own death by making it appear that he drowned off an isolated Martha's Vineyard beach (no body was ever found, of course), I tracked him down by locating the woman he had run away with; a few weeks later, he was arrested in Reno, Nevada, by postal authorities on charges of allowing his unwitting "widow" to use the mail to claim $300,000 in life insurance. In December 1977, I covered his trial in the U.S. District Court in Boston, where he was convicted. (There is even a bookish coda to the story: While in prison, the man, John Corbin, became a librarian.)

In the course of all this, I mastered the fine art of following paper trails in courthouses, city halls, state and federal repositories, and registries of deeds. I cultivated sources, conducted hundreds of interviews, and always took pride in the quality of my writing. It was all part of an apprenticeship that I knew, intuitively, would make me the author I always wanted to be. And how that finally came about is a true story of serendipity, one that came ten years after I arrived on what I like to think of as the book beat. In 1978, I was named literary editor of the *Sunday Telegram* in Worcester, a dream job for a person who has always nourished a lifelong love of reading with a steady diet of book acquisitions. New titles flooded in, and I took full advantage of what was made readily available to me. Editing the *Telegram's* weekly book-review section placed me squarely within an industry that I found totally absorbing.

Just as important, because it allowed me to continue writing on a regular basis, was the column I wrote once a week, usually centered on a personal interview with an author. From the very beginning of that undertaking—indeed, it became a labor of love over a twenty-two-year span—my idea was to write a literary feature that combined the critical acumen of a book reviewer with the seasoned skills of a trained journalist. My pleasure in this assignment knew no bounds, and I accepted every interesting offer that was proposed to me. When I left the *Telegram & Gazette* in 1991 to devote more time to the writing of my first book, I maintained my publishing contacts and syndicated the column to other newspapers around the country. By 2000, I had written, by rough estimate, more than a thousand of these features. (In 2008, the best of these interviews will be included in a companion volume to this collection.)

But that is getting ahead of the story. In 1988, a press release came across my desk announcing a forthcoming exhibition of rare books in Philadelphia called *Legacies of Genius*. There was an invitation to attend a press viewing, and on a whim—I am unable, honestly, to explain what possessed me to do so—I accepted. My managing editor, thankfully, agreed to pick up the expenses, and off I went on a day trip to the City of Brotherly Love. The exhibition's concept, developed by a noted bookman, the late Edwin Wolf 2nd, was straightforward enough but brilliant in its simplicity. I was especially intrigued by the claim that only Philadelphia had the resources to mount such a show, and after writing a straight news story of the event for my newspaper, I queried *Bostonia* magazine about writing a piece that would challenge that assertion. Because *Bostonia* is owned by Boston University, I made plain in my pitch letter my intention to highlight the dynamic work being done there by the flamboyant librarian Howard Gotlieb.

My approach to the story, which appears in this volume, was to use profiles of driven bibliophiles as a device to discuss the development of great institutional book collections in Boston. My wife, Connie, suggested I take the premise a step further and consider a longer work that would examine the phenomenon on a broader basis. "This is the book you were born to write," she told me. With the *Bostonia* essay serving as an example of what I had in mind, I retained an agent, who soon found a publisher excited by the idea of *A Gentle Madness*. My original contract with Random House was to write a book of ninety thousand words and to have it done in eighteen months. No one realized at the time that I would crisscross the United States repeatedly and make multiple trips to Europe before I was finished seven years later. Why the final product took so much longer to complete, why it came in at more than twice the projected length, and why the book was ultimately published by Henry Holt are matters too complicated to discuss in detail here, but the short of it all is that once I got started on the project, my reporter's instincts kicked in, and what I had envisioned at first as a tidy little history of bibliomania over two millennia became an obsessive adventure in contemporary journalism that sought out untold stories that were fresh and new.

A second critical moment came about halfway into the project with yet another bit of good luck. During a casual conversation in 1990 at an American Booksellers Association convention in Las Vegas, I mentioned my book project to Rebecca Sinkler, then the editor of the *New York Times Book Review*. She was particularly taken by three of the stories I sketched out for her with light brushstrokes—the exploits of the book thief Stephen Blumberg, the creation in a few frenetic years of the Humanities Research Center at the University of Texas, and the spectacular rise and fall of a mysterious collector known as Haven O'More (a name that with different spacing reads *have no more*)—and invited me to write a discursive essay for the *Review*. The piece I subsequently submitted began on the front page of the section and filled four inside pages (it, too, appears in this volume). Prominent publication in such a distinguished journal gave me not only national exposure but also immediate credibility in the book world. More important, it gave me access to people, libraries, and wonderful stories that a few weeks earlier I would have thought unimaginable.

Through all of this, my dedication to the book beat has continued without interruption. Indeed, one of the reasons I agreed in 1996 to write a column for the now-defunct periodical *Biblio* was the opportunity it gave me to work out in print some of the material I was then gathering for *Patience and Fortitude*. Because I regard the book beat to embrace all of book culture, the essays that follow encompass profiles I have written of fascinating people, be they collectors, dealers, librarians, archivists, authors, scholars, pop-up engineers, dust-jacket designers, or readers; impressions of the various places I have visited in the pursuit of compelling stories; and ruminations on the role of books in society. In every instance, it should be obvious that the process of journalism is part of the way I write.

While I have used a good number of the stories that I have written for various publications over the years as a kind of finger exercise for my books, I selected essays for this collection precisely because they are not replicated in any substantial way in my other published work. Unlike book manuscripts, which can expand as needed, pieces written for magazines and newspapers tend to be constrained by space. Roughly one-third of the essays printed here are markedly longer than their magazine counterparts. Where possible, I reverted to the stories as I originally wrote them, before they underwent editorial pruning. One story about New York was cut in its entirety and has never appeared in print at all.

Let me conclude by saying that I have learned mightily from the people I have interviewed over the years. John Updike, in my view the outstanding man of letters of our time and the subject of a literary interview that will appear next year in the second volume of these selected pieces, wrote in the foreword to a 1983 collection of his essays and reviews that, for him, writing criticism "is to writing fiction and poetry as hugging the shore is to sailing in the open sea." Out on the ocean, he explained, "we have that beautiful blankness all around, a cold bright wind, and the occasional thrill of a dolphin-back or the synchronized leap of silverfish; hugging the shore, one can always come about and draw even closer to the land with another nine-point quotation." In the quarter century that has transpired since he wrote those words, Updike has filled two more stout volumes with his miscellaneous work, proof positive that regardless of the genre or the medium—or the depth of the waters around him, for that matter—the pleasure never fades. Writers, it seems, are always compelled to write.

Nicholas A. Basbanes
North Grafton, Massachusetts
August 22, 2007

BOOK CULTURE

Bibliophilia
The Love of Books

"In Search of the Great Books," Bostonia 61, no. 5 (September/October 1988).

I f you were lucky enough to view *Legacies of Genius* this summer in Philadelphia, you were treated to a literary extravaganza that included James Joyce's handwritten manuscript of *Ulysses*, a 1472 first edition of Dante's *Divine Comedy*, Lewis Carroll's own copy of *Alice's Adventures in Wonderland*, and General Ulysses S. Grant's draft telegram announcing Robert E. Lee's surrender. The impressive exhibit of 250 rare books and manuscripts ran in the adjoining galleries of the Historical Society of Pennsylvania and the Library Company of Philadelphia and, by all accounts, was a blockbuster.

But can Philadelphia justify the bold claim it made in announcing the exhibit a few weeks earlier? According to Marie Korey, chairwoman of the consortium that organized the event, "the quality and quantity of rare books and manuscripts in Philadelphia is unsurpassed in this country." Perhaps this was a bit of local pride at work—who knows?—though as a native New Englander with some knowledge of these matters, it did make me wonder. So on the opening day of the show, I asked Edwin Wolf 2nd, guest curator of the exhibit and an internationally respected authority on rare books, what he thought about the claim. "Oh, Lord," he said with a kind smile and a knowing wink. "You could do this sort of thing quite easily up in Boston."

Indeed, the more salient question is where would you start? At Harvard, where the Houghton Library houses the widest collection of John Keats's autograph manuscripts, letters, and publications any-where? Or how about near the summit of Beacon Hill, where the Boston Athenæum maintains thousands of seminal documents relat-ing to American history, among them the finest assemblage of Con-federate States imprints on either side of the Mason-Dixon Line?

You only have to drive a short distance to where the Fenway meets Boylston Street to find a team of Massachusetts Historical Society scholars working on a project that will continue well into the next century—the editing of four generations of Adams family papers. This archive is just a fragment of what is widely esteemed to be one of the leading collections of historical manuscripts maintained in the country.

Nearby, off Copley Square, visitors to the rare-book room of the Boston Public Library (BPL) can consult any of 260,000 scarce books or one million manuscripts that range in variety and scope from Ptolemy's 1477 Cosmography to the papers of Nathan-iel Bowditch, the noted mathematician whose 1802 work, *The New American Practical Navigator*, remains a standard source for ship handlers; in a secure case under protective glass are the most cov-eted jewels of the collection, two copies of the first book printed in North America, a hymnal published in 1640 known as the Bay Psalm Book.

Five minutes away, in the Mugar Memorial Library, Boston University's (BU) constantly expanding twentieth-century archives make available the raw materials of the social history of our time. The repository, which is currently celebrating the twenty-fifth anniversary of its founding, is renowned for its collection of the papers of luminaries such as George Bernard Shaw and Isaac Asimov and memorabilia such as Fred Astaire's dancing shoes and Bette Davis's scrapbooks.

The treasure trail, in fact, seems never ending. Farther west on Commonwealth Avenue, Boston College's recently restored Burns Memorial Library displays collections that illumine Irish and Jesuitical history and British Catholic authors; the Clapp Library of Wellesley College holds the original love letters of Robert and Elizabeth Barrett Browning; forty-odd miles west, in Worcester, the American Antiquarian Society has an unparalleled run of early American newspapers and imprints; and north to Salem, the Essex Institute includes a vast collection of Nathaniel Hawthorne's works among its holdings.

It makes sense, when you think about it, that the educational center of America could lay claim to the most extensive rare-book and manuscript collections on the continent. Any urban area that has as many colleges and independent research libraries as Greater Boston is bound to have its share of prized books and manuscripts. Indeed, the deeper you look, what becomes obvious is just how rich the repositories are.

Yes, it is true, there is no Gutenberg Bible in Boston, nor is there a copy of Edgar Allan Poe's *Tamerlane and Other Poems*, published here in 1827, and regarded today as the elusive "black tulip" of American literature, a copy of which sold for $198,000 at a Sotheby's auction in June. As every curator and archivist will tell you, however, it is the depth of a research collection, not the individual high spots that make a library strong and relevant. And while there is some overlap, most of the local special-collections libraries have staked out distinct interests, some reassuringly predictable, others delightfully surprising.

If you were going to mount a show similar to *Legacies of Genius*, Harvard's collections would command center stage, hands down. The library dates to 1638, when British-born clergyman John Harvard left his books and half his estate to a newly founded college in Cambridge. What survives of that original collection is now a showpiece for the institution later named for him. Since the seventeenth century, many benefactors have helped build the Harvard University collections, a complex that now includes ninety-five libraries and some twelve million books.

Rarities abound in virtually every field of scholarly pursuit. The incomparable John Keats collection, for instance, was started in 1925 by the wealthy poet and biographer Amy Lowell and later augmented by gifts from John Gregory, Louis A. Holman, and the man for whom the special-collections library is named, Arthur A. Houghton Jr., class of 1929.

Perhaps the university's most consequential benefactor of all was a young man named Harry Elkins Widener, a member of the class of 1907, whose love for rare books brought him in contact with the most celebrated dealer of the twentieth century, Dr. A. S. W. Rosenbach of Philadelphia. In 1912, during a trip abroad with his parents, Widener bought many items in London, among them the 1598 edition of Francis Bacon's *Essaies*.

"I think I'll take that little Bacon with me in my pocket," legend has him saying, "and if I am shipwrecked, it will go with me." As events turned out, on April 15, 1912, Harry, his father—and presumably the little Bacon—went to the bottom of the North Atlantic with the *Titanic*.

Mrs. Widener, who escaped in a lifeboat, knew that her son had wanted his collection ultimately in the safekeeping of his alma mater, so she decided that a suitable "wing" to house it would be an appropriate memorial. Her $2 million gift brought much more than an addition; the Widener Library, opened in 1915, remains the central storehouse for books at the university, and the example young Harry set became a beacon of inspiration for future Harvard graduates.

In 1940, the Houghton Library, nestled between the Widener and Lamont libraries, was opened strictly for the housing of special collections, though a few of the Harvard libraries have opted to keep their proud possessions right where they are. The law library, for example, has been acquiring books since 1817 and numbers among its possessions more than five hundred works printed in the latter half of the fifteenth century as well as some twelve thousand sixteenth-century editions. Over at the Francis A. Countway Library of Medicine, Richard J. Wolfe, curator of special collections, points to nine hundred books of medicinal science printed before 1500 as one of the highlights of the collection. The Kress Collection at the

Harvard Business School houses the largest collection of Adam Smith's work in the world, including a 1776 first edition of *The Wealth of Nations.*

These, as Houghton's curator of rare books Roger E. Stoddard said, comprise some of the "fascinating pockets" to be found throughout the university. Yet the mother lode is still safeguarded in the Houghton Library, where acquisitions continue at a steady pace. Stoddard told me he spends $300,000 annually on rare books, and on those occasions when something of unusual interest becomes available, he calls on a network of well-heeled "friends of the college" for additional assistance. When acquiring for the Houghton, Stoddard said he is always mindful of what other area institutions already own. "The Boston Public Library has a great Defoe collection, and so does Harvard. While replication is not always bad—several strong collections on the same subject in the same area can be irresistible to a scholar—I will still try not to buy a Defoe that is at the public library."

In contrast to Harvard, the BPL has no generous alumni to turn to, as Laura V. Monti, curator of rare books and manuscripts, pointed out. Still, there have been many wonderful bequests all the same. "We are by definition a public institution, and while I have about $100,000 to $150,000 available, what we have comes mostly from gifts." She said that the most she has ever paid for one item was about $20,000 for "a particularly beautiful page" from an illuminated manuscript.

Monti said her major problem is obtaining sufficient public funding to maintain an adequate staff. "We have all these rare books and manuscripts, and we are just five people. We have one person who has been working off and on for three years just trying to catalog our Sacco and Vanzetti papers of two hundred thousand pieces."

Unlike the Boston Public Library, which always has been open to everyone, the Boston Athenæum was established in 1807 as a private reading club for gentlemen. Dues have always been assessed and initial acquisitions were made for the entertainment and enlightenment of the membership. "The idea at first was to get popular and interesting things for the members to read," John H. Lannon, director of acquisitions and special collections, told me. "So many of the books we bought in the early 1800s became important with the passage of time. Before we knew it, we had become a research library by default."

By 1851, the Athenæum was one of the five largest libraries in the country. Since then, its members have been alert to locating desirable items. The great body of six thousand Confederate imprints is an apt example. Francis Parkman, the noted nineteenth-century historian whose papers may be found at the Massachusetts Historical Society, was a prominent member of the Athenæum. As the Civil War was drawing to a close, he mobilized an effort to gather regional books, periodicals, broadsides, and music printed in the rebel states during the war.

"Parkman was following his historian's instincts," Lannon said. "He knew that once the war was over, these materials would be destroyed or lost or suppressed. What is important is not which items are so rare, but that the collection is so comprehensive. This is the Confederate collection by which all others are compared."

What is easily the Athenæum's most important possession is a set of four hundred books once owned by George Washington and kept in his study at Mount Vernon. In 1849, they were acquired by a dealer who planned to sell them to the British Museum. A group of seventy horrified Bostonians raised the $3,800 necessary to buy the books and place them permanently in the Athenæum.

Undoubtedly the Athenæum's most bizarre possession is a book with a fairly innocuous title, *Narrative of the Life of James Allen.* It is the memoir of a notorious early nineteenth-century highwayman who was finally brought to justice after robbing a stagecoach. Allen was sentenced to twenty years in prison, where he began to work on his life story. On his deathbed, he asked that a copy of his book be bound with his own hide and given to his captor, John Fenno, who was also an Athenæum member. Published in 1837—and bound as stipulated—the book was removed from public display several years ago. "It has no literary merit whatsoever," Lannon deadpanned. "It's the binding that makes it interesting."

While the Athenæum has been gathering treasures for 181 years, it is by no means the only independent library in the region with a venerable heritage. In fact, the Massachusetts Historical Society, founded in 1791, is the oldest such institution in the country. And in Worcester, the American Antiquarian Society has been maintaining material of a similar nature since 1812, while the Essex Institute of Salem has been at the task since 1821.

From the beginning of its existence, the Massachusetts Historical Society has aggressively persuaded prominent figures to donate their papers. "There is nothing like having a good repository and keeping a good lookout, not just waiting at home for things to fall into your lap, but prowling about like a wolf for prey," the society's colorful founder, the Reverend Jeremy Belknap, wrote to a friend in 1795. Belknap is said to have badgered Paul Revere into writing for the society a formal account of his midnight ride. He also picked out choice items from the estate of John Hancock.

"We have so many things because we started early, before anyone had any idea they would be so desirable," Stephen T. Riley, the society's director emeritus, said during an informal tour of the holdings. "We don't pay a lot of money for anything, and never have. The real trick is to get people to give things to you. How could we ever buy a collection like this?"

Riley pointed out six manuscript containers, each bearing the title *Biblia Americana*, each containing a folio-sized volume with incisive commentary on all books of the New and Old Testaments. "This is a great church history in the hand of Cotton Mather that has never been published, not because it isn't worthy, but because it would mean a lifetime of work for somebody," he said. The sheer size of the 4,500-page manuscript, written over a thirty-year period in double columns by the leading theologian in Colonial America, would have to be examined, transcribed, and closely edited before it could be published for a modern readership, a tedious undertaking that has scared away more than one scholar. "I had one fellow coming in here to work on it, then he disappeared, and I didn't blame him one bit. You take a look at it, and you'll understand why people steer clear of it. But it's here, and someday somebody's going to get it done."

Among the historical society's other archives is the extensive collection of Thomas Jefferson's papers. "We have more of Jefferson's papers than the University of Virginia and maybe as many as the Library of Congress. We have the greatest collection of his architectural drawings. And you know why? After he died, Jefferson's family needed money, and in 1898, a Boston man—Thomas Jefferson Coolidge—bought them up and brought them here to us."

Riley paused for a moment, and then spread his arms in wonder. "There's *so* much here," he said. "Then once in a while, a single little volume will make your mouth water." To illustrate the point, he reached out for a file that contains what he considers the greatest exchange of correspondence in American history: Edward Everett's letter of congratulations sent to Abraham Lincoln on November 20, 1863, for his succinct Gettysburg Address of 269 words delivered the day before, and Lincoln's gracious reply to the famed Massachusetts orator, whose two-hour speech had formally dedicated the battleground cemetery. "In our respective parts yesterday," the president wrote, "you could not have been excused to make a short address, nor I a long one."

As these various treasures suggest, the richness of cultural materials preserved in and around Boston is abundant, and if there is any wisdom to be gleaned for other institutions that aspire to become major participants in the process, it is the staggering realization that the competition has been at it collectively for about 1,200 years. It was with that knowledge that Howard B. Gotlieb, a professional historian and archivist, came to Boston University in 1963 from Yale University. "I was brought here for one reason and that was to create a major collection," he said matter-of-factly as we sat down to talk in his office on the fifth floor of the Mugar Memorial Library.

"When I came here, there was no manuscript collection, no rare-book collection. Our sister institution across the river had been collecting for three hundred years, though we were starting from scratch. Well, my idea was to collect the papers of people who were living, which was pretty radical at the time. The general feeling out there was why take a chance on the reputation of someone who, through the patina of time or reputation, might not be collectable?"

Gotlieb said he began to think about gathering contemporary materials while he was still at Yale. "I could see the holes in so many collections," he said, and cited a few examples of what can happen to important materials through indifference or neglect. "Andrew Johnson's wife burned many of his papers in order to protect his reputation. Abraham Lincoln's family destroyed many of his papers. I began to worry about people taking care of their own papers."

When the twentieth-century archives were established at BU, Gotlieb knew that he had to be imaginative, and that he had to gather much more than literature. "If we were going to document the twentieth century, we would also have to collect theater, film, journalism, politics, diplomacy, civil rights—whatever the student of social history needs to get a rounded picture of our time and culture. My one rule is that I always follow the curriculum. That is why we do not collect architecture: Boston University does not have a school of architecture."

Gotlieb said he has been able to persuade important people that even the minutiae of their lives are worth preserving. "I have attempted to be a Boswell at the side of the public figures of our time. What I tell them is this: 'Don't throw anything away; let us make that decision.' If someone had paid this much attention to Charles Dickens during his lifetime, today we would surely have an excellent biography of Charles Dickens."

In the quarter century since he articulated this concept and defined its scope, Gotlieb has acquired the archives of more than 1,400 notables, from George Abbe, novelist and naturalist, to Paul Zindel, Pulitzer Prize–winning dramatist, with major contributions from such diverse figures as Isaac Asimov, Alistair Cooke, Martin Luther King Jr., Dan Rather, Rex Harrison, Cab Callaway, Nathaniel Benchley, Oriana Fallaci, and Simon Brett.

Gotlieb said that four thousand to five thousand people use the twentieth-century archives for research each year and that the competition has become intense in the genre, with a number of other institutions, most notably the University of Texas, Indiana University, UCLA, and the University of Wisconsin, frequently vying with him to acquire the same material. "I was amused recently to see that Yale is creating a contemporary authors collection," he said. "My ideas, it seems, are now acceptable."

Gotlieb believes he must get to know people if he is going to coax them into parting with their prize possessions. "One of the reasons we've been so successful is that we have made it a very personal operation." He recalled one of many visits he made to the home of Claude Rains. "I picked up a Shaw play he had there and saw that it was inscribed to him by the playwright. 'To my favorite actor,' it said. I didn't know he knew Shaw. He knew him very well it turned out, and he had a superb collection of correspondence and books. When I left, the whole collection departed with me."

A less-productive friendship developed with Gloria Swanson, the late actress. "I would stay with her for days at a time," Gotlieb said. "I ate macrobiotic food until it was coming out of my ears. I was wooing her because her archive was tremendous. She had kept everything, from the coming of sound in film right up to the present day, and she virtually promised it all to me. Nevertheless, one morning I turn on the radio and hear that the Swanson collection is going to the University of Texas at Austin. I later found out they did something we could not do: they paid her a million dollars."[*]

Gotlieb said that he has about $300,000 a year to use for acquisitions, and that if something "irresistible" becomes available

---

[*] *See endnote.*

unexpectedly, "all I have to do is say that I must have this," and the Friends of the Boston University Libraries unfailingly come to his aid. "This is an expensive enterprise. It costs a lot of money to do this," he said, then explained why he never goes to auctions: "They see me walk through the door and the price will go up. But I do have other people go for us. It's important not only for us to see what is selling and for how much, but where it is going. Sometimes it is much more important to know whom we lost to than it is to win the lot."

It is worth noting that Boston University is not the only local institution to join the hunt for rare books in recent years and that respected collections have emerged at other area universities. In 1986, Boston College dedicated the John J. Burns Library of rare books, a major restoration of a wing in the Bapst Library that features a number of impressive exhibits.

"We've got a specific focus here," according to Robert K. O'Neill, the Burns librarian. "We are aggressively building what we intend to be the definitive Irish collection in the United States." The college's collection of British Catholic writers—Hilaire Belloc, Graham Greene, Francis Thompson, and Evelyn Waugh among them—is solid, and its archive of Jesuitiana includes an original letter from St. Francis Xavier to Don Juan III, the king of Portugal, written in 1552. The biggest surprise of the Burns Library may be the Nicholas M. Williams Memorial Ethnological Collection, which includes ten thousand books, pamphlets, and other narrative items that document West African and Caribbean folklore and oral literature.

For the *Legacies of Genius* show in Philadelphia, each participating institution contributed anywhere from six to twenty choice items for display. If Boston were to consider mounting a similar event, it would be difficult to choose among the thousands of breathtaking items available. "Boston has ten times what Philadelphia has," the BPL's Laura Monti said without a trace of exaggeration. "To be honest, the collection is so large, I can't even keep track. But after all these years of collecting, we'd *have* to be rich, don't you think?"

°∘⟨⟩∘°

NOTE

Two decades is a long time, especially with a piece of contemporary journalism, and this essay—the one that persuaded me to write a proposal for what became *A Gentle Madness*—is no exception. There are, as a consequence, a number of important updates to report.

By far the most dramatic is the total holdings of the Harvard University libraries, which, according to the Association of Research Libraries, had reached 15,586,234 volumes by 2005, an increase of 3.5 million since this article was published in 1988.

The person who introduced me to Harvard's incomparable repository of special collections, Roger E. Stoddard, retired in 2004 as curator of rare books. His service at Harvard from 1965 to 2003, a period in which he acquired sixty-five thousand rare books for the institution, was commemorated by an exhibition at the Houghton Library, one that he curated himself. I developed a friendship with Stoddard as a result of this interview, one in which he served as a valued mentor in a world filled with many nuances. In gratitude, I described him in my book *Among the Gently Mad* as "a kind of Socrates for me."

For those planning a bibliographical excursion to the North Shore of Massachusetts, it is worth noting that, in 1992, the Essex Institute merged with the Peabody Museum of Salem to become the Peabody Essex Museum, a true example of cultural partnership at work.

In response to the pressing need to protect decaying books at the Boston Public Library—a crisis expressed passionately to me two decades ago by former director of special collections Laura V. Monti—the Pulitzer Prize–winning historian David McCullough, a trustee of the institution from 1995 to 2000, established a conservation fund in 2001 that at last report had raised close to $1 million.

Stephen T. Riley, librarian of the Massachusetts Historical Society from 1947 to 1976 and one of the outstanding book people of his time, died in 1997 at the age of eighty-nine. Riley's prediction in this piece that scholarship would ultimately take a crack at bringing out an edition of Cotton Mather's unpublished magnum opus, *Biblia Americana,* was realized in 2001 with the establishment of a collaborative editorial project under the direction of Reiner Smolinski, a professor of English at Georgia State University. The first volume—ten are projected—is expected to be released online in 2010, with print-on-demand copies available soon thereafter.

Finally, Howard B. Gotlieb, founder of the archival research center at Boston University that now bears his name, died in 2005 at seventy-nine. Gotlieb was a towering presence at BU during his four-decade tenure, with a formidable ego to match his stature. (It can now be told that he was referred to privately among some staff members as "His Eminence.") A good bit of that swagger may have been responsible for his somewhat-petulant assertion to me that the only reason he lost the Gloria Swanson archive to the University of Texas was because the oil-rich institution gave the actress $1 million. "Howard got that all wrong," Thomas F. Staley, director of the Harry Ransom Humanities Research Center, told me in February 1990, when I arrived on the Austin campus for a series of interviews that would appear in the chapter "Instant Ivy" of *A Gentle Madness.* "It was only $100,000," he said. Along with the money, however, was a further inducement—a commitment to hire Swanson's personal assistant as curator of her archive.

Bibliomania
An Obsession with Books

*"A Major Book Sale—Up Close and Personal," Telegram & Gazette
(Worcester, Massachusetts), January 13, 1991.*

It was ten fifteen on the morning of Tuesday, December 11, 1990, and there was little time for me to ponder the business at hand. The last major book sale of the year was ready to begin in the third-floor auction room of Sotheby's at York Avenue and Seventy-second Street in New York City, and I had barely caught my breath.

Driving down from Worcester, I arrived in the cavernous East Side building minutes before the scheduled opening, excited by the prospect of bidding on twenty-one lots.

For two years now, I have been doing research on the book trade and have followed many auctions, the sale of Estelle Doheny's library at Christie's, the Bradley Martin extravaganza at Sotheby's, and some smaller though no less exciting events at Swann Galleries among them.

But on this day—because an acquaintance who is an antiquarian bookseller had urgent business to resolve elsewhere—I was attending as a participant, prepared to lock horns with such stalwarts as Quaritch of London, Pierre Berès of Paris, Heritage Book Shop of Los Angeles, and H. P. Kraus of New York.

My friend, in essence, was offering me an opportunity to compete for some of the most coveted books in the world. I have bid at book auctions before—some of my fondest experiences have come at the small country sales put on periodically by Roland Boutwell in the

Southbridge basement of the First Methodist Church—but this was Yankee Stadium, and I was in the lineup. How could I refuse?

The dealer, needless to say, gave me some guidelines. Booksellers, as a rule, do not like to say whether they ever have any limits going into an auction—why let anyone know how much they are willing to spend?—though all of them surely have definite ideas on what something is worth and know just how far they might go to acquire it.

Because I was new at this, and because I would be on my own, the dealer gave me some pretty specific marching orders; no "gut feelings" would be allowed. Still, during the drive down, toying with the numbers, I squirmed when I realized I would be putting about a quarter of a million dollars into play.

At this level of competition, your identification number isn't scribbled on the back of a paper plate with a Magic Marker. Here, you express your intentions by thrusting an impressive plastic paddle in the air.

My first target—the second lot being offered in the opening session—was a gorgeous religious treatise with thirty-eight illuminated initials that was presented in 1523 by Baldassare Acquaviva, the author, to Pope Clement VII, the dedicatee.

The book is described on the first page of the handsome catalog that highlights 350 choice items from the estate of John M. Schiff, a noted connoisseur whose collection of rare printed books, fine bindings, breathtaking illuminations, and important manuscripts was being sold by his heirs.

The first lot of the sale, an 1812 history of the University of Oxford with 115 aquatints, was knocked down in under a minute for $3,000. Since the presale estimate for this book was $1,200 to $1,800, the feeling was that everyone here was very serious about the proceedings.

"Lot Number 2, the Acquaviva," David Redden, the auctioneer, announced. "And—I have $15,000 at the desk—do I hear $16,000?"

No fewer than six paddles went up, and the bids moved along smartly by $1,000 advances.

At $25,000, I entered the contest.

Bids, meanwhile, came in quickly from around the room, while others were being relayed in by telephone.

At $40,000, advances were now coming in at $2,500 a shot, and my paddle stayed in the air.

At $60,000, a new bidder entered the contest from the left, and at $70,000, the advances had been raised yet again, to $5,000 a pop.

By then, however, I had folded.

"We have $100,000 in the back row now, bidding at $100,000, is there any advance over $100,000?" Redden implored, then sold the lot at that price, which was $50,000 above its highest presale estimate.

But there was hardly enough time to brood, because my next target was coming along in minutes. As it turned out, I had no reason to fret; the bidding zoomed past my limit before I even had a chance to raise my paddle.

For our next target, I decided to change strategy and come out slugging early. The bidding opened at $3,000. I was in right away and held tough to the end, when a well-known New York dealer who specializes in fine bindings secured the final nod with an offer of $21,000.

This was turning out to be a pretty fast track, and a few lots later, I began to wonder what it would take to get anything for my friend. At $6,500, we were underbidders on a lot of nine assorted items—in other words, we were pretty close—but I had been certain this one was a lock. The presale estimate there was $1,500 to $2,500. I went a full $4,000 above that, yet still couldn't get it.

What transpired next, though, proves that you can never predict what is going to happen at an auction. Lot 48, a French Book of Hours with illuminations on vellum so splendid it rated a full-page color reproduction in the catalog, had a presale estimate of $20,000 to $30,000. We were willing to go to considerable lengths for this one, but the way things were developing, I had no confidence at all we could get it.

So what happens?

"It's on the right, then, at $28,000—fair warning, "Redden said after a brisk but energetic contest. "Sold," he declared—and then he called out my number—"for $28,000."

Finally, I had broken through, and a while after that came lot 142, four assorted eighteenth-century works in five volumes estimated to sell somewhere between $900 and $1,200. It was ours for $500.

But the absolute shocker of the day came on lot 183, a series of ninety-four Old Testament scenes in woodcut by Hans Holbein the Younger, estimated to sell for $10,000 to $15,000. We were ready to go well beyond that, and I figured it was ours in a walk, a piece of cake.

Entering at $10,000, I fought for about forty-five spirited seconds before lowering my paddle. Offers came in from all over the room and from four callers on telephone hookups. At $50,000, someone altogether new—I couldn't see who it was, he was toward the back of the room—took over, and when it seemed he was about to triumph at $70,000, a telephone bidder forced what was now a two-person duel to $100,000.

When the prize finally was knocked down for $120,000—the 10 percent buyer's premium would nudge that higher, to $132,000—there was scattered applause and incredulous laughter.

"That's a whole lot of yen," the man sitting next to me said with a knowing grin.

"You think so?" I asked.

"Oh, yes, I certainly think so," he said.

The buyer of record was later said by Sotheby's to be a French dealer, who chose not to be identified. Be it yen, dollars, or francs, however, this was still big money, and considerably more than the auction house had estimated.

"You see this often with single owner collections," a Sotheby's official would explain to me later. "The material was fresh on the market—nobody had seen any of it for years—so it generated tons of excitement."

The Schiff Library was expected to bring in $1.4 million. The $2 million total, more than 30 percent greater than that, was further evidence that while prices in the paintings market have gone into a tailspin, rare books have held their own.

For my part, before the day was out, I had emerged victorious on five lots, spending $54,250. The 10 percent buyer's premium brought the final figure to $59,625.

This wasn't my money, but I have to admit, it was a kick.

Reality resumes for me at 6:30 P.M. on Thursday, January 17, in the basement of United Methodist Church, right next to the Kentucky Fried Chicken on Main Street in Southbridge.

Roland Boutwell promises that some nice modern firsts, along with plenty of ephemera, old magazines, regional history, and stereoview slides, will be on the block. As usual, the buck-a-book table will be open from 4:30 to 6:30 P.M.

Roland leaves for Pennsylvania in March. We wish this fine and knowledgeable bookman all the luck in the world. And we will miss his laid-back country auctions. Every time I pick up *The Sketch Book of Geoffrey Crayon, Gent.*, I savor that rainy night four years ago when I saw a line of type on the title-page of a book that everyone else in the hall had missed. This collection of stories was published in 1820 by C. S. *Van Winkle*, of 101 Greenwich Street, New York. Geoffrey Crayon was a pseudonym for Washington Irving, and a fast glance through the contents determined the presence of the short story "The Legend of Sleepy Hollow," its first appearance between hard covers, I correctly surmised.

The prize was mine for $24, proof, yet again, that a book hunter doesn't need a fat bankbook to achieve fun and satisfaction.

⁂

NOTE
The bookseller I bid for at Sotheby's in 1990, I am at liberty now to report, was Priscilla Juvelis, based then in Cambridge, Massachusetts, and now in Kennebunkport, Maine.

Bibliokleptomania

The Obsessive
Theft of Books

*"The Quintessential Case of Bibliokleptomania," Telegram & Gazette
(Worcester, Massachusetts), February 17, 1991.*

If you study the criminal complaint lodged against the notorious
book thief Stephen Blumberg last year by federal prosecutors,
you see a pretty straightforward case of conspiracy to transport
stolen goods across state lines, nothing more, nothing less.

As a legal proceeding, it was not extraordinary at all, and the
evidence presented by Assistant U.S. Attorney Linda R. Reade in
a Des Moines, Iowa, courtroom last month was pretty clear-cut
and convincing to the jury, which returned a verdict of guilty on all
counts after a few hours of deliberation.

But two central elements at issue in the trial—hoarded books
and purported madness—made the seven-day trial one of the most
fascinating chapters in the history of bibliomania, a word never
more appropriate than in the matter of *United States v. Stephen
Carrie Blumberg*, docket number 90-63 for the Southern District
of Iowa.

Blumberg's lawyers, it must be stressed, did not argue that
the crimes were never committed. Instead, their strategy was to
suggest *why* their client had stalked and stolen more than twenty-
one thousand rare books and manuscripts from as many as 327
libraries and institutions throughout the United States and Canada
over a twenty-year period, and *why* he stashed them away in an

old Victorian house in Ottumwa, a quiet town eighty-five miles southeast of Des Moines.

Bolstered by detailed testimony from a psychologist and a Menninger Clinic forensic psychiatrist, the defense asserted that Blumberg, forty-two, suffers from a severe disillusionment disorder that forces him to believe he must rescue the past and protect it from an indifferent environment.

"He came to view himself as the savior of these objects," Dr. James S. Logan testified, stressing that Blumberg never sold any of the books but hoarded them all and committed himself to their well being. Logan outlined an extensive history of treatment for mental illness that began in 1965 and includes six separate diagnoses that seem to corroborate his evaluation of a chronic condition.

Reade, however, insisted that Blumberg's cunning acts were carried out with great care and consummate skill. "Just like any cat burglar," she said, "the man is a thief."

In her final argument to a jury of three men and nine women, Reade asked: "Can a man who committed crimes the way he did possibly have been suffering from a severe mental illness?"

Though no acts of violence were involved, Reade insisted that Blumberg "is a more hardened criminal that many others" she has seen. "He didn't just steal a few library books, he stole our cultural history. How can you justify that?"

That contention—that Blumberg stole a priceless segment of America's cultural heritage—is what lured me out to Iowa in the middle of a cold and blustery winter to attend his trial.

I am writing a book about the formation of great, interesting, and eccentric book collections. Typical collectors, of course, preserve the relics of creativity and shared experience, and though bibliomania certainly involves obsession, it can be productive, so long as it is held reasonably in check.

Blumberg, on the other hand, is an example of bibliomania out of control, a truly incredible instance of a collector who has gone over the edge in spectacular fashion. What we see in him, more precisely, is an uncommon case of bibliokleptomania, certainly the most sensational example of the condition recorded in this century.

For one full day and halfway into another, librarian after librarian came to the witness stand and outlined the extent of their losses. A clear pattern was established: Americana, history, travel, architecture, expansion, exploration, and in no fewer than one hundred cases, incunables, or books published before the year 1501, when printing was in its infancy.

Most dramatic, perhaps, was the account given by Fraser Cocks, curator of special collections at the University of Oregon, who told about the loss of the Applegate Collection, twenty linear feet of manuscript material dating from 1842 to 1876. The papers, he said, relate to the settlement and early statehood of Oregon, and are "absolutely unique."

The Oregon archive—seized by the FBI in the Ottumwa house owned by Blumberg—was independently valued at $649,940. "These materials contain the information from which history books are written," Cocks said. "The people who write these books get their information from materials like this."

Susan M. Allen, head of special collections for the six Claremont Colleges in Claremont, California, said she identified 648 books recovered by the FBI as items reported missing from her institution, including a 1493 Nuremberg Chronicle, the last major world history that did not mention the discovery of America by Columbus.

Glen Dawson, a well-known Los Angeles book dealer, estimated the value of Claremont's purloined books at $644,000.

Lynn Newell, director of preservation for Connecticut's governmental library system, said her agency's losses were valued at $225,280 and included *The Confession of Faith* (1708), the state's own copy of the first book printed in Connecticut. The stolen materials, kept in seventeen locked vaults, were not known to be lost until the FBI contacted state officials.

Since most of the books recovered were altered in ways that obscure original ownership, identification has been difficult. Typically, labels were removed, shelf numbers were sanded off, embossed stamps were sliced out by razor blades. In many cases, new bookplates had been glued on, some of them bearing the seal of an invented institution, the Columbian Library, while others were given new numbers from a classification system known only to the defendant.

Roger E. Stoddard, a librarian from Harvard University, said he was able to identify many of the 670 books taken from Widener Library by their green leather bindings, and in other cases by a distinctive brand of repair tape used by the university. Harvard's losses were estimated at $75,185.

The University of Southern California in Los Angeles, once the repository for the collection of the Zamorano Club, a prestigious group of Los Angeles area bibliophiles, reported losses totaling $251,450.

Among the more noteworthy items identified were most of the Zamorano Club's own collection of the Zamorano Eighty, a group of eighty rare books said to be the most important titles associated with the exploration and settlement of California.

Only two collections are known to have all eighty, the Beinecke Library at Yale and a private collector in Pasadena. Blumberg had managed to acquire seventy-eight, and was thinking of ways, according to several former friends who testified for the prosecution, to get the two he lacked from the home of the private collector.

Two of these friends helped Blumberg load and transport much of the material from the various states to Iowa and had been charged as accomplices. They worked out plea bargains with the government in exchange for their testimony.

Nobody, not even the prosecution, denied that Blumberg was absorbed with the past. In addition to the books, he had amassed hundreds of stained glass windows from abandoned houses in Minneapolis, his hometown, and throughout the Midwest. Another passion was old doorknobs, as many as fifty thousand of them, and 78 rpm records, "thousand and thousands and thousands of them," according to one witness. Many of these items he sold at flea markets in Texas and at the Brimfield antiques fair in Massachusetts.

But the books were sacred. Kenneth Rhodes—the informant who testified he was paid $56,000 by the government to "drop the dime" on Blumberg—told how he once suggested "there was money to be made" on some of the books: "It was the maddest I ever saw Stephen get."

Blumberg did not testify in his own behalf, but his former associates gave ample testimony on just how books were taken. When Blumberg entered the general stacks, he would locate the books he wanted. "He would lick the old labels off," Rhodes said, and affix new ones. Once, when he thought he was about to be discovered in the University of California at Riverside Library, he ate the rubber stamp he had with him.

Rhodes also recalled his experiences "crisscrossing" the county with Blumberg, "buying, selling, stealing, and acquiring books." One time, when they were in Texas, "Steve took out books every night for a week in Houston."

After stealing the identity card of a University of Minnesota professor, Blumberg was able to assume the persona of a scholar and, in a sense, elevate the level of his collecting by gaining entry to secure areas where the rarest books are housed. He also stole and made copies of keys that allowed him to enter libraries after hours.

It is a story filled with ironies, too many to relate here. Personal appearance, hygiene, and modern conveniences like televisions and microwave ovens are anathema to Blumberg, though he is not an impoverished man. Testimony disclosed that he receives $72,000 a year from a family trust fund, much of which he disperses among the homeless and destitute. He has never held a job, but by his own estimate he has traveled "at least a million" miles on the road over the past twenty years, going from town to town, working flea markets, studying local history, collecting books.

The Iowa jury took about three hours to decide that Blumberg was not insane when he committed these crimes and returned a verdict of guilty on all counts. Despite the jury's refusal to accept his defense of not guilty by reason of insanity, however, few can argue that the man doesn't need some kind of psychiatric attention.

For her part, Reade insisted she is going for the maximum penalty, which could be as many as thirty-five years imprisonment.

"The federal prison system is fully equipped to offer appropriate medical care," she said when pressed on the subject.

NOTE

I wrote at length about Stephen C. Blumberg in chapter 13 of *A Gentle Madness,* and I have tried to stay abreast of his fortunes over the past decade. After serving four and a half years in a succession of federal penitentiaries and paying a $200,000 fine, he was released in 1995, only to be arrested two years later in Des Moines on charges of third-degree burglary—he had stolen antique doorknobs and assorted lighting fixtures from an abandoned Victorian house. He served two and a half years of a five-year sentence in state prison. In 2003, he was arrested in another abandoned house, this time in the Mississippi River town of Keokuk, Iowa, with a doorknob in his pocket. After entering a guilty plea to burglary charges, he was fined $7,500 and released with five years' probation. At this writing, he is free, said to be living in St. Paul, Minnesota, his hometown, and traveling about the country in a secondhand yellow truck.

BIBLIOPHILIA II

"Bibliophilia: Still No Cure in Sight," New York Times, April 14, 1991.

On April 24, 1911, Henry E. Huntington confirmed his intention to form one of the world's finest libraries by spending $50,000 for a Gutenberg Bible, the most anyone had ever bid on a printed book.

His bold victory came on the first day of a landmark auction that dispersed some sixteen thousand books and manuscripts gathered over half a century by Robert Hoe III, a New Yorker whose family made a fortune in the manufacture of high-speed newspaper presses.

That first night, by every contemporary account, was a dazzling event. All four hundred seats in the Madison Avenue gallery were reserved well in advance, and the most important people in the book world attended. Before that day, the highest price ever paid for one volume was the $24,000 spent by J. Pierpont Morgan for an illuminated treasure known as the Mainz Psalter. When Huntington set a new record by purchasing his copy of the Gutenberg Bible, the *New York Times*, like many other publications around the country, carried the story on page 1. In fact, just about every bang of the auctioneer's hammer at the sale was big news.

Often called the golden age of American book collecting, this was a time when a premium was placed on refinement, when the importance of a book collector was measured as much by discrimination and taste as it was by wealth. This giddy epoch, which had begun in the mid-nineteenth century, didn't end until another sale hit even dizzier heights in January 1929, just nine months before the great crash, with the sale of the composer Jerome Kern's compact collection of 1,484 books and manuscripts, many of them unique "association" items like Shelley's own annotated copy of his poem "Queen Mab" or an Edgar Allan Poe letter in which Poe quotes Elizabeth Barrett Browning's enthusiastic response to his poem "The Raven." In all, some $1.7 million was spent, an astounding figure that averaged about $1,165 an entry. On the first night, when Kern learned of the frenzied battles being waged for his treasures, he wired Mitchell Kennerley, the auctioneer: "MY GOD WHAT'S GOING ON?"

With the Depression, the golden age collapsed, and though collecting came back, the noble sport has never been the same. Gone are the days when flamboyant dealers like George D. Smith and A. S. W. Rosenbach routinely bought the scarcest books and manuscripts for their general stock, and gone too, for the most part, are the opulent showrooms and vast inventories maintained by the celebrated booksellers, replaced now by smaller operations that specialize in finely focused fields of interest.

Yet despite its leaner and less visible profile, book collecting continues to thrive quietly. Consider the sale of the splendid Garden Ltd. collection at Sotheby's in New York in November 1989, an electrifying event occasioned by a bitter civil suit between the two owners that was so sensitive a judge in Massachusetts has impounded all files relating to the case. The auction's most dramatic moment came when a New York collector spent $2.1 million for a set of the first four Shakespeare folios, but there also were 311 other choice offerings, a veritable panoply of high spots in world literature, all in remarkably fine condition.

An exceptional set of the two-volume first edition of *Don Quixote*, estimated to bring up to $300,000, sold for $1.65 million to Bernard Quaritch Ltd., of London, representing, informed gossip had it, a reclusive Spanish collector. A first complete issue of William Blake's *Songs of Innocence and Experience* in a contemporary straight-grain morocco binding sold for $1.32 million; a Kelmscott Chaucer went for $176,000; the first recorded printings of Homer, Aristotle, Cicero, Euclid, Dante, Copernicus, Erasmus, John Milton, Charles Darwin, Herman Melville, and Walt Whitman; manuscripts by William Butler Yeats and James Joyce; a notebook kept by John Locke; and Vaslav Nijinsky's unpublished diary were sold as well. The Sotheby's auction brought in an impressive $16.2 million for the Garden Ltd. collection, yet earned barely a footnote in local press accounts.

Even more instructive is what happened in the two most important book auctions of the past twenty years in the United States: Christie's disposition of Estelle Doheny's library in a series of six sales held in the period from October 27, 1987, to May 19, 1989; and Sotheby's sale of H. Bradley Martin's books from June 6, 1989, to June 14, 1990. These were libraries in the grand tradition, collections assembled lovingly over many years by two fabulously wealthy connoisseurs.

Doheny, widow of a California oil baron, built a collection that included many books (known collectively as incunables) published during the infancy of printing, including the Old Testament volume of a Gutenberg Bible in its original binding and St. Jerome's *Epistolary*, printed on vellum by Peter Schöffer in 1470. Other volumes reflected her keen interest in English and American literature and in the exploration and settlement of California and the West.

Midway through the Doheny sale, H. Bradley Martin, a native New Yorker who started gathering books while attending Christ Church College at Oxford during the 1920s, died at the age of eighty-two. Blessed from birth with great wealth, Martin maintained two libraries, one in Manhattan, the other at Rose Hill, a Georgian estate in Virginia.

On June 6, 1989—barely a month after Christie's sold the last of Doheny's books—Sotheby's opened the Martin sale by offering what was regarded as the finest collection of ornithology to be found anywhere, including a complete run of the classic illustrated books, beginning in the sixteenth century, and a pristine set of John James

Audubon's *Birds of America* that sold for $3.96 million. Subsequent sessions featured such rarities as Poe's *Tamerlane*, Herman Melville's famous letter to Sophia Hawthorne discussing the writing of his novel *Moby-Dick*, George Washington's inscribed copy of *The Federalist Papers*, and an extremely scarce July 4, 1776, first issue of the Declaration of Independence.

In all, $35.7 million was spent for more than ten thousand books and manuscripts, just short of the $37.4 million record for the contents of one library established in the Doheny sale.

Unquestionably, this was serious money. Yet it is pocket change when compared to all the other action that goes on in Manhattan auction houses.

Just three weeks before the Martin sale concluded last spring, one Japanese collector had paid a little more than $160 million for two paintings, $82.5 million for Vincent van Gogh's *Portrait of Dr. Gachet* at Christie's on May 15 and $78.1 million for Pierre-Auguste Renoir's *At the Moulin de la Galette* at Sotheby's on May 17.

"Let's just say that this guy's artistic passion was inclined toward books," a New York book dealer, Bart Auerbach, mused during lunch on the final day of the Martin sale. "In just three years, for what he paid for those two master paintings, he could have built one of the finest private libraries in the world. A Gutenberg Bible, Poe manuscripts, Shakespeare folios, a papyrus fragment from the Book of the Dead, you name it, hundreds of extraordinary things, the highest of high spots. And he would have had more than $50 million left over. All he had to tell his agent was one thing: 'Keep your paddle in the air.' It would have all been his. Instead of a man who has two nice paintings on the wall, he could have gone down as one of the great book collectors of the twentieth century."

Is such a scenario preposterous?

Well, there is a precedent. When Henry Huntington acknowledged the applause of an appreciative audience eighty years ago with a triumphant bow after buying Robert Hoe's Gutenberg Bible, he had only just begun. Another seventy-seven sessions in the sale

were conducted through November 22, 1912, and just about everything the California railroad magnate wanted for the dream library
he planned for his San Marino ranch, he got. Of the $1.9 million
spent, Huntington committed $1 million for 5,500 of the choicest
selections.

Huntington, who became a serious collector after observing his
fifty-fifth birthday, was determined to form a superior collection. He
knew exactly what he wanted—a voluminous body of correspondence
preserved at the Rosenbach Library in Philadelphia leaves no doubt
about his immediate involvement in every acquisition—and he had
no qualms about applying the same decisive methods to collecting
that had helped him consolidate control of vast California land,
power, and transportation interests and ownership of numerous
railroads, the streetcar lines of Los Angeles among them.

To eliminate the competition, Huntington used a tactic known
as the en bloc purchase. By making bold preemptive offers, he acquired many notable collections. A few decades later, the University
of Texas adopted a similar strategy to build what is arguably the
strongest archive of twentieth-century primary manuscript material to be found anywhere. In 1956, the university's special collections were, by any yardstick, modest to the extreme; fourteen years
later, the British bibliographer and rare-book specialist Anthony
Hobson included the Humanities Research Center in his influential survey of the world's major collections, *Great Libraries*. In 1973,
the *New York Times* ranked it among the top five research collections in the world.

Down in Austin, when people talk about the university's
former chancellor Harry H. Ransom, they use the word *vision* to
describe the frenetic zeal that characterized his efforts to build a
major repository in Texas. These were oil boom years for the state,
and it was a time for greatness.

To achieve it, Ransom made a shrewd decision. He knew he
could never achieve parity with Harvard, Yale, or the New York
Public Library in traditional fields, but what he could do was exploit

areas they had deemed unworthy of their attention. Ransom chose to document the twentieth century in all its cultural richness, which largely meant buying the papers of people still alive and still producing. Many, like Graham Greene, Tennessee Williams, Robert Graves, and Evelyn Waugh, were already secure in their reputations; others were virtually unknown. Cyril Connolly wrote in 1962 that, because such a program "will not only pay for what an author has written but what he has tried to throw away," it was "probably the best thing that has happened to writers for many years."

But it wasn't just money Texas offered, and it wasn't just money that every prospective benefactor coveted. "These people want to be wanted," a former curator at the research center explained.

For Erle Stanley Gardner, a redwood replica of the mystery writer's California study was built to house his memorabilia. Alfred A. Knopf's enormous personal library not only has its own room but also an area for selected pieces of furniture from his Manhattan apartment. When Gloria Swanson agreed to send her papers to Austin, she was assured that her assistant would be offered a job at the center.

F. Warren Roberts, director of the Humanities Research Center from 1961 to 1978, worked closely with Ransom and often bore the brunt of attacks in the United States and abroad that criticized what were perceived as aggressive tactics. He still lives in Austin, not far from the huge campus.

"Harry Ransom had a great talent for getting money out of the board of regents," Roberts said. "He was a man with the kind of personality that could make people believe anything was possible, even if it wasn't."

Just how much Texas spent during those wild years is uncertain. Some observers say as much as $40 million, others suggest even more. Nobody will say for sure because money not only came from the state but also came from private benefactors Ransom had wooed, and the purchasing procedures he used were decidedly unorthodox.

"I would be very surprised, to tell you the truth, if it's as much as $20 million," Roberts said, when pressed for a figure. "But whatever it is, my theory anyway has always been that money is only money, and you can't believe the way people spend money for other things. You know how much money they spend over there for scientific research without even thinking about it? They'll spend $5 million for a machine that is obsolete before they even get it operating. What has gone into the humanities is practically nothing by comparison, nothing. And everything we bought will increase in value."

At a time when the American economy has softened, that assertion seems more valid now than ever. Nobody suggests that books and literary material are recession proof, but they certainly have held their own, especially when compared to the disappointing sales recorded recently in the art market. On November 20, the *New York Times* reported that a "sharp decline in prices" had persuaded many prospective sellers to turn away from the "glamorous world of auction houses" and place their paintings with private dealers. In the article, Diane D. Brooks, the president of Sotheby's in New York, noted that "there certainly is a shakedown" underway.

There was no mention of books, however, once again probably because the amount of money being spent for them is comparatively small. But every book and manuscript sale conducted last fall and into this year at Sotheby's, Christie's, and Swann Galleries either met or exceeded its estimates, however modest those estimates may have been.

The November 9 sale at Christie's of 119 books decorated with handcrafted leather and jeweled bindings from the Paul Chevalier collection sold for $1 million, well above expectations. The December 11 sale at Sotheby's of 350 choice lots from the library of the late John M. Schiff sold for $2 million, $600,000 more than the high estimate. Swann Galleries, which deals exclusively in books, prints, photographs, and manuscripts, conducted a series of successful sales throughout the fall and into February. On Valentine's Day, a collection of colonial and revolutionary period British and American books, pamphlets, and broadsides sold for $299,000 at Swann, almost twice the high estimate.

George S. Lowry, president of Swann Galleries, stressed in an interview that books represent "something of a sleepy backwater" in the collecting world. "Books have appreciated at a steady pace over the years, and they're relatively unaffected by what goes on in the real world. The art world now is looking at a fairly severe drought over the next year or so. The worst that will happen in the book business is that it will level off. Here at Swann, our bread and butter is the item that sells in the area of $500 to $2,000."

Book collecting, in other words, is not restricted to the very rich. Indeed, the beauty is that satisfaction is possible at any level, even with items that sell for a few dollars at flea markets; every collector has a story to tell about making a miraculous find. My hero is not the person who paid $198,000 for Poe's anonymously published *Tamerlane and Other Poems* at auction in 1988, but the commercial fisherman who spotted this rarity of rarities buried beneath a pile of agricultural pamphlets a few months earlier in a New Hampshire antiques barn; he bought it, on a hunch, for $15.

As in any enterprise that depends to some degree on intuition, there is always a wild card, and most elusive in rare-book collecting is the concept of rarity itself. Marcia McGhee Carter, co-owner of an antiquarian book store in Washington with the author Larry McMurtry, recalls attending a dinner where she was asked by Paul A. Volcker, then the chairman of the Federal Reserve Board, what qualities make one book more valuable than another: "Suddenly, nine heads turned toward me, and I was deeply embarrassed, and I said, 'Well, Mr. Chairman, it's really just a matter of supply and demand.' Which, really, is all it is."

Right now, Stephen King, the author of many wildly successful horror novels, is one of the hottest properties among living writers. Literary merit—whatever it may be—has little to do with the currency he enjoys among his legions of fans and the extraordinary prices fine copies of his relatively scarce early books command.

On February 7, a Florida collector purchased a ten-page manuscript written in longhand by King for $5,610 at Swann Galleries, well above the upper estimate of $3,000. Is that an investment, though, or merely an example of a collector indulging his hobby in the face of stiff competition? More to the point, will Stephen King retain this value over time, and will the demand for his material be there fifty years from now? The answers to these questions will determine how much future collectors will be willing to spend on him.

To some extent, of course, prices will always depend on literary merit, which means that scholars can have an impact on the rare-book marketplace. Daniel Aaron, a professor emeritus of English at Harvard University, has been a principal consultant to the Library of America since its founding twelve years ago, and in that capacity makes key decisions on which works deserve inclusion in what amounts to an official canon of our literary heritage.

"I, for one, have never been a collector," Aaron said. "I would just as soon have a very good edition of a writer on good paper than a signed first edition or a manuscript that more properly belongs in a library where it is available to scholars. Having said that, I would say that it is obvious there's a kind of financial canon that goes along with the literary canon. The literary canon chooses the best writers. And I suppose the value of a manuscript and copies of the writer's books in the marketplace then depend to some extent on the literary canon."

In recent weeks, the vagaries of value have turned up in the unlikeliest of places. A case in Iowa involves methods used to appraise a cache of twenty-one thousand rare books and manuscripts stolen over twenty years by Stephen C. Blumberg, an acknowledged bibliomaniac who was convicted in February by a federal jury in Des Moines on four counts of conspiracy and interstate transportation of stolen property. Stephen Blumberg's lawyers never denied that their client stole rare books from as many as 327 institutions throughout the United States and Canada. They argued that he had been driven by a delusional fantasy that forced him to "rescue" these treasures from what he perceived as their indifferent owners. Their defense of not guilty by reason of insanity was rejected.

Since the sentencing will be influenced partly by the extent of losses, it behooved the prosecution to demonstrate just how valuable the books are. The government claimed the entire hoard to be worth anywhere from $10 million to $20 million. Blumberg's lawyers challenged that assertion at every opportunity.

A prominent Los Angeles dealer, Glen Dawson, testifying as an expert witness for the government, described how he determined such a book as the Claremont Colleges copy of the 1493 edition of the Nuremberg Chronicle is worth $35,000, and how 271 items taken from the Connecticut State Library—including Connecticut's own copy of the first book printed in the state—are worth $225,280.

"A book is worth what someone is willing to pay for it," Dawson explained. "The best way to learn that is to list a book in a catalog and see what happens, or place it in an auction and let it take its chances. I appraised these books, wherever I could, at prices they sold for at public auction."

Dawson added that such a determination is not always possible, and that his professional specialty is to evaluate items for which there are no published records. He does that, he said, by making comparisons with "other books of similar quality and subject." But, he stressed, "appraisal is not an exact science. What it comes down to most of the time is that a book is worth what it's worth on a particular day at a particular time."

Blumberg never took the stand in his own defense, but midway through the trial, on a frigid Saturday when court was in recess, I spent nine hours with him, talking about books, talking about his "collection." We drove the eighty-seven miles from Des Moines to Ottumwa and went through the old Victorian house where he kept the books recovered last year by the Federal Bureau of Investigation.

On the way back to Des Moines, he told how, shortly after his arrest, he was sent to a federal medical facility for a psychiatric evaluation. He recalled the day he was summoned by a prominent Mafia boss, there at the same time for minor surgery.

"Everybody wanted to meet the guy who took $20 million worth of books," Blumberg said, but what the high-ranking mobster really wanted to know was why he hadn't concentrated his considerable skills on "things that were more liquid," like gold or diamonds.

"You don't understand," Blumberg told him. "I never took the books to sell them. The idea was to keep them."

The man was incredulous.

"When he heard that," Blumberg said, "I think he decided I really was crazy."

T astes change and fashion is fickle, but the most prized twentieth-century American authors among collectors continue to be William Faulkner and Ernest Hemingway. "Both are still as hot as a pistol," according to Allen Ahearn of Rockville, Maryland, a coauthor of *Collected Books: The Guide to Values*, which lists current prices for twenty thousand first editions. "A mint copy of *The Sound and the Fury* is about as rare a modern book as there is; I know people who would pay $15,000 to get one." Ahearn, who has been cataloging books with his wife since 1963, adds that even copies that are less than perfect can sell for up to $3,500.

Especially popular among living authors is Anne Tyler. Fine copies of *If Morning Ever Comes*, her first book, can cost as much as $1,000, while *The Clock Winder* can reach $750, and *The Tin Can Tree* $650. Also demonstrating continued strength is Larry McMurtry, whose first novel, *Horseman, Pass By*, now lists for around $750.

John Kennedy Toole's novel *A Confederacy of Dunces* was rejected by almost every trade publishing house. In 1980, at the urging of Walker Percy, Louisiana State University Press issued the novel posthumously in an initial printing of 2,500 copies. The comic novel was awarded a Pulitzer Prize in 1981. The first printing now sells for about $300.

While the fortunes of writers like James Whitcomb Riley, John Galsworthy, Christopher Morley, Henry Van Dyke, James Branch Cabell, and Erskine Caldwell have declined in recent years, collectors will still pay respectable prices for their most important books, a practice called high-spot collecting. "John O'Hara is the perfect example," Ahearn said. "Most of his books you can pick up anywhere for next to nothing, but you're still going to pay $1,000 for a nice copy of *Appointment in Samarra*."

Some collectors, he added, will pay $850 for Walker Percy's novel *The Moviegoer* and $500 for Joseph Heller's *Catch-22*, but considerably less for their other books. "I'd say that the really great high spots have been going up about 50 percent a year since 1988 or so," he said. Today, *Gone with the Wind* in a first-issue dust jacket sells for $3,000. "Just last year, we sold one at the New York fair for $2,000."

Showing tremendous strength in recent New York auctions have been T. E. Lawrence, Edgar Rice Burroughs, and Lafcadio Hearn, who is especially popular among Japanese collectors.

First issues of important books by Poe, Melville, Whitman, Dickinson, and Hawthorne, of course, remain exceedingly desirable and exceedingly expensive. Henry James is strong, while the fireside poets—Longfellow, Whittier, Holmes—are weak.

"King of the hill right now is Anthony Trollope," according to Glenn Horowitz, a New York dealer. "He's gone from zero to sixty in the last five years. He was vastly underrated, but no more; he's being collected up and down Park Avenue."

Pretty much out of favor today, Horowitz said, is Charles Lamb, who "at one time, back in the twenties, was probably as sought-after a writer as the major romantics. Nobody's really collecting Thackeray or Hazlitt either, and I don't know of any great interest in Carlyle."

Horowitz's hot tip for the nineties: "Anything to do with nineteenth-century baseball."

Peter Howard, a bookseller in Berkeley, California, declined to speculate on which authors are in and which ones are out. "I know a man who collects Opie Read [a turn-of-the-century Southern humorist] and I know people who collect Bret Harte," he said.

"What you have to understand is that the whole book business is not about who's in and who's out. What is a rare book, anyway? If you're only going to find one of anything in a lifetime, to me that means rare. If you can't get a particular book for money, that's *really* rare."

NOTE

The appearance of this lengthy essay in the *New York Times Book Review* signaled, in a very palpable way, what I had been up to in what by then was a three-year research project. I still had another four years to go before *A Gentle Madness* would see its way into print, but from this point on I gained access to people who might otherwise have declined my requests to see them. The disclosure, meanwhile, that I had spent a day in the company of Stephen Blumberg halfway through his trial caused a minor sensation back in Des Moines, where the bibliokleptomaniac had not taken the witness stand in his own defense and had spoken to no other representative of the press.

Bibliolatry
The Worship of Books

"An Enterprising Passion," Biblio 2, no. 8 (August 1997).

T o create a private library is to enter an ever-expanding world of wonder, a gathering of artifacts based as much on accumulated wisdom as on provenance and condition.

"Collecting books is often thought of in terms of rarities and landmarks, including first books and early books dealing with a particular subject," Sinclair H. Hitchings, keeper of prints at the Boston Public Library, told a meeting of the Friends of the Dartmouth College Library a few years ago.

"It is thought of in terms of first editions, association copies, and lavish and luxurious presentation copies," he continued. "I appreciate such books, but I am not much interested in collecting them, as far as our home library is concerned—nor do I have the budget to collect them."

No, Hitchings explained, the books he desires most are those that "bring me encounters with personalities I could know in no other way. It is the human beings I am after, what they can share of their own discoveries in life." And it is in that context, he said, that the library he has formed for his personal use "is filled with clues to the art of living. I buy books to nourish my interests."

There are purists who might argue that this is not collecting at all, that a collection needs a focus that is sufficiently theme related or subject driven to unify the mass and give it direction. True enough, but there also has to be room for people who actually treasure books for the knowledge they contain.

Hitchings's remarks, recently encountered in the November 1995 issue of the *Dartmouth College Library Bulletin*, brought to mind an anecdote told by John Carter some years ago about the famed collector Frederick Locker-Lampson's complaint to Francis Bedford, an eminent British binder, that a newly adorned volume did not close properly. "Why bless me, sir," Bedford is said to have replied with delighted surprise, "you've been reading it!"

Consider this remark from Sir Francis Bacon: "Some books are to be tasted, others to be swallowed, and some few to be chewed and digested." A good number of the books Bacon was describing were books he undoubtedly owned himself. Indeed, there was a time not so long ago when professional historians had to be collectors, especially in the United States, where the first public libraries were not established until the 1850s. John Quincy Adams is reported by Luther Farnham in *A Glance at Private Libraries* to have undertaken the acquisition of all books referenced by Edward Gibbon in *The History of the Decline and Fall of the Roman Empire*, "not half of which were then, probably, to be found on this side of the water."

Just how daunting a task that might have been is suggested by Geoffrey Keynes in *The Library of Edward Gibbon*. Keynes tells us that Gibbon's thirst for books was such that he had to wait until the death of his father, and the inheritance it occasioned, to indulge his passion fully. "To a lover of books," Gibbon wrote in his memoirs, "the shops and sales of London present irresistible temptations; and the manufacture of my History required a various and growing stock of materials."

For Sir Isaac Newton, books were purely the means to satisfying his intellectual curiosity. "The delights of mere collecting did not appeal to him," John Harrison writes in *The Library of Isaac Newton*. "His library was a set of working books most of which he came to know well and in some cases used extensively: the well-thumbed books are evidence of this. For Newton everything had its place in a regulated state of apparent disorder and so presumably he saw no advantage in making extensive booklists or catalogs—nor in asking anyone else to compile them for him."

Gibbon and Newton were fortunate in that they had extensive research collections available to them at Oxford and Cambridge universities. The obstacles encountered by American scholars through most of the nineteenth century were far more intimidating. In order for William Prescott, George Ticknor, Francis Parkman, and George Bancroft to write their various histories, personal libraries had to be assembled, often through the efforts of booksellers working abroad.

Today, professional writers have vast libraries available to them, not only in repositories of primary materials maintained in their home countries but also, in many cases, electronically through online sources. It is no longer necessary, in other words, for a writer to construct what amounts to the bibliography of a work being planned—unless, of course, the writer also happens to be a book hunter whose most satisfying forays are those that locate material that can function in the preparation of new books.

Nikolai Tolstoy, Robert K. Massie, Stephen Jay Gould, and Umberto Eco—four authors I have interviewed over the years for my syndicated literary column—each confided how some of their most accomplished works have been shaped by books which reside in their own libraries. Count Nikolai Tolstoy—a distant relative of Leo Tolstoy whose family has lived in England since the days of the Russian Revolution—is an authority on Arthurian lore. "I have a twenty-thousand-volume library of Celtic history," he told me, one factor that persuaded him to write *The Coming of the King*, a bestseller in England.

Robert K. Massie, a historian whose books include *Nicholas and Alexandra* and *Peter the Great*, winner of a Pulitzer Prize, spent more than ten years researching *Dreadnought*, a mammoth examination of the historical forces and monumental egos that led to the outbreak of the First World War. "I became a bibliophile to write this book," Massie said during our interview. "That may be one of the reasons it took me so long to get it done; I became absorbed in my research material."

Stephen Jay Gould, an eminent paleontologist whose numerous books about natural history provide the kind of exciting accessibility for general readers that Carl Sagan's writings about the heavens have done for astronomy, is an enthusiastic collector of old scientific books and monographs, as attendees at a talk he gave at the Grolier Club in New York two years ago will readily attest. Gould told me in an interview that he derives some of his greatest inspiration from original manuscripts and first editions. "Don't ask me what it is, I can't say for sure, but I get something special out of handling the real things," he said.

The premise for *The Name of the Rose*, one of the great biblioadventures of our time, was inspired in part by a sixteenth-century volume of Aristotle that Umberto Eco had acquired twenty years earlier and deposited on a remote shelf in his home library of thirty thousand volumes. "It was a book I had paid one thousand lira for, about seventy cents when I bought it," he said. "It is not a handsome book by any means—water stained, soiled, very unpleasant to the touch—which explains why I had hidden it away. I believed I was inventing a manuscript in the novel, when in fact I was describing that printed book in my library. I had it up here all the time," he said, tapping his forehead.

Researching a book depends as much on serendipity as it does on discovery, and the author never knows when something useful will come along. There is a generalized sense of pursuit propelling the search, but the one element that makes every day an adventure is the expectation that something totally unknown will be located along the way. Disciplined research in institutional libraries is essential, but the unexpected finds that come in bookstores, flea markets, and antiquarian fairs can be just as rewarding. An added advantage is that books acquired in this manner not only become sources for research but also become prized additions to a bona fide collection of knowledge.

I offer as a recent example my own experiences at the thirty-seventh annual New York Antiquarian Book Fair held at the Seventh Regiment Armory on Park Avenue. In an essay in *Biblio* magazine, Sidney E. Berger provided a thorough overview of book-fair protocol, based on his many experiences attending these spectacles that he calls "the most public version of the book hunt." Towards the end of his essay, Berger offers this sage observation: "For some collectors, knowing when to call it a day poses the greatest challenge. One day you'll be able to spend ten hours or more looking at the books, with equal energy on the morrow. Another time, you'll find yourself simply overwhelmed at the enormity of it all."

I would like to add a footnote to Berger's caveat: If you are driving to a book fair, try not to park your car at a meter that needs to be fed at frequent intervals. The prospect of parking legally in Manhattan for $1 an hour is a truly seductive enticement, to be sure. But leaving the exhibition hall every sixty minutes can wreak havoc on your acquisition budget, since each visit to the meter facilitates the deposit of freshly captured game in the trunk, thereby liberating hands that might otherwise be burdened with too much weight.

My first acquisition at the New York fair was *The Treasures of Mount Athos: Illuminated Manuscripts*, two huge folios in English and Greek compiled and written by a team of eminent scholars, illustrated throughout with six-color reproductions, and weighing in at thirteen pounds. The relevance of these volumes to my work can best be explained by quoting from my copy of *Visits to Monasteries in the Levant*, by Robert Curzon, one of the greatest accounts of bibliographical globe-trotting ever written and recently found lying in a wooden fruit box at a Massachusetts flea market. Curzon describes several trips he made during the 1830s throughout the regions bordering the eastern Mediterranean Sea known as the Levant in search of old books and manuscripts.

Before he was granted entry to an ancient library in one of the monasteries on Mount Athos in Greece, Curzon tells how he was required by the abbot in charge to eat a breakfast of pulverized raw garlic mixed with olive oil, sugar, and a shredded cheese "which almost takes the skin off your fingers." This "savoury mess" left him "sorely troubled in spirit" for many years afterward. "Who could have expected so dreadful a martyrdom as this?" he writes. "Was ever an unfortunate bibliomaniac dosed with such a medicine before? It would have been enough to have cured the whole Roxburghe Club from meddling with libraries and books for ever and ever."

Despite his delicate constitution, Curzon consumed the food nonetheless, and many of the treasures he thereupon was allowed to handle are reproduced in the lovely books I found in New York. They made their way to my car on Madison Avenue seconds before a Manhattan meter maid arrived on the scene and were joined an hour later by Adrian Wilson's *The Making of the Nuremberg Chronicle* and *Bookmaking & Kindred Amenities*, a collection of excellent essays on the state of book culture during the Second World War, edited by Earl Schenck Miers and Richard Ellis. Daniel Berkeley Updike's two-volume opus, *Printing Types: Their History, Forms, and Use* came next, followed by a cluster of smaller items sure to reward their new owner with useful nuggets of information for many years to come.

My final acquisition of the day was an elegant little volume printed by the Ward Ritchie Press in 1954 for the Zamorano Club of Los Angeles. Titled *A Chinese Printing Manual*, the twenty-page duodecimo publishes a translation by Richard C. Rudolph of an important guide for the printing of books in the Imperial Manuscript Library in China, prepared by the Superintendent of the Royal Printing Office in 1776. My enthusiasm for the item was sharpened in no small measure by the fact that it weighs slightly less than four ounces and posed no undue hardship on the final trek to the car.

This was the kind of book-hunting day, as Sid Berger pointed out in his *Biblio* essay, that provides "vivid memories of the books you wish you could have bought and with delight in the ones you did." And just as interesting as the books that entered my working collection were the leads, tips, and suggestions I gathered for active and future writing projects. Altogether a most-satisfying day at the fair.

Biblioclasm

The Deliberate
Destruction of Books

"Fragile Guardians of Culture," Los Angeles Times, January 12, 2004.

The phrase most frequently associated with George Orwell's *1984* is the chilling caveat "Big Brother Is Watching You."
However, as a writer concerned with the life cycle of books and the institutions that contain them, I think the most consequential sentence in *1984* is this one trumpeted by the ironically named Ministry of Truth: "Who controls the present controls the past; who controls the past controls the future."

This suggests why tyrants and ideologues bent on a final solution go beyond physically annihilating their enemies to eradicating the artifacts that document their existence.

The surreal goal of controlling the past has been with us throughout recorded time, as the Roman Senate understood when it ordered the legions of Scipio Aemelianus to reduce Carthage to rubble in 146 B.C.—and to obliterate every standing remnant of its intellectual vitality while they were at it.

The best way to do that? *Biblioclasm*, which the *Oxford English Dictionary* defines as the deliberate destruction of books, a cultural offense of incalculable consequence.

If there is any constant to biblioclasm, it is that it has no geographical boundaries, no historical limitations, no philosophical or theological restraints.

Was it a Christian mob acting on the orders of the Roman emperor Theodosius I in the fourth century or Muslim followers of the caliph Omar in the seventh century who destroyed the great library at Alexandria and all the "pagan" masterpieces from classical antiquity that it contained? Nobody can say for sure, because the likelihood is that both inflicted damage on the collections.

The late twentieth century was a banner era for biblioclasm. China's Red Guard wiped out artifacts and books in the takeover of Tibet in the 1960s. Pol Pot did the same in Cambodia in the 1970s. And on August 25, 1992, the Serbs extended ethnic cleansing to the National and University Library of Bosnia and Herzegovina in Sarajevo, resulting in 1.5 million books and manuscripts being incinerated in one night.

And the twenty-first century? Just last month, 150 members of a group called the Sambhaji Brigade ransacked the Bhandarkar Oriental Research Institute in Pune, India, 130 miles from Mumbai (formerly Bombay). The provocation? The institute was used in research for an Oxford University Press book that questioned aspects of the story of the Hindu warrior-king Shivaji. One of the most grievous losses was a clay tablet dating back to the Assyrian period of 600 B.C.

There is an upside to all this: Book culture has a way of surviving calamities both natural and deliberate.

Thousands of books made from the bark of trees and bearing the wisdom of Mayan culture went up in smoke on a single day in 1562 in Mexico, the victims of a Spanish friar's zealous attempt to cleanse the natives of devilish thoughts. Yet four codices were saved from the flames as curiosities, and from them came the key to unlocking the mystery of the Mayan hieroglyphs in the latter years of the twentieth century.

Contemporary horrors are also being remedied.

The national collection of Cambodia is being "reseeded" with help from Cornell University's rich collection of Southeast Asian materials; the Tibetan Buddhist Resource Center is building an

Internet archive of works rescued out of the diaspora; and two curators at Harvard's Fine Arts Library have mobilized a worldwide effort to restore fragments of what was lost in Sarajevo.

When an arsonist's match ignited Los Angeles's downtown Central Library on April 30, 1986, about 375,000 books were destroyed outright and another 700,000 were damaged by smoke and water. About 1,500 volunteers joined weary staff in an inspirational effort to save the imperiled volumes, prompting the California librarian, author, and all-around bookman Lawrence Clark Powell to write in the *Los Angeles Times* that, although damage to the revered building was lamentable, "saving most of the books matters more." It is, in fact, a happy reality that books multiply: One archive begets more archives; one collection can save another. In that spirit, the poet Archibald MacLeish, librarian of Congress during the Second World War, observed in 1972: "What is more important in a library than anything else—than everything else—is that it exists."

Biblioclasm II

"A Bitter End for HUB Gem," The Boston Globe, February 29, 2004.

O
n a frigid winter morning when all New England was saluting the Patriots on their thrilling triumph in the Super Bowl, I was in an airplane, on my way to see a single book at the Chicago Botanic Garden. The purpose of this day trip to the Windy City was to pay my respects to the remains of a great rarity that had become a victim of its own fragile beauty, a book that had been stripped to the bare bone for its 248 copperplate engravings. Fourteen months earlier, this copy had been described as "one of the most celebrated eighteenth-century fruit books" in the world by the New York auction firm Christie's, which was retained by the Massachusetts Horticultural Society to sell it off to the highest bidder.

Known by a shortened form of its lengthy title as the *Nurnbergische hesperides*, the book was assembled between 1708 and 1714 in two volumes by Johann Christoph Volkamer, a prominent Nuremberg merchant and citrus farmer. Though by no means the most coveted prize put on the block by Christie's on December 18, 2002—indeed, it was offered as lot 127 among 132 "important botanical books" that had been culled from the society's once-legendary collections for the sale—it did fetch $50,190, more than $10,000 above its presale estimate.

Acquired by a buyer who chose to remain anonymous, the two volumes were taken to Europe and shorn of their plates and calfskin bindings. Once disassembled, the black-and-white engravings were colored in by hand, a process that makes them more appealing as wall adornments, and thus more salable at prices from $500 to $1,500 each, as numerous Internet searches have confirmed.

Though not illegal, tearing apart a perfectly serviceable work of scholarly importance in order to extract its illustrations is roundly reviled as an egregious form of cultural vandalism. When the financially beleaguered Horticultural Society proceeded with a two-tiered plan in 2002 to replenish its coffers, there were dissenters who warned that just such an eventuality might happen to some of the books.

Phase one involved selling 2,219 books and 2,000 journals to the Chicago Botanic Garden for $3 million. Then, to maximize its return, the society consigned its most spectacular holdings to Christie's, a strategy that brought in an additional $2.45 million.

Unable to secure everything—and fearing for what was about to be scattered to the four winds—Chicago Botanic Garden librarian Edward J. Valauskas quietly put the word out among colleagues to look for cannibalized books from the Christie's sale, which he thought might show up on the antiquarian market.

A few months ago, a Chicago bookseller located what was left of the *Nurnbergische hesperides* in Great Britain and acquired it for $2,000; along with the detached pages of print came ten of the newly colored plates.

Though the bindings and bookplates had been discarded, a positive identification was still possible since the Horticultural Society call numbers remained in place on two interior pages, along with the notations, "Bur. Oct. 1934," an unambiguous reference to Albert Cameron Burrage, a Boston tycoon who gave these books—and many others—to the society.

Just eight copies of the *Nurnbergische hesperides* are reported in institutional collections worldwide, and only one in New England, at Yale. No facsimile edition has ever been produced, which is why even a truncated version is worth having in Chicago.

Valauskas explained that the illustrations were never meant as decorations, but as integral elements of the text. "Without the images," he said, "you lose the life of the book." But his anxiety extends well beyond what happened to this single object. "How many other books from that auction," he wondered, "have met the same fate?"

Robert H. Fraker, of Lanesboro, Massachusetts, a specialist in natural history books who appraised the library in the 1990s and argued vehemently against its breakup, offered this reaction when informed of the desecration: "Albert Burrage bequeathed his collection to the Massachusetts Horticultural Society with the good faith expectation that it would be held there in perpetuity. While the ultimate villain is the person who put the knife to the book, the Christie's sale represents a fundamental betrayal of patrimony."

John C. Peterson, president and CEO of the society at the time of the sale, justified the dispersal then by asserting that the books "hadn't been used in decades." That will not be the case for the volumes now under Chicago stewardship. *Plants in Print: The Age of Botanical Discovery*, an exhibition featuring many of the Boston acquisitions, will be on view from April 1 to July 15 at the U.S. Botanical Garden in Washington, D.C., and travel from there to Glencoe, Illinois, for an opening in September. In October, *Plants in Print*, an international symposium, will be held at the Chicago Botanic Garden, with the Massachusetts titles occupying center stage.

PEOPLE

OTTO BETTMANN

"Sixteen Million Images, One Vision," Biblio 2, no. 1 (January 1997).

When a private company based in Bellevue, Washington,
known as Corbis Corporation acquired the legendary
Bettmann Archive of 16 million images in 1995, the
New York Times trumpeted details of the unprecedented deal on
page 1 under the headline, "Huge Photo Archive Bought by Software
Billionaire Gates."

With the purchase, said to be a "multi-million dollar transaction," William H. Gates III, the chairman of Microsoft Corporation and owner of Corbis, announced his intention of creating the
world's foremost collection of digitally stored images. The service
provides visual materials to book publishers, magazines, newspapers, and commercial clients.

Printed alongside the October 11, 1995, *Times* article was a
sampling of images contained in the massive collection: baseball
great Joe DiMaggio kissing Marilyn Monroe, a dapper Winston
Churchill flashing his trademark "V for Victory" sign, and the
drawing of a floppy-eared dog cocking his head toward an RCA
Victor record player emitting the sound of "His Master's Voice."
Aptly, the Bettmann Archive—which included 11.5 million news
photographs from the files of United Press International—has been
described as "a visual chronicle of the twentieth century." The deal
with Corbis was consummated with the Kraus Organization Ltd.,
of New York, a company founded by the late bookseller Hans P.
Kraus, which had bought the archive from Otto Bettmann fourteen
years earlier.

For Gates, the purchase made a bold statement on the direction this modern visionary feels the world is taking in what has been widely proclaimed as the information age. Corbis has acquired licensing rights to half a million other images, negotiated with such institutions as the Library of Congress, the Barnes Foundation in Philadelphia, and the National Gallery in London. Since then, deals have been worked out with additional sources, including the State Hermitage Museum in St. Petersburg, Russia, and the estate of the late outdoor photographer Ansel Adams. How the implications of this new technology will influence the way visual information is stored, transmitted, used, and digested in the years to come, and how it will affect the future of printed books themselves, remains, of course, to be determined.

Almost lost in all of the excitement, however, was the role played by the man who originated the collection sixty years ago and whose life has touched every decade of the twentieth century. Appearing in a small sidebar to the main story reporting the acquisition, at the bottom of an inside page in the *New York Times*, was a brief piece that teased readers with this headline: "From One Vision to 16 Million Images." William Grimes's piece began with these two succinct paragraphs:

> The Bettmann Archive, the world's largest commercial photo collection, originated with the private collection of a single man.
> That collector, Otto L. Bettmann, was born into a prosperous family in Leipzig, Germany, in 1903. His father was an orthopedic surgeon who transmitted his love of books to his son. As early as age 12, Otto began rooting through the family's wastebaskets and stockpiling medical illustrations.

After earning a doctorate in history at Leipzig University in 1927, Bettmann spent several years as a curator of rare books in the Prussian State Art Library in Berlin, where he began using a new invention—the 35-millimeter Leica camera—to photograph manuscripts in the national collections. When the Nazis took power, Bettmann, a Jew, was forced to leave his job. In 1935, he emigrated to the United States, carrying with him ten marks in his wallet and two steamer trunks full of photographs, a haphazard trove that became the foundation of a commercial picture library that would provide images to such publishing outlets as the Book-of-the-Month Club, *Life* and *Look* magazines, and commercial clients that variously included cereal manufacturers, soup makers, and T-shirt printers—anyone and everyone with a pressing need for a particular image.

Retired since 1981 and a widower since 1988, Bettmann lives alone in a condominium in Deerfield Beach, Florida. Identified often over the years as the "Picture Man," he is uncommonly articulate about the events, trends, and developments he has witnessed, and about the place of books in civilized society. Luckily for me, this gentle, self-effacing man had a listed telephone number, and I wasted no time getting in touch with him. A few months later, we met for two days in Florida to discuss these matters and to talk about his thoughts on the eve of a new millennium.

It is mildly ironic, he agreed, that his archive is now identified with the relentless trend technology is making toward the digitization of words and the compression of images onto microchips. "It is a new world, but the amazing thing is that it doesn't make much for literacy," he said in precisely phrased, though heavily accented, English. "Pictures, I am afraid, do not make us civilized. They are very nice, but they do not lead us, like words, toward understanding. We have created picture repositories that show us the outer life, but only books can convey to us the inner life. I declare war, I am sad to say, against the very medium that has kept me alive; I bite the hand that fed me." As a gesture of solidarity with the printed word, he arranged to have all royalties from a book he wrote in 1987, *The Delights of Reading: Quotes, Notes & Anecdotes*, donated to the Library of Congress Center for the Book, and as an activity to enjoy during his retirement, he accepted an offer in 1978 to serve part-time as curator of rare books at Florida Atlantic University in nearby Boca Raton.

Had the political crisis in Europe not forced him to flee his native land sixty-one years ago, Bettmann said he undoubtedly would have pursued a life among books. "I come from a very bookish background. My father was a great bibliophile in Leipzig, where I was born, and I worked as a curator of rare books at the art museum in Berlin. Reading has always been my great passion. I wrote my doctoral dissertation on the eighteenth-century German book trade, and had I stayed in Germany I probably would have become a publisher. I was a bookman from day one." Translated into English, the title of his dissertation is "Development of Ideals in the German Book Trade." In addition to his Ph.D. in history, Bettmann earned another degree as a master librarian.

But when he did leave for the United States, it was his collection of photographs that determined his destiny. "My idea was simply that art was not only the reflection of the artist's own feelings or beliefs, but that these things also give us a history of how people lived. People rather thought me a little crazy for pursuing this in America. They said America is oriented toward the future, not the past; that the past plays absolutely no role there. But when I got here, I started to make a little living, setting up an archive and getting pictures that people could use for commercial use. I found the interest in historical things quite remarkable here."

Once settled in the United States, Bettmann immersed himself in American life, refusing for six decades to visit the land of his birth. Finally, at the behest of the German government, he agreed to return in May 1995 for a brief visit. "My coming to America was simply a miracle," he said. "It was as if God held out a hand and took me out of this terrible, hopeless situation. Had I not left when I did, I would have been among the first to be picked up and sent to a concentration camp."

Although he was proficient in the use of cameras, Bettmann never considered himself a photographer. "I regard myself as a graphic historian, an archivist." The founding by Henry Luce of *Life* magazine in 1936, just a year after Bettmann's arrival in the United States, and the explosion of interest in photojournalism that brought about, created an immediate demand for the material he had to offer. By renting pictures to clients on a onetime basis, Bettmann was able to generate income without sacrificing inventory. As the collection grew, he published catalogs for his clients, with categories ranging from games and toys to sun, moon, and stars; and from opera, medicine, and popular music to yachting, weather, and radio.

Essential to the success of his operation was careful cataloging, a skill he developed during his years as a curator in Berlin. A ruthless judge of relevance, Bettmann prided himself as much on what material he rejected for inclusion as on what he acquired. An essential goal, though, was to achieve a state of critical mass and to have readily available whatever image a client might need, "right now today," as Bettmann put it.

"The pictures come to us as a message from the past, but there are no pictures that I really, definitely love and find fulfilling. It isn't quite enough. It's all surface stuff. The pictorial material covers just the outside of things. You need the deepening; at least intellectually interested people need the deepening of the world. Only reading does that. And that is the power of the book." Smartly dressed in a sport coat and ascot, his trim white beard neatly groomed, Bettmann projects an impeccable image of care and organization. A skilled musician, he is devoted to the works of Bach, who, like him, is a native of Leipzig. Among Bettmann's dozen published books is *Johann Sebastian Bach: As His World Knew Him*, released last year. Before we left his apartment for lunch, the Picture Man played a minuet from one of Bach's piano suites on the small organ in his living room, a delightful interlude that I captured on my tape recorder.

"It is my conviction that Bach was sent here to make a little order out of the chaos," Bettmann explained. "He starts with a theme and develops it. It must always be in the same tonality and in the same spirit. The theme is carried forth, it goes up, up into forms of variation, but it always comes back to where it started. Bach always brings us back to life. Beethoven doesn't do that; he starts out, and he shoots into outer space. Bach is confined, small in his melodic inventions perhaps, but then he gets hold of a theme, and everything is always in such wonderful order. What did God do when he started the world? He made order out of chaos. I get this wonderful feeling of order in everything Bach writes."

NOTE
Otto Bettmann died in 1998, at the age of ninety-four. Three years later, Corbis announced that it would move the Bettmann Archive out of New York City to a site sixty miles northwest of Pittsburgh, where it would be stored more than two hundred feet beneath the ground in a low-humidity storage area carved from an old limestone mine. "The objective," according to a company official, "is to preserve the originals for thousands of years."

Matthew Bruccoli

"An Obligatory and Mandatory Occupation," Fine Books & Collections, no. 15 (May/June 2005).

Matthew J. Bruccoli (pronounced "brook-lee") is one of the most intense bookmen I have ever been privileged to meet, and I have met quite a few over the past twenty-five years. I had occasion recently to spend a day at the University of South Carolina (USC) with this man, described by the *New York Times* last year in a front-page story as the "senior pack rat of American letters," a description that barely begins to do him justice.

He is a collector, but his tenacious pursuit of literary treasure is only the beginning and has been just one part of a grand scheme that began more than a half century ago, when Bruccoli, now seventy-three, was a student at Yale and hopelessly hooked on the fiction of F. Scott Fitzgerald.

Bruccoli dates his antiquarian interest in his favorite author to the week he graduated, when he made a purchase in a New Haven, Connecticut, bookstore of two Fitzgerald first editions, one for $5, the other for $7.50. Later, as a graduate student at the University of Virginia, he found a magnificent first printing in dust jacket of *The Great Gatsby*, which remains the centerpiece of a collection that now numbers three thousand printed books and eleven thousand documents. "I bought it from Henry Wenning for $30," he said, "and I didn't have the $30. I paid it off $5 at a time."

The collection became the property of USC in 1994, when Bruccoli agreed to sell it for less than half its market value, pegged then at just under $2 million. Impressive as all these treasures may be, it is the scope and the nature of the holdings that make them supremely important to scholars doing research in the history of American literature.

"Everything I do, everything I write, everything I buy, everything I collect," Bruccoli told me, "has to do with the role of the book in American culture and the profession of authorship." Exhibit A: the Matthew J. and Arlyn Bruccoli Collection of F. Scott Fitzgerald, which occupies a prime location in USC's Thomas Cooper Library.

What Bruccoli declared to be his flat-out favorite spot in the Fitzgerald Room is twelve linear feet of floor-to-ceiling shelving. "Every one of those books you see there is inscribed *by* Fitzgerald or *to* Fitzgerald," he said. "Every one of those books Fitzgerald held and may have read. There are more books inscribed by Fitzgerald on those shelves than any place else in the world."

Some of the books he bought from established antiquarian booksellers and in the major auction galleries; others he turned up in basements, attics, junk shops, and barns. Last year, Bruccoli acquired a rich collection of movie scripts written by Fitzgerald over an eighteen-month period in 1937 and 1938 for the Metro-Goldwyn-Mayer studio.

"I regard book collecting as the obligatory and mandatory occupation of a scholar," Bruccoli stressed, adding his frank dismissal of people "claiming to be scholars" who disdain "access to the great books" in their fields. "I think most of the teaching of literature today is flawed because the author is ignored. All of this nonsense about postmodernism—the idea that the author is dead—actually injures the work, and it certainly injures the students." Students taking any of Bruccoli's courses learn this firsthand. Rare books have been used as essential teaching tools since he arrived on USC's Columbia campus as a professor of literature in 1968.

Access, in Bruccoli's view, means consulting every available version of a favored author's writings, which is why the catalog of his Fitzgerald collection lists 148 entries for *The Great Gatsby*, including a unique set of galley proofs that bear the running title of

Trimalchio, which was Fitzgerald's original title. Another sixty-five entries identify copies of *Tender Is the Night,* thirty-nine more cite *The Beautiful and Damned,* and fifty-four list copies of *This Side of Paradise.* There are even four for *Fie! Fie! Fi-Fi!,* a musical comedy presented by the Triangle Club at Princeton University in 1914, with lyrics written by Fitzgerald when he was a college freshman.

Bruccoli wrote to every surviving student who attended Princeton while Fitzgerald was there. "I told them, 'I would not presume to offer you money, but if you have any material relating to the Triangle Club productions for 1914, 1915, and 1916, I would be very happy to make a generous donation to Princeton University in your name,'" Bruccoli said, explaining how he located *Fie! Fie! Fi-Fi!* The strategy was so successful that he used it again, this time to acquire a run of St. Paul Academy's *Now and Then* for the period between 1908 and 1911, when Fitzgerald was writing his first fictional works as a student in St. Paul, Minnesota. "I got hold of a Minneapolis phone book and a St. Paul phone book, and I wrote to every name that had a Fitzgerald connection, and I wrote and I wrote and I wrote, and finally, somebody said, 'Yes, I have one.'"

One item in particular that Bruccoli showed me is a perfect example of what is prized today in research libraries as a material object, an artifact that offers unexpected insight into artistic expression. It is the brown leather briefcase Fitzgerald had with him when he was writing screenplays in Hollywood. Bruccoli bought it at a Sotheby's auction in 1973 for reasons, he insisted, that have a bearing on the creative process. "If you notice the gold stamping, it says 'Scott Fitzgerald, 597 5th Ave., New York.' Well, that's the Scribner Building. Fitzgerald didn't have a home, much less one on Fifth Avenue in Manhattan. Fitzgerald's home was the Scribner Building. What does that tell you about the man who wrote *The Great Gatsby?*"

Knowing everything he can about the man who wrote what is arguably the most outstanding American novel of the twentieth century and documenting whatever he can about the creation of lasting literature in general is central to the mission Bruccoli has fashioned for himself. It is an endeavor that has resulted in the release of more than sixty works of literary biography and bibliography, a good number of them published by Bruccoli Clark, an imprint he established with C. E. Frazer Clark Jr. in 1962. Known since 1976 as Bruccoli Clark Layman, the company produces works of scholarly nonfiction and reference.

As a sideline, Bruccoli has assembled, over the years, two collections of British and American posters, literary works, sheet music, broadsides, manuscripts, ephemera, movies, and photographs related to the First World War. He named both collections in honor of his father, Joseph M. Bruccoli, a veteran of the Great War. The first archive was installed in the University of Virginia; the second was created after Bruccoli moved to South Carolina.

Another consequence of Bruccoli's zeal is a near-complete run of Armed Services Editions, which were published between 1943 and 1947. Of the 1,322 titles issued by the publishing industry during the Second World War to bring a bit of America to the troops overseas, Bruccoli has rounded up 1,309. "There were two Fitzgerald books—*Gatsby* and *The Diamond as Big as the Ritz and Other Stories*—issued in the series. When I started looking for them, I saw merit in looking for them all."

Other research collections he has gathered illuminate the life and works of Ernest Hemingway, Joseph Heller, James Gould Cozzens, John O'Hara, James Dickey, Ring Lardner, H. L. Mencken, Thomas Wolfe, Budd Schulberg, Maxwell Perkins, and others. "Everything connects," Bruccoli repeats as a mantra. "Research begets research. Books beget books."

CARTER BURDEN

*"You Can't Be Too Thin, Too Rich, or Have Too Many
Books," Biblio 1, no. 2 (September/October 1996).*

The sudden death of Carter Burden on January 23, 1996, marked
the passing of a bibliophile whose bold declaration a decade and
a half ago to build the greatest collection of twentieth-century
American literature ever assembled sent shock waves through the
antiquarian book world that continue rippling to this day.

A handsome, witty, charismatic man of wealth and refinement,
Burden possessed that rare combination of qualities so essential to
collecting at the highest levels of accomplishment—ample means
and impeccable taste. The fifty-four-year-old great-great-great-
grandson of Commodore Cornelius W. Vanderbilt died of a heart
attack in his Manhattan apartment. In the lead sentence of a four-
column obituary, the *New York Times* described him as a person
"who epitomized the young patrician party giver of the early 1960s,
who flashed across the political firmament as a progressive New
York City Councilman a few years later and who spent his latter
years as a publisher, founder of a broadcasting empire and benefactor
of the arts."

A glamorous fixture among Manhattan's social elite, Burden
was a major patron of the New York Public Library, the Pierpont
Morgan Library, and the New York City Ballet. During the 1960s, he
and his first wife, Amanda, were described as "the young locomotives"
and the Big Apple's leading "fun couple," appearing often in gossip
columns and in the pages of *Vogue*, *Harper's Bazaar*, and *Women's
Wear Daily*. Party guests at their elegant apartment in the Dakota
included such luminaries as Norman Mailer, Truman Capote, Andy

Warhol, George Plimpton, Larry Rivers, Robert and Ethel Kennedy, and Prince Philip of Great Britain. The Burdens divorced in 1972, three years after Carter was elected to the first of three terms he would serve on the New York City Council. An unsuccessful effort to succeed Edward I. Koch in the U.S. House of Representatives ended his political career in 1978, two years before he embarked on becoming a book collector.

Born in Beverly Hills on August 25, 1941, Shirley Carter Burden Jr.—he dropped the Shirley from his name when he entered New York politics—grew up on the periphery of the film colony in a house formerly owned by Fredric March. He once remarked that his first serious girlfriend was Geraldine Chaplin. Flobelle Fairbanks, Burden's mother, was a niece of the actor Douglas Fairbanks and played small parts in a number of movies. Burden majored in English at Harvard College in the early 1960s and wrote his senior thesis on Henry Miller; years later, he gave an inscribed copy of the paper to California bookseller Ralph Sipper of Joseph the Provider Inc., of Santa Barbara, as an expression of gratitude for finding a number of particularly coveted titles. In 1966, Burden received a bachelor of laws degree from Columbia University Law School, stayed in New York, and entered Manhattan society in a big way.

During the early 1990s, I conducted three interviews with Carter Burden for my book *A Gentle Madness*, and in each one he declared his conviction that "the urge to collect is innate," and that he could never remember not having a lot of "things" gathered around him. "I started collecting toy soldiers and baseball cards when I was six years old," he told me. "That's not especially significant, but I think the fact that I have kept the toy soldiers all these years probably is."

From toy soldiers and baseball cards, Burden's attention turned variously to sculptures, bronzes, drawings, clocks, antiques, Indian miniatures, glass bells, wooden snuffboxes, even old English ballot boxes. In the 1960s, he started collecting the paintings of living artists such as Frank Stella and Jasper Johns, a move that proved especially

perceptive when prices for contemporary art exploded in the early
1980s. "I never paid more than $10,000 for a single painting," Burden
asserted, and when he saw what other collectors were suddenly
willing to pay for his prize pieces, he began selling most of them off
at the height of the market and promptly considered other ways to
satisfy his passion to accumulate.

One obvious choice was twentieth-century American literature,
a field previously ignored by most major collectors, and one that
Burden determined he not only could enter but also could dominate
in a fairly short period of time. "I basically paid for my books with
the profits I made on my paintings," he insisted, although the
key word in that sentence is *basically*. According to some reliable
estimates, he pumped anywhere from $15 million to $20 million
into his newfound interest, a veritable fortune in a field where "value"
is measured usually in the hundreds of dollars, and sometimes
in the thousands—but never in the millions. He began quietly
enough in 1981, around the time of his fortieth birthday, dealing
at first with Marguerite A. "Margie" Cohn, the late owner of the
House of Books in New York and a pioneer in the field of modern
first editions. As good as Cohn's sources and contacts were—and
they were renowned—she knew that she could never supply what
Burden had in mind by herself, so she began taking him around
to antiquarian book fairs and introducing him to other prominent
booksellers.

Burden's concept was simple enough, but awesome in its scope.
What he wanted, essentially, was to document the full sweep of
American literature during the twentieth century, picking up
where the noted steamship magnate and collector of nineteenth-
century American authors Clifton Waller Barrett had left off. The
Clifton Waller Barrett Library, given to the University of Virginia
in Charlottesville in 1960, spanned the full range of literature
produced in the United States prior to 1900 and focused on the
books, manuscripts, journals, and correspondence of one thousand
writers, five hundred of them in great depth. In addition to the

unquestioned giants of American letters, figures like Henry James, Mark Twain, and Harriet Beecher Stowe, Barrett's list included lesser-known names like Charles Brockden Brown, John Neal, William Gilmore Simms, and Robert Montgomery Bird. At Barrett's death five years ago at age ninety, his bequest totaled 112,000 manuscripts and 35,000 books.

Peter B. Howard, owner of Serendipity Books in Berkeley, California, and a past president of the Antiquarian Booksellers' Association of America, became one of Burden's principal suppliers and admits candidly that he benefited from the relationship in a big way. "The joy was that Carter wanted one of every book by every serious twentieth-century author," he said. "He collected the primary editions, he collected significant inscribed and biographical editions, and he collected representative autograph material."

By 1987, when Burden wrote an article for *House & Garden* titled "Voluminous Obsession," some seventy thousand books by six thousand authors had already been amassed. In the essay, he stressed how he had applied several fundamental rules to the way he proceeded.

> I wanted my entire collection to meet the highest bibliographic standards. I insisted on first editions, pristine condition, original dust jackets. I wanted all the rarities and high spots, but more than anything, I sought comprehensiveness and depth. I was determined to collect not just the acknowledged giants of American letters but writers like Booth Tarkington and Pearl Buck, whom nobody has paid attention to in years. Not just novelists, poets, and dramatists but critics, humorists, detective writers, science fiction writers, Western writers, black writers, political writers. Moreover, I was committed to collecting the work of every important writer in depth—proofs, limited editions, variant issues, pamphlets, broadsides, English editions, magazine appearances.

When he wrote that piece, Burden was still living in a thirty-five-room apartment overlooking the East River, and happily surrounded by his beloved objects. "Books do not merely furnish my rooms," he exclaimed, "they engulf them. They are everywhere—in my study, the library, the kitchen, the corridors, the bathrooms, the children's rooms. My family is rebellious, but I don't care. As far as I'm concerned, you can't be too thin, too rich, or have too many books."

When I first interviewed Burden in 1990, we met in the offices of the family investment firm, William A. M. Burden & Co., where he was the managing partner. By that time, the frenetic pace of acquisition had slowed down dramatically. Carter and his second wife, Susan, had sold their large apartment on the East Side and were living in temporary quarters while renovations were being completed on a new suite across Fifth Avenue from the Metropolitan Museum of Art. All the books were in storage, he said, and all new purchases had been put on hold. Indeed, along with the realization that he could never own every book written by every twentieth-century American writer, a winnowing process had begun.

"I made a manful effort, but what you quickly learn is that no collection is ever complete," he told me. "So, yes, I was defeated. The point, I guess, is that I tried. If I were starting today, I certainly would never attempt to be as broad as I was in the beginning. Six thousand authors, in every issue of every book? Periodical appearances and signed limited editions? And uncorrected proofs. That was a mistake, trying to collect all those proofs."

In the summer of 1992, Burden showed me through his spectacular new apartment, magnificently designed by Mark Hampton and profiled a few months earlier in the pages of *Vogue* and *House & Garden*. The antiques and artworks, needless to say, were magnificent; a George III writing table, William IV armchairs, sculptures, bronzes, porcelain, bronzes, drawings, clocks, but it was the books that were overwhelming, room after room of them, with shelves rising fourteen feet high, starting with James Agee in the living room and continuing on through Tennessee Williams. There were, he speculated, about twelve thousand volumes displayed, with the rest in storage. "The original scheme is finished," he said. "I finally realized that I can't do it all."

But did that mean he had stopped collecting altogether? He answered that question by recalling his purchase—at Swann Auction Galleries just a few weeks earlier—of an exceedingly scarce copy of Sinclair Lewis's first book, *Hike and the Aeroplane*, published in 1912 in an edition of one thousand copies under the pseudonym of Tom Graham, and almost impossible to find with a wrapper. The presale estimate was $3,000 to $5,000; Burden paid $19,250. "I already had a copy of the book," he said. "It was the dust jacket I needed."

So Burden, obviously, had every intention of keeping the core collection intact, although he was vague about what plans were being formulated for the books he no longer wanted. Well before his death, there was strong evidence that moderate dispersion was already taking place. A considerable amount of science fiction material had been presented to the New York Public Library. His collections of W. H. Auden, Edgar Rice Burroughs, Ambrose Bierce, Charles Bukowski, E. E. Cummings, and Robinson Jeffers were consigned to Sipper for sale, while the T. S. Eliot and Marianne Moore material went to Glenn Horowitz in New York.

Peter Howard, meanwhile, had negotiated the most extensive transaction of all, the purchase of seventeen thousand volumes, representing the work of two thousand authors. "He kept the cream," Howard said. "I got the dross. But I'm ecstatic, because what I got is still important." Asked to cite a few examples, Howard named the authors Michael McClure, William Heyen, Mary Austin, Gertrude Atherton, and George Ade.

Remarking on Burden's contribution in general to American book collecting, Howard said simply, "He revitalized the book trade; he made it possible. He pumped millions of dollars into the market, and that money enabled every bookseller of modern first editions, whether they were a direct vendor to Carter or not, to solidify their businesses." As for Burden's scheme, Howard said, "He did not traverse unknown territory because he collected established authors. But within the area of known authors, he focused on unusual materials. He bought radio scripts, film scripts, he bought in great depth, and in doing this he caused all of his sources and dealers to look more closely at previously unappreciated material. And he was extremely well served by the booksellers. He wanted everything—and everything was made available to him. Basically, he was a millionaire who bought $30 books. He didn't want to buy $10,000 books, although at the end he did buy some."

Massachusetts bookseller Priscilla Juvelis, who started out in the business as an associate of the late John Fleming, placed Burden in a special category of "extremely wealthy, well-educated people who do not necessarily have to work for a living, people like Bradley Martin who have the time, the intellect, and the money to devote to their collecting. I sold Carter first editions and variants of Edith Wharton, for instance, and even though he wasn't my only customer for these items, he would usually get first refusal because he was the one who had those perquisites. You could always count on Carter to understand how important an item might be—and be willing to pay for it."

Sarah Baldwin, owner of E. Wharton & Co., of Oakton, Virginia, said Burden's greatest achievement was to "create an en-tirely new standard of what collecting modern firsts should be. He saw American literature in its entirety. When he talked about mod-ern American literature, he wanted every good writer published in this century, and what he was creating was a profile of modern American literature."

Ralph Sipper agreed that much of what Burden accomplished can be credited to intelligence, but he said that discipline also was a factor.

"Carter collected on a broad scale, yet he was also fastidious. Along with the desire and having the means to build a great collection, he understood how money worked. And having been a collector of other things from early on, he understood the mechanism of how to function as a collector, and how to interact with the sources. One of Carter's greatest achievements, I think, was that no book was too small to escape his attention or interest. After he had almost everything, it became apparent that he had to winnow down, but there is no doubt in my mind that he wanted to keep the heart of the collection intact."

Glenn Horowitz, an East Side bookseller who handled numerous transactions for Burden and represented his interests at many New York auctions, expressed his belief that Burden not only wanted to keep the central collection together but also in all likelihood would have worked to improve it. "This was a long-term project, and he was gearing up to make a major push forward," he said. "I believe that he was about to focus on the seventy-five or one hundred most important authors of the century, and that what he had in mind was building what would amount to the definitive canonical collection of these authors."

As for the future of what remains of the library, Horowitz said he has no direct knowledge of what Burden's heirs plan to do with it, but he would be surprised if it were to be broken up and dispersed. "Knowing the family, I believe that if circumstances permit them to keep the collection together and see it installed in a research institution not unlike the New York Public Library, that is what they would like to do." In addition to the twelve thousand or so volumes housed in the Fifth Avenue apartment, Horowitz said that about another twenty-three thousand remain in storage. "I would define the core collection as thirty-five thousand volumes," he said.

"We all watched open jawed as Carter embarked on this Herculean task," Horowitz concluded. "There's no question that if Carter's collection were to be deposited into a research facility, that institution, if it didn't already own a single modern first edition, would be a significant player overnight. His collection has the armature for that because it helps to define the twentieth century in America."

NOTE
In February 1998, Carter Burden's family presented the core of the collection—thirty thousand books, manuscripts, letters, and assorted papers valued at $10 million—to the Pierpont Morgan Library, along with an additional gift of $1.5 million to endow a fund to care for the materials. "This is the greatest collection of American literature in private hands," Charles E. Pierce Jr., director of the library, said in accepting the gift. "It represents a mega-leap in terms of strengthening our American holdings and particularly in strengthening our holdings in the twentieth century." The remainder of the library was dispersed through booksellers.

Anne Fadiman

"A Common Reader, An Uncommon Passion," Biblio 3, no. 12 (December 1998).

N ot many bibliophiles would consider their love of books to be "carnal" in nature, but then not many bibliophiles grew up in a "literary hothouse" where an unqualified passion for reading was nurtured almost from birth.

Here is how Anne Fadiman, the recently appointed editor of *American Scholar* magazine and the winner of a National Book Critics Circle Award for an exceptional work of literary journalism, describes what she and her older brother, Kim, share among their earliest memories:

"Between them, our parents had about seven thousand books," she writes in *Ex Libris*, a charming collection of personal essays released by Farrar, Straus, and Giroux. "Whenever we moved to a new house, a carpenter would build a quarter of a mile of shelves; whenever we left, the new owners would rip them out. Other people's walls looked naked to me. Ours weren't flat white backdrops for pictures. They were works of art themselves, floor-to-ceiling mosaics whose vividly pigmented tiles were all tall skinny rectangles, pleasant to the touch and even, if one liked the dusty fragrance of old paper, to the sniff."

Clifton Fadiman, now ninety-four and the father of Anne and Kim, is a writer, editor, critic, and noted anthologist who has been a judge for the Book-of-the-Month Club since 1944. His wife, Annalee Jacoby Fadiman, eighty-two, is a former journalist who covered China for *Time* magazine during the Second World War. She was also a onetime scriptwriter for Metro-Goldwyn-Mayer and, with Theodore H. White, was coauthor of *Thunder Out of China*, a 1946 bestseller that remains in print to this day.

"Our father's library spanned the globe and three millennia, although it was particularly strong in English poetry and fiction of the eighteenth and nineteenth centuries," Fadiman continues in *Ex Libris*. "Our mother's library was narrower, focusing almost entirely on China and the Philippines." One reason for the decided difference in content, she points out, was the nature of their work. "Our father, who often boasted that he had never actually done anything but think, was still the same person he had been when he started collecting books in the early 1920s. He and his library had never diverged. Our mother, on the other hand, had once led a life of action."

As children, Anne and Kim were allowed complete access to the two libraries. "My brother and I were able to fantasize far more extravagantly about our parents' tastes and desires, their aspirations and their vices, by scanning their bookcases than by snooping in their closets. Their selves were on their shelves." When she was four, Anne built castles with her father's pocket-sized, twenty-two-volume set of Anthony Trollope, "because they were so much thinner than they were tall, perfect, as cards are, for constructing gates and drawbridges." When the elder Fadimans moved from California to Florida a few years ago, these tiny tomes passed on to Anne.

On Sunday nights in the 1960s, when a television program remembered fondly by people of a certain age as the *General Electric College Bowl* went on the air live from New York, the Fadiman family took assigned seats in their Los Angeles living room, fully prepared to match wits with some of the sharpest young minds in the country. They called themselves Fadiman U., and in six years of spirited competition that tested their knowledge of literature, history, science, sports, and current events, the foursome "lost only to Brandeis and Colorado College."

The opportunity to compete one-on-one with kindred spirits was certainly part of the family's motivation. But a lot of it was nourished simply by living every day in a supercharged atmosphere where all forms of intellectual competition were viewed "as a sacrament, a kind of holy water, as it were, to be slathered on at every opportunity with the largest possible aspergill."

A 1974 honors graduate from Harvard University, Fadiman followed initially in the footsteps of her mother, opting for the lure of journalism and a life of adventure. After spending some time as a mountaineering instructor in Wyoming, she became a writer for *Life* magazine, traveling the world in search of stories. For a 1984 piece, she profiled her father on the occasion of his eightieth birthday. "He sits in a big, black reclining chair, turning pages at an average rate of 80 an hour," she wrote. "In the last 76 years, he estimates he has read about 25,000 books." Because their father always worked at home, the children considered him "infinitely interruptible," and that his "chief occupation was serving as our private storyteller."

Books were revered for their content, not as artifacts. "To us, a book's *words* were holy, but the paper, cloth, cardboard, glue, thread, and ink that contained them were a mere vessel, and it was not sacrilege to treat them as wantonly as desire and pragmatism dictated. Hard use was a sign not of disrespect but of intimacy." Indeed, it is on this point where Fadiman parts ways with what she believes is the "platonic" love for books evidenced by so many antiquarians and collectors who insist on pristine condition with uncut pages.

"I don't believe that books should be sacred," she said pointedly in an interview, and she tapped the spine of a volume bound in green cloth that was lying close at hand. We met on an August afternoon on Cape Cod in Massachusetts, where Fadiman was vacationing with her husband and two young children, Susanna and Henry. Because it was such a gorgeous day, our wide-ranging conversation took place at an outside picnic table, with Buzzards Bay sparkling in the background. "The wonderful thing about this book," she said of the bulky quarto by her elbow—it was a forty-fifth birthday present she had just received from her husband, George Howe Colt—"is that you can see it was loved, and that it will continue to be loved." Titled *The Friendly Arctic*, the book was written by a Scandinavian explorer named Vilhjalmur Stefansson and published in 1922 by Macmillan; her husband had found it at Titcomb's in East Sandwich, one of the cape's finest secondhand bookstores. A great admirer of polar exploration, Fadiman said the book would be added to her "odd shelf" of expedition narratives, journals, photograph collections, and naval manuals. There is no doubt that this new addition had been consulted often by a former owner, whose name is embossed on the half title-page. The condition is good, but there is evidence of continued use; inserted between two pages was a green leaf plucked from a nearby tree.

"I manhandle my books," Fadiman said. "I turn down the pages, I scribble notes in the margins, and if a bookmark isn't handy to mark my place, then I will use an oak leaf. I think there's something to be said about not being too respectful. For me, it's carnal love." Collectors, she believes, too often tremble at the thought of handling fragile pieces and fall into a category she likens to "courtly love" and the platonic ideal. "Courtly lovers always remove their bookmarks when the assignation is over," she writes in *Ex Libris*, and their goal is "a noble but doomed attempt to conserve forever the state of perfect chastity in which it had left the bookseller."

As we learn in *Ex Libris*, Fadiman's husband is just as obsessed with books as she is. "I couldn't imagine marrying anyone who wasn't a reader," she said. "As soon as I walked into George's apartment and saw that there were books everywhere, and that he had floor to ceiling bookcases, I knew that this was a kindred spirit." The couple met in the 1980s at *Life* magazine. "We also have mutual interests in the literature of suicide, which becomes an extremely gloomy romantic bond. I was working on a long piece for *Life* about the right to die, and George was writing a book, *The Enigma of Suicide*, which was published by Summit in 1991. So we read all the same books."

A good deal of the charm in *Ex Libris* is that the eighteen essays produce a kind of personal reflection, a particularly notable feat since they were all written between 1994 and 1997 as "The Common Reader" column in *Civilization*, the magazine of the Library of Congress. Each one develops a different aspect of Fadiman's life as a reader and read as chapters in a memoir that does not take itself too seriously. "I always knew that these pieces were going to be a book, right from the start," she said. "That's why there are the same characters throughout. It's really a series of linked essays."

The title of the *Civilization* column—which has been incorporated into the subtitle of the book as "Confessions of a Common Reader"—emphasizes the word *common* and is prefaced with a reverential nod in the direction of Virginia Woolf, who wrote a celebrated book titled *The Common Reader* in 1925. Woolf paid tribute to "all those rooms, too humble to be called libraries, yet full of books, where the pursuit of reading is carried on by private people." She defined a common reader as one who differs from the critic and the scholar by reading for individual pleasure "rather than to impart knowledge or correct the opinions of others." Fadiman is quick to emphasize that while she is "no Woolf," she is nonetheless, by that definition, a common reader.

"I am simply writing these essays about books from the point of view of an ordinary reader who likes to read, not someone who brings any special academic qualifications, not someone who brings any particular brilliance to the act of reading, simply someone whose life is furnished by books," she said. "I am a person who brings nothing special to my reading except my love of it. It permeates my life, yet it becomes a circle because the more I read, the better qualified I am for that tradition of common reader."

Because the pieces are personal essays, it bears noting that they are written in the tradition of Fadiman's father, an influence she readily acknowledges. "The essay was my father's specialty, and I had to pass the age of forty before I felt I had the self-confidence to venture into a genre that I knew I was really made for, but that I wouldn't do earlier because I didn't want to compete with someone I knew I couldn't surpass," she said. "I also believe that a person's first book should not be an exercise of looking into the mirror. I think it's a mistake when people write a memoir for their first book."

Fadiman's first book was a work of literary journalism, *The Spirit Catches You and You Fall Down: A Hmong Child, Her American Doctors, and the Collision of Two Cultures*, a detailed examination of what happens when modern American medicine comes into direct conflict with the traditional beliefs of a Laotian family living in the United States as exiles. Resolute in its belief that illness and healing are spiritual concerns, a Hmong family refuses to allow California pediatricians to treat their three-month-old epileptic daughter with anticonvulsants, preferring animal sacrifices to be performed instead. The conflict—scrupulously researched and painstakingly reported—earned widespread praise from critics and won the National Book Critics Circle Award in nonfiction.

"A lot of people wondered where that book came from, but this was a work of reportage, and I was very much following in my mother's footsteps," Fadiman said. "She was a reporter, but because she had done her major work before I was born, I didn't actually see her working when I was growing up. Her work was not intimidating to me in the same way that my father's was. I could actually see him write. I would see him holding his pencil and then read the essays he wrote. I think I actually had to reach middle age before I could venture into what I felt was his territory."

Fadiman's latest foray into uncharted territory began a year ago when she assumed the editorship of *American Scholar* magazine, the sixty-six-year-old quarterly journal published by the Phi Beta Kappa Society and named after Ralph Waldo Emerson's 1837 oration of the same title at Harvard University. Fadiman's appointment followed the abrupt dismissal of the noted essayist Joseph Epstein, a lecturer at Northwestern University and editor of the journal for twenty-three years. Why Epstein was terminated was not disclosed, although there were mumblings that his cultural conservatism was too entrenched for some tastes and that it was time for an infusion of new blood.

Epstein, for his part, has declined requests to be interviewed on the subject, preferring to let his final essay for the magazine be his last word on the subject. Titled "I'm History," he compared the Phi Beta Kappa senate that let him go to the Russian Duma, where a radical Bolshevik minority defeated a moderate majority. The overall response to his successor's first efforts, however, has been positive, and Fadiman takes pains to stay out of the culture wars that continue to flare around her.

"Although I think Mr. Epstein was very angry at Phi Beta Kappa for dismissing him, he is large spirited enough to know that my being chosen editor had nothing to do with his being dismissed," she said. "He has never taken out his anger at Phi Beta Kappa on me. He is a real gentleman."

As to the direction she would like to take the journal, Fadiman said she is "not interested in making the *Scholar* political" at all. "I think perhaps there was a feeling of wanting someone younger. I was the youngest of the short list, although I don't think that age or gender was particularly important to them. Some were academics, some were journalists, some were older, some younger, some women, some men; it was a very interesting and heterogeneous list. Why they finally settled on me? Who knows?"

NOTE

In 2004, Anne Fadiman was dismissed as editor of *The American Scholar* in a disagreement with the Phi Beta Kappa Society over a continuing budget deficit and the editorial direction of the journal. During her six-year tenure, the publication won three National Magazine Awards, among other distinguished prizes.

Victor Gulotta

"Once a Collector..." Fine Books & Collections, no. 23 (September/October 2006).

This is a story about a book collector who said good-bye to it all after emerging triumphant in one area of pursuit and then took up the hunt in another direction entirely when the urge to resume proved irresistible.

In July 2001, the Houghton Library of rare books and manuscripts at Harvard University paid Victor Gulotta of Newton, Massachusetts, a figure reported to be in the middle six figures for a collection of books, photographs, posters, calendars, lithographs, broadsides, busts, letters, and various ephemeral objects related to the life and work of the nineteenth-century New England poet Henry Wadsworth Longfellow. What especially piqued my interest about the transaction was curiosity as to why an institution that already held the world's foremost Longfellow archive would commit such a sum for objects that in another time might be regarded as peripheral at best.

When told by William P. Stoneman, the Florence Fearrington Librarian at Houghton Library, that "material artifacts" have become increasingly coveted in recent years by research libraries seeking to "fill gaps" in their principal holdings, I decided to learn more about what is sometimes referred to as "realia" with the idea of using it in *Among the Gently Mad*, the discursive guide I was then writing about strategies and perspectives for book hunting in the twenty-first century.

Shortly thereafter I contacted Gulotta, owner of Gulotta Communications Inc., a one-man publicity firm that arranges promotion for authors on tour, with a client list that has included Isaac Asimov, Margaret Thatcher, and Richard Brodie (the original author of Microsoft Word). In time, he would help out on a couple of my books, but five years ago, all I knew about Victor Gulotta was that he had built an eclectic collection of interesting materials "in and around" a notable literary figure on a modest acquisition budget and that he had placed what he had gathered in one of the world's foremost rare book repositories.

Given the little that I knew about Gulotta at the time, I frankly expected to meet an older man who, after decades of indulging a passion for all things Longfellow, had decided at long last to let his treasures find a new life with someone else. What I didn't expect was a forty-seven-year-old bibliophile who showed very little separation anxiety after having just packed up his coveted materials and shipped them off to Harvard.

"First of all, I hadn't planned to amass the largest Longfellow collection in private hands in half a century; it just happened," Gulotta told me, noting that he learned the skills of bibliography in the early 1990s while working as cataloger and sales director for Bromer Booksellers, of Boston. After starting his publicity business in 1993, he kept his hand in the trade on a part-time basis, primarily through Internet and eBay sales, as a means to finance his own collecting.

A native of Brooklyn, Gulotta studied English literature at the State University of New York, in Buffalo. He took some courses with the noted poet Robert Creeley, who inspired in him a love of nineteenth-century American fiction and poetry, which in turn nurtured a desire to collect. "I wanted to focus on a single author, and I chose Longfellow precisely because his reputation had been in decline," he said. "I could see that material was everywhere on the market, and available at very good prices. I saw a lot of opportunity, and I jumped at it."

From the beginning, Gulotta said, he wanted a collection that "wasn't all books," one that gave depth to the life and works.

"I wanted a collection that would reflect on the life of the first superstar in American literature. It became a quest, and I put it all together in about fifteen years. It just dazzled me that I could own an original letter by Longfellow for $250. I found Longfellow cigar wrappers; there was Longfellow beer, dishes, posters, beautiful signed engravings, a publisher's contract he had signed for the book *Poets and Poetry of Europe.*"

And just as easily as he assembled everything, Gulotta was able to let it all go. "I got a call one day from the 19th Century Shop in Baltimore asking me if I was interested in selling my Longfellow material to a client of theirs who wanted to make a gift of a ready-made collection to an institution. I was intrigued by the offer, so I prepared a detailed catalog of my holdings. I came up with a price that they chose not to accept, but which I thought was eminently fair. Once I had the catalog, I decided to see if anyone else might be interested, and it turned out that Harvard was the perfect home."

Normally, that would be the end of this story. A collection had been built with verve and originality; it had value that can be measured on aesthetic, cultural, and monetary scales; it moved along to new custodians who love and respect it; and everyone was happy.

"But once a collector, always a collector," Gulotta told me in a recent visit to his home, and for emphasis he waved proudly at the dozens of maps; medieval manuscript leaves; sixteenth-century Albrecht Dürer engravings; nineteenth-century photographs of Charles Dickens, Mark Twain, and Alfred, Lord Tennyson; and original engravings by Anthony Van Dyck, Peter Paul Rubens, and William Hogarth that grace the walls of his charming Victorian house in the Boston suburbs, every one framed to museum standards in his own basement studio.

In glazed cabinets nearby, Gulotta has what he calls his antiquities collection. Each item part of a continuum that reflects an aspect of writing through history. "What drives me in all this, I believe—I don't know for sure just yet, but I'm working on an understanding as to why I've switched gears—is the deep love I have for archaeology. I always wanted to be an archaeologist when I was a kid, but I don't like to travel. I just don't enjoy flying. Isaac Asimov and I had that in common. He had a deep dread of flying, and I do too. As a scientist he understood the mechanics of aviation so much that it terrified him, and I feel the same way. But I am able to travel through history with my collections."

After making his deal with Harvard, Gulotta said he thought briefly about starting a Washington Irving collection—"another author who is considered passé"—but he wanted to be more expansive in his new approach. "Once I sold the Longfellow collection, I felt that now the floodgates were opened, and I that had the freedom to collect anything within the limits of affordability. I really wanted to diversify."

The range he chose is vast. He has several examples of cuneiform dating from the third millennium B.C., pictograms from the Indus Valley region that are even older, an ancient Roman grave marker honoring a slave who died at the age of twenty-five, a fragment of an Egyptian mummy covering that pictures the goddesses Isis and Neftis in a form of plaster called gesso. "The antiquities number about thirty pieces, and every one has a recorded provenance. Without that, I won't touch them. I have gone back five thousand years, and I have to wonder—am I going to collect cave art?"

Among traditional books in his collection, there is a massive Gradual, a fifteenth-century Spanish choir book in Latin that weighs twenty-seven pounds. There are numerous incunables and some very nice editions of English authors. And yes, there is a very strong single-author collection that includes a number of fascinating realia objects, along with most first appearances of Charles Dickens in books and monthly serials known as parts. "Dickens and Longfellow became friends, they visited each other, and both were the superstars of their time," he said, "so there is a natural connection."

And what will happen in time to all these collections? Gulotta and his wife, Donna, a university professor, have a thirteen-year-old daughter, Emily. "I see some serious tuition payments in my future," he said, and left it at that.

Gulotta's best tip to fellow collectors is worth stressing: "Every time I acquire a new book or object, I research it thoroughly and I acquire new knowledge. I pull books off the shelves; I read about literary history; I catalog carefully and in depth. When you write descriptive catalogs, you are going to learn an awful lot. You become the authority."

ARTHUR JAFFE

"Risk Your Opinions," Fine Books & Collections, no. 27 (May/June 2007).

My overwhelming view has always been that books, fundamentally, are carriers of knowledge and that so many of us become mad about possessing them by virtue of the wisdom, insight, comfort, and wonder they bring to our lives. But books are also extraordinarily resilient objects capable of performing many worthwhile functions, not least among them the magical way they can become things of beauty and artistic expression in and of themselves.

I was reminded of this reality during a recent visit to the Arthur and Mata Jaffe Collection at Florida Atlantic University (FAU) in Boca Raton, a gathering of twelve thousand books, works of art, and pieces of ephemera for which text is an almost-incidental consideration. Even Arthur Jaffe, the prime mover of this diverse gathering, admits that what is seen in a collection like this takes precedence over what is read.

"It is a visual collection," Jaffe told me cheerfully during a walking tour of his pride and joy, assembled so lovingly over the past half century, which remains very much a growing entity that he oversees as curator and frequent contributor. He also teaches courses that use the books as teaching tools. "There are words and text, but they are secondary to the aesthetics. Think of this primarily as a book-arts collection—fine bindings, handmade papers, unique artist's books, exquisite typography, book sculptures, and the like. Here, the aesthetic trumps the content. What you see around you are books that are artworks, and we begin to appreciate them on that level."

Jaffe stressed several times during our talk that he likes to think of these pieces as a "happy collection," or something I like to think of as a feel-good collection, not unlike the wonderful assortment of Christmas books assembled by the late Jock Elliott, who I profiled in my book *Among the Gently Mad*. (A major selection of Elliott's books sold at Christie's for just under half-a-million dollars.)

Some of the qualities that make the collection happy are immediately evident, even to the most sanguine of observers. There are books made out of wood, fabric, metal, glass, string, even potato sacking; there are accordion books that unfold, books with three covers known as dos-à-dos (back-to-back) books; there are upside-down books and tête-à-tête books that allow people to look at the same volume while facing each other. There are altered books where an artist has made significant changes to the structure of a regularly published book, and tunnel books that lie flat until opened, when they reveal tiny figures inside. There is a book made by the late conceptual artist John Cage out of mud, and there are dozens of pop-up—or movable—books, created by paper engineers such as Robert Sabuda, and a generous selection of miniature books.

Particularly striking is *Working Philosophy, Volume I*, a large, almost impressionistic sculpture of a book shaped from handmade paper by Chicago artist Melissa Jay Craig. Another sculpture, *Check Book*, by Florida artist Barbara Brandt, is a clever construction in the form of a chess table, complete with pieces, each one of them a book bearing calligraphic text.

Another Florida artist, Marianne Haycook, was inspired by a fourteenth-century Persian tapestry to fashion a book with acrylic and oil paint on handmade antique tablet paper decorated with peacock feathers; she called it, aptly enough, *The Peacock's Tail*. A truly striking "painted book" called *The Brooklyn Bridge: A Love Song*, by the estimable West Coast book artist Don Glaister, features five paintings of the venerable East River span seen from different angles, each done on sanded aluminum sheets and attached to a paper hinge; the quarter-leather binding is made of Nigerian goatskin. The longest book in the collection folds out to thirty-three feet; the largest stands seven feet tall; the tiniest, barely two inches in height, fits comfortably in the palm of a hand. What is for all intents and purposes a gumball machine is *Book for a Buck*, a device designed and built by FAU staffer Nancine Thompson that dispenses—in exchange for four quarters—a tiny book enclosed in a plastic case.

But well beyond the unusual texture of the objects is their functionality as an archive at the university and the role they have played in helping a growing institution achieve credibility as a research center. Presented to FAU in 1998, the Jaffe collection is housed in its own wing on the third floor of the S. E. Wimberly Library, with a permanent exhibition of some 250 objects that attracts hundreds of visitors each year. Displays change often, and special presentations are mounted frequently. On the instructional level, various workshops are offered to the general public, and book-arts courses for students enrolled in the university make regular use of the materials

Jaffe, eighty-six, said he began by acquiring woodcut engravings in the years following the Second World War as a hobby undertaken for pure pleasure. "Every book in the collection has something uniquely memorable about it," Jaffe told me. "I never thought of myself as a collector in the conventional sense, and I still don't. A collector means that you have a particular goal, that you have a focus. I saw things that I liked that I bought and enjoyed. I know what I like when I see it, and I buy books, basically, to look at them. I don't particularly covet old books either. I like to support the work of living artists, and regional artists. So is it eclectic? Eccentric? Idiosyncratic? Yes, yes, and yes."

A native of Butler, a small city in western Pennsylvania, Jaffe moved to Florida in 1978 after spending a successful career as a partner in a chain of family department stores and began a new life as a professional fundraiser for numerous charitable enterprises. As residents of Boca Raton, he and his late wife, Mata—who he credits with bringing "a lot of color and life" to the collection—looked to the nearby university as a possible home for their collection. "There were a number of institutions that made overtures," Jaffe said, "but FAU was a fairly new school that opened its doors in 1962 and was growing quickly. They needed special collections for their research programs, and we were pleased to work with them."

William Miller, director of libraries at FAU, told me that a key element in his talks with Jaffe was the assurance that the collection would become a centerpiece of the library. "We were very familiar with his collection and very taken with it," Miller said. "As a new library, we did not have any significantly large special collections," he said. When Jaffe suggested donating his treasures to the library, Miller jumped at the chance. "He felt that his collection would have been given short shrift in a larger institution. Here, it is a featured signature of our library. And he has been happy with the venue and the freedom he has here to teach and promote."

Another plus, Miller said, has been the willingness of other donors to give their prized collections to the university. Last year, a Florida couple, Marvin and Sybil Weiner, donated a major collection of colonial-era imprints to the library. "The Weiner family saw how the Jaffe collection was being treated and decided that we had the capacity to house and promote the use of their collection. Again, they wanted it featured and used, not just stuck away in a rare-book room."

The Jaffe-FAU match, to use a shopworn phrase, has been a perfect fit. For Jaffe, the objects he loves so deeply have a home where they are valued and respected, and where he has a hand in directing their future. The university, meanwhile, has become a player in the world of special collections, a necessary ingredient for a college that seeks to attract independent scholars and graduate students to do research.

Never one to consider charging admission to see his collection, Jaffe said he requests two considerations from visitors. "Your curiosity and a willingness to risk your opinions," he said. "If you don't have those two, you can't come. I have a tendency to fall in love easily, and I trust my instincts when I see a book. A book belongs in this collection because it will be in company with other books. They will live together well. They will be happy together. I think it's as simple as all that."

MITCHELL KAPLAN

"Saint Mitch of Miami," Fine Books & Collections, no. 20 (March/April 2006).

itchell Kaplan, of Miami, is living proof that if you care
deeply enough about books, you can do something
meaningful to keep the culture that celebrates, nurtures,
and preserves them thriving at a time when so many forces seem to
be marginalizing their importance.

Now completing his second term as president of the American
Booksellers Association, the trade group for independent sellers of
new books, Kaplan is the owner of three bookstores in southern
Florida. That is, in itself, an achievement of consequence during
these days of increasing dominance by mammoth chains, like Barnes
& Noble and Borders, and the muscular arrival of online retailers,
such as Amazon.com, that eliminate entirely the notion of the
bookstore as a gathering place staffed by flesh-and-blood people
who are eager to attend to your literary needs.

Also of note is the bond Kaplan has established with his community as cofounder and guiding spirit of Miami Book Fair International, an annual event that invites hundreds of authors to the city
that Jackie Gleason once called the "sun-and-fun capital of the world."
Its eight days of literary festivity feature a bustling street fair complete with ethnic food and music and dozens of engaging presentations with an appeal broad enough to attract the city's richly varied
population. A true measure of its success is the number of volunteers—now numbering more than a thousand—who freely give their
time and energy each year to ensure the continued survival of what
has become a local institution and a model for others to imitate.

For the twenty-second renewal of the extravaganza this past November, a quarter million people entered the urban campus of Miami Dade College, where the fair has been held since 1984. None of them were deterred by the $5 admission fee that Kaplan and his associates felt required to charge adults for the first time, a decision hastened by the demise of similar events elsewhere in the United States.

Among recent casualties is the Boston Globe Book Festival, which closed down in 2003 after a thirty-six-year run. The following year, New York Is Book Country folded its tent after twenty-six years of holding court on Fifth Avenue in midtown Manhattan. Neither closed due to low attendance, which was always enthusiastic. In the end, there was a lack of financial sponsors.

From the beginning of its existence, Miami Book Fair International has emphasized the cosmopolitan nature of the city it serves. In 1984, Cuban exiles were the dominant minority, but today there are immigrant communities from such places as Colombia, Nicaragua, Mexico, Haiti, Brazil, and Spain. In addition to dozens of American authors, the 2005 fair featured programs with writers from Argentina, Bolivia, Chile, Venezuela, Costa Rica, Ecuador, Guatemala, Nigeria, China, Croatia, and France. "We've got programs that take place in Spanish, in French, in Creole," Kaplan told me. "What has always been a hallmark of the fair has been the recognition that Miami is an extremely diverse city. The notion of a big tent at the center of everything we have going on is a metaphor that resonates for everyone."

A tall, lanky man with a soft baritone voice, the fifty-year-old Kaplan came into the book business by the unlikeliest of ways. A native of Miami Beach, he studied English literature at the University of Colorado and then entered Antioch Law School in Washington, D.C., in 1976 with every intention of becoming an attorney. But there was something truly magnetic about the bookstores he had always enjoyed visiting, and the thought that he could do something special proved sufficiently seductive for him to drop out of law school, return home, pursue a master's degree in English at the University of Miami, and teach literature at a local high school.

"It just dawned on me at one point that somewhere in the center of so many twentieth-century literary movements you could usually find a bookseller," he said. He ticked off a few salient examples—the most notable being Sylvia Beach and Shakespeare & Company in 1920s and 1930s Paris; Frances Steloff and the Gotham Book Mart in New York during the 1930s, 1940s, and 1950s; and the poet Lawrence Ferlinghetti, whose City Lights bookstore opened in San Francisco in 1953 and remains a vibrant cultural force in the City by the Bay to this day.

In 1982, Kaplan took over the lease of a five-hundred-square-foot storefront in Coral Gables, stocked it with two thousand carefully chosen titles, and called the hopeful enterprise Books & Books. From the beginning, his personal goal was to serve as a kind of enabler who would provide a welcoming place where writers and readers could meet on common ground and books would be at the center of the discourse.

When Kaplan first opened for business, Miami, in his words, was a "beleaguered city" that had lost a good deal of its focus, partly a result of the Mariel boat lift in 1980, which brought 125,000 exiles to a city that was unprepared to handle so many people at one time. Soon after, a traumatic race riot followed, occasioned by the beating death of a black man by white police officers. The city suffered a severe identity crisis, and outsiders took notice.

"*Time* magazine ran a cover story calling Miami 'Paradise Lost,'" Kaplan said. "Through all of this I felt there would be a cultural renaissance and that Miami could use a bookshop and a fair that would help break the clichéd notions of what the city was all about. I had absolute confidence in the literary community here. I found intelligent people coming to the store and buying books of a nature that convinced me we had as serious a literary community as any other in the country."

Today, home base for Books & Books is 265 Aragon Avenue in chic Coral Gables, an eight-thousand-square-foot building of elegant Spanish design that boasts hardwood floors, an inner courtyard café, a large children's section, local artworks—all of them appealing complements to the store's staple offerings of books, books, and more books, a good many of them in Spanish, since half of Kaplan's customers are bilingual Spanish speakers. His two other locations are in the upscale Bal Harbour Shops and on Lincoln Road in South Beach, which also features a three-star restaurant, Café at Books & Books, that serves breakfast, lunch, and dinner.

Through all these subtle concessions to changing times, Kaplan's dedication to the writers of his region remains the stuff of local legend, prompting the *Miami Herald* to proclaim him "Saint Mitch" in the headline of a lengthy feature published in 1996. It doesn't matter whether the authors he supports are national best-sellers, like Dave Barry, Carl Hiaasen, Edna Buchanan, Dan Wakefield, James Hall, or Les Standiford, or writers still striving to hit their stride and find their voice—all are invited to do readings, sign books, and foster a core readership. Kaplan estimates that Books & Books mounts between four hundred and five hundred literary events a year, "pretty much one every day."

Throughout the store's impressive expansion and diversification, it is worth noting that the name of the store is not simply cute. "I had a heck of time back then, figuring out what I was going to call the place," Kaplan said. "So I finally asked myself, what is it that I'm going to sell? The answer was that I'm going to sell books—and *books*. And that's what I called it."

CHIP KIDD

"Whiz Kidd," Fine Books & Collections, no. 24 (November/December 2006).

When all is said and done, a dust jacket is successful if a browser is persuaded to pick a volume up in a bookstore and give it nothing more than a momentary glance. "That is it in a nutshell," agreed the estimable Chip Kidd, whose clever literary adornments have become something of a status symbol among authors over the past twenty years, prompting John Updike to declare him "second to none, and singular in the complexity of the comment his book jackets sometimes deliver upon the text they enwrap." And Kidd manages to do all this, Updike, emphasized, in a world "where edge, zip, and instant impact are sine qua non."

While not minimizing the role a jacket plays in giving a literary product a kind of visual identity, Kidd—who is associate art director at the New York publishing firm of Alfred A. Knopf and a freelance designer for numerous other publishers—nevertheless downplays its importance in marketing. "We can talk about art, we can talk about color, we can talk about type, all those things, but in the end, all the real ideas are in the book itself," he told me in a lively interview that encompassed his multiple creative interests and his unending passion for popular culture. Among his own books are an academic satire, *The Cheese Monkeys*, and a catalog of his obsession for Caped Crusader paraphernalia, *Batman Collected*.

"I am a great believer in the adage that jackets don't sell books; bookstores sell books," he said. "What a really good jacket will do is capture your attention amidst a sea of other books. It will tease you to pick it up. But persuade you to buy it? No way. There are many, many different factors as to why books sell or don't sell, and I have no idea what they are. I'm glad, actually, that it remains a relatively mysterious process. The last thing I need to have is a formula to guide what I do."

Dust jackets have been with us in one form or other for the better part of two centuries, though in earlier manifestations their function was strictly utilitarian, and they often met the same fate as the candy-bar wrapper—crumpled and tossed in the trash can once the treat is opened and consumed. Over the past eighty years or so, jackets emerged as an essential marketing tool for books, and there have been a number of designers whose work is sufficiently accomplished to be known outside publishing circles and esteemed in its own right.

Among the more venerable practitioners from past decades are William A. Dwiggins, Arthur Hawkins Jr., Ernst Reichl, Paul Rand, George Salter, and Paul Bacon. My personal favorite from that period is Alvin Lustig, creator of a truly splendid series of jackets for the incomparable playwright Tennessee Williams, whose complete oeuvre of searing drama in first-issue copies, I am pleased to say, is among my proudest of possessions.

Lustig's body of work included equally distinctive covers for editions of William Carlos Williams, Franz Kafka, Henry Miller, and Djuna Barnes. They were notable for having introduced graphic techniques from modern art that embodied the frequent use of montage. "Whatever the medium," James Laughlin, the founder of New Directions, marveled in a 1956 tribute to his colleague, who had died the previous year at forty, "he could make it do new things, make it extend itself under the prodding of his imagination." It is partly, perhaps, due to this quality—an exuberant willingness to experiment with media in daringly inventive ways—that accounts for the comparisons that are sometimes made between Lustig's pioneering work from half a century ago, and the trendsetting contributions of Chip Kidd today.

Last year, Kidd celebrated his first two decades in the business with release of a zany retrospective, *Chip Kidd: Book One Work: 1986–2006*, confidently identified as the first installment of an obviously open-ended compilation. Though the book depicts just a sampling of the twelve hundred or so jackets Kidd estimates he has produced over the years for such authors as Cormac McCarthy, Bobbie Ann Mason, Don DeLillo, Michael Ondaatje, Anne Rice, Martin Amis, James Ellroy, Elmore Leonard, Larry McMurtry, Kazuo Ishiguro, Gish Jen, and John le Carré, those pictured are, nonetheless, representative of his reach and versatility.

While dust jackets are indisputably intended to supplement the creative output of someone else—it is the author's work, after all, that is being presented to the reading public for its acclaim and approbation—Kidd's covers have acquired a spirited following, as witnessed at several exhibitions featuring his work, most recently a retrospective at Cooper Union in New York earlier this year. His contributions have even been the subject of a scholarly monograph, *Chip Kidd*, from Yale University Press. The author Véronique Vienne asserts that Chip Kidd—born Charles I. Kidd in 1964, in Shillington, Pennsylvania, the very same Shillington, Pennsylvania, that was the birthplace of John Updike—is "today a figurehead in the highbrow world of literary book jacket design" whose "greatest design influence was daytime television."

Kidd's covers, she writes, are breathtaking for the ways they engage a reader's intelligence and imagination. "Indeed, some of his best jackets are capable of triggering a moment of sheer insight into the nature of the text stowed between the covers. Others are simply elegant collages that suggest that this is the latest offering by a new talented writer."

In some instances—Katherine Dunn's *Geek Love*, for instance, or Rupert Thomson's *The Five Gates of Hell*—Kidd will only use type to project a sense of the content. For William Boyd's novel *Brazzaville Beach*, Kidd came up with a design that suggested an exotic brand of cigarettes, the brand, perhaps, that the heroine

smokes. For Irina Ratushinskaya's memoir of activism in the old Soviet Union, the cover is a collage of scrap paper—the medium used
by the author while confined to prison. Every once in a while one
of Kidd's jackets—the dinosaur silhouette on Michael Crichton's
Jurassic Park is probably the most dramatic example—will become
synonymous with the work itself.

Visual puns, the enlargement of images to the point of abstraction, the manipulation of color, and tinkering with type are
all grist for Kidd's creative mill as well. The one constant he applies—and it is almost embarrassing to have to state it—is that he
always reads the books he is encapsulating visually, a practice that
most of the authors who wrote tributes for his retrospective noted
with gratitude and relief.

"All of the ideas come from the author, and all books are
different, so I take it one case at a time, and everything is in play,"
Kidd told me. "You have to ask yourself: What's it all about? How
is the author approaching the subject matter? Sometimes I might
take a novel and not make it look like a work of fiction at all. And
that approach can work both ways. There was a work of nonfiction
a while back by Robert Polito about the pulp author Jim Thompson.
When you're doing a biography the impulse generally is to find an
interesting picture of the subject, do a type treatment, and that's that.
But Jim Thompson was this crime-writing guy who elevated what he
did into an art form. So for that cover, I could basically deconstruct
and then reconstruct some pulp covers of his books."

The idea that "everything is in play" is another way of acknowl-
edging John Updike's description of him as a "hunter-gatherer" who
is unafraid to exploit "every resource of modern printing," be it
archival photography, digital scans, cutouts, or fluorescent colors.
"There is a playful thinginess and stern dimension of concreteness
to Kidd's designs," he marveled. "In an edgy field, he is not only
edgy but deep."

Appreciative as he is of those words, Kidd does not regard himself as "all that avant-garde or edgy. I do like to think that someone

won't look at a jacket of mine five or ten years from now and say, oh my, that is so dated. That definitely goes into my thought process when designing a book jacket, which is why, to tell you the truth, I think my stuff is rather tame."

HENRY WADSWORTH LONGFELLOW

"Famous Once Again," Smithsonian 37, no. 11 (February 2007).

Even in his later years, Henry Wadsworth Longfellow did not mind birthdays. He inspired others to celebrate right along with him. His seventieth, for example, took on the air of a national holiday, with parades, speeches, and lots of his poetry. "My study is a garden of flowers," he wrote in his journal on February 27, 1877, with "salutations and friendly greetings from far and near" filling his house in Cambridge, Massachusetts.

By then, Longfellow was the superstar of his generation—"the object of a national adulation enjoyed by few poets before or since," according to Andrew R. Hilen, the scholar who edited and annotated an edition of the poet's correspondence. For his seventy-second birthday, local schoolchildren presented him with an armchair crafted from the wood of "the spreading chestnut tree" he had made famous in "The Village Blacksmith."

And the gestures of respect were repeated with regularity. On Longfellow's seventy-fifth birthday, observances were held in such cities as Lockport, New York; Media, Pennsylvania; Westminster, Minnesota; St. Louis, Missouri; and Hiawatha, Kansas, a prairie community that had been named twenty-three years earlier for one of his most endearing literary characters. In Atlanta, some five thousand children participated in various recitations of his poetry. The Boston *Evening Transcript* printed details of similar exercises in Maryland, Illinois, Wisconsin, California, Texas, Alabama, Louisiana, and Maine.

He was dazzlingly prolific, equally adept at prose, drama, and poetry, and a scholar as well; his translation of Dante's *Divine Comedy* was the first in America. He also had the good fortune to come along just as the United States was forming a distinctive cultural identity. "Longfellow did as much as any author or politician of his time to shape the way nineteenth-century Americans saw themselves, their nation and their past," Dana Gioia, chairman of the National Endowment for the Arts, has asserted.

Today, people of a certain age can still recall the Longfellow poetry they memorized as schoolchildren, perhaps passages from "Paul Revere's Ride" or "The Wreck of the Hesperus" or "The Children's Hour." Many more speak of "the patter of little feet" or "ships that pass in the night," or declare, "I shot an arrow into the air," or proclaim that "into each life some rain must fall," without realizing that those words, too, are his. And there are numerous other phrases that slip so easily off the tongue—"One, if by land, and two, if by sea," "Why don't you speak for yourself, John," "When she was good, she was very, very good," "Sail on, O Ship of State!"—that also claim Longfellow as their maker.

At the height of his celebrity, Longfellow's fame was without parallel for a public figure in the United States, and though there were some detractors among his contemporaries—Edgar Allan Poe and Margaret Fuller were among the most critical—the overwhelming consensus was that he was a true American bard. These days, however, even Longfellow's most ardent of admirers acknowledge that his verses were of a particular time, and he has spent the better part of the past century at the margins of public consciousness; if his contemporaries revered him, subsequent generations pushed him aside as a relic.

How Longfellow rose to such dizzying heights—and how the exponents of modernism and new criticism expunged him from the American literary canon several decades after his death—is a case study in the ephemeral nature of celebrity. Yet in light of his two-hundredth birthday this month, Longfellow is looking fresh once again, and while his name is not likely to ever regain its former glory, he is enjoying a modest renaissance in some corners of academe, and his influence on our culture remains rock solid.

To celebrate his bicentennial, the U.S. Postal Service has issued a commemorative stamp—the second to bear his likeness; Herman Melville is the only writer similarly honored. At Harvard University, an exhibition of rare books, documents, correspondence, engravings, photographs, and various artifacts called *Public Poet, Private Man: Henry Wadsworth Longfellow at 200* has been mounted at the Houghton Library. Notable among the curiosities on display is a Chinese folding fan from 1865 with the words of Longfellow's poem "Psalm of Life" written in Chinese characters on the paper folds. In another display case is an ornate pitcher manufactured in England in 1880 by Josiah Wedgwood & Sons; an oval portrait of Longfellow appears on the front, a seven-line excerpt from the poem "Kéramos" is on the rear

A central thrust of the Harvard show, according to Christoph Irmscher, the curator, is to document "the poet's connection with his audience and his efforts to give an international dimension to American literature." Longfellow was not a "stuffy Victorian," he stressed, but a highly motivated writer who "worked hard to professionalize the business of literature and to earn his status as America's first—and most successful to date—celebrity poet." Irmscher is a professor of English at Indiana University and the author of *Longfellow Redux*, a scholarly monograph that argues for a reevaluation of the poet's work.

Curiously, in his ambition, in his approach to fame, and in his connection with his audience, Longfellow can appear quite contemporary, even now, and while his verse may seem somewhat stilted to modern sensibilities, it has not been forgotten. In 2000, the Library of America issued a collection of Longfellow's poems and other writings, the 118th volume issued in its series of canonical works. The editor of the volume was J. D. McClatchy, the noted poet, critic, and lecturer at Yale University who from 1996 to 2003 served as a chancellor of the Academy of American Poets. McClatchy has become a kind of champion of writers who have fallen out of favor, people like Edna St. Vincent Millay and Thornton Wilder, and most assuredly Longfellow.

"Millay and Longfellow are very similar in that they fascinated the people of their own time, enjoyed enormous reputations, and then, when tastes changed, seem to have been not just forgotten, but despised by the modernists, T. S. Eliot and Ezra Pound in particular," McClatchy told me. "With modernism, taste in poetry shifted from history to psychology, from narrative to lyric. All this left Longfellow's achievements high and dry. Victorian poetry in general, and everything that Victorianism stood for—sentimentality, a certain sense of narrative that precluded deep psychologizing—contributed to his decline. Unwittingly, he became the enemy of the new." Yet by the end of 2006, the Library of America edition of his works had gone through four printings, with thirty-seven thousand copies in print. "He wrote poems that have become indelibly fixed in our collective American imagination," McClatchey said. "And that is something that no critic can repudiate or take away."

One of Longfellow's six children, Annie, once compared her father's line of work to that of the commercial fishermen in nearby Nahant, Massachusetts, where the family spent many pleasant summers. "The trade of poet is better," she said, "because you can do it all winter." Longfellow undoubtedly agreed with the precocious child, since he entered her cheerful observation in his daily journal. It was a welcome form of approbation for a man who quite easily could have been a country lawyer like his father, Stephen, who represented Maine in Congress from 1823 to 1825, but Henry had other ideas. "I most eagerly aspire after future eminence in literature, my whole soul burns most ardently for it, and every earthly thought centers on it," he wrote home during his senior year at Bowdoin College.

Born in Portland, Maine, in 1807, he would cite Washington Irving's *Sketchbook of Geoffrey Crayon* as the most influential book of his youth. By the time he was thirteen, he was reading Shakespeare,

Samuel Johnson, John Milton, Alexander Pope, and Edward Gibbon; he had even published his first poem, "The Battle of Lovell's Pond," in the Portland *Gazette*. His Bowdoin acquaintances included Nathaniel Hawthorne, who would become a lifelong friend, and Franklin Pierce, who would become the fourteenth president of the United States.

After receiving his bachelor's degree in 1825, Longfellow spent three years in Europe learning French, Italian, Spanish, German, and Portuguese, then five years teaching European languages at Bowdoin and translating various scholarly texts for classroom use. In 1831, he married Mary Storer Potter, a nineteen-year-old neighbor from Portland, and the daughter of a prominent judge. Three years after that, Harvard College named him Smith Professor of Modern Languages and Belles Lettres. To prepare himself for this exciting new assignment, Longfellow made another trip abroad, this time with his wife. Over the next two years, he added Swedish, Danish, Finnish, Old Icelandic, and Dutch to his repertoire but suffered a grievous loss as well. In 1834, Mary died in Rotterdam after having a miscarriage. It wasn't until 1836 that Longfellow reported to Cambridge, taking a room in an elegant old house on Brattle Street that had served as General Washington's headquarters during the siege of Boston.

As at Bowdoin, he was a popular teacher and energetic scholar, introducing his students to the European forms he had mastered, all the while honing his own literary skills. In 1839, he published two books, *Hyperion: A Romance* and *Voices of the Night*, followed in 1841 by *Ballads and Other Poems*. And he married again, exchanging vows with Frances "Fanny" Appleton. She came from money—her father, the Boston industrialist Nathan Appleton, bought the house on Brattle Street for them as a wedding present—but soon Longfellow was making his own way as a distinguished man of letters.

In 1847, Longfellow published *Evangeline*, the story in verse of an Acadian woman's heartbreaking separation from her bridegroom on their wedding day. It generated six printings in six months. Other successful works followed—*Kavanagh*, a short novel; *The Seaside and the Fireside*, another collection of poetry; and *The Golden Legend*, a medieval tale in verse. By the mid-1850s, Longfellow was financially secure enough to leave Harvard and concentrate on writing. In 1857, *The Song of Hiawatha*, arguably his best-known poem, sold fifty thousand copies, blockbuster numbers for its time. A year after that, *The Courtship of Miles Standish*, a story based loosely on his own Pilgrim ancestors, sold twenty-five thousand copies in the United States within two months—and ten thousand copies in London in a single day. But his sales figures only begin to suggest the impact Longfellow had on nineteenth-century thought; his books remained in print year after year, and many were translated into no fewer than ten foreign languages.

In *Evangeline*, Longfellow created a character whose experiences were based on the expulsion of French-speaking Acadians from modern-day Nova Scotia by the British in 1755; inspired by the wanderings of Homer's Odysseus and Virgil's Aeneas, he gave an epic structure to a local theme. Similarly, Miles Standish and Hiawatha brought a human dimension to the lives of the continent's European settlers and its indigenous people—and let Longfellow achieve his goal of explaining America to Americans through poetry.

Moreover, he proved a shrewd manager of his literary properties. He insisted that inexpensive paperbacks be made readily available and that his poems be widely reproduced in newspapers and on broadsides. His image appeared on cigar boxes, beer bottle labels, inkwells, bookends, lithographic engravings, and even fine china. His magnificent house became a tourist magnet; he kept a stack of autographed cards handy to distribute to the hundreds who came to call. "There is never an hour in the day, when someone is not pounding at the brass knocker of my door," he wrote in a letter to the poet Paul Hamilton Hayne, "never a moment when some unanswered letter is not beckoning to me with its pallid finger."

That grumbling notwithstanding, Longfellow scrupulously answered his mail, sometimes writing up to twenty responses a day. (More than five thousand of his letters were gathered in six volumes published between 1966 and 1982.) He also knew the value of a fascinating new medium, photography: Twelve thousand images, including many of him and his family, are among the some eight hundred thousand documents, household items, artworks, and furnishings maintained by the National Park Service, custodian of his home, called Craigie House, since 1972, when his descendants turned it over to the nation.

Though his celebrity spread to every reach of society, Longfellow enjoyed keeping rarefied company. Among the luminaries to drop by over the years were Mark Twain, Julia Ward Howe, Harriet Beecher Stowe, Anthony Trollope, Ralph Waldo Emerson, and Oscar Wilde; even Dom Pedro II, the emperor of Brazil, and the famous singer Jenny Lind came calling. On November 28, 1867, the most famous novelist on either side of the Atlantic, Charles Dickens, spent Thanksgiving Day with Longfellow, renewing a friendship they had established twenty-five years earlier when the novelist made his first reading tour of the United States and the two men had already achieved international acclaim.

The Englishman had returned to the United States that fall to give a farewell series of readings, and while good cheer was evident everywhere he went, the get-together with Longfellow was bittersweet, at least for Dickens. Six years earlier, Fanny Longfellow had burned to death, apparently after her dress was ignited by wax from a dripping candle as she was sealing a snippet of hair from one of her children in an envelope, though the precise cause was never determined. The accident had occurred in the spacious living room where the two writers gathered to exchange pleasantries.

"He is now white-haired and, white-bearded, but remarkably handsome," Dickens confided in a letter to his son. "He still lives in his old house, where his beautiful wife was burned to death. I dined with him the other day, and could not get the terrific scene out of my imagination."

Indeed, the reason Longfellow grew the long beard Dickens had mentioned—he was clean shaven up until the deadly mishap—was to hide scars suffered while frantically trying to smother the flames with a rug. Another twelve years would pass from the time of Dickens's visit before he was able to deal with the loss in a poem. Here is how "The Cross of Snow" opens:

> In the long, sleepless watches of the night,
> A gentle face—the face of one long dead—
> Looks at me from the wall, where round its head
> The night-lamp casts a halo of pale light.
> Here in this room she died; and soul more white
> Never through martyrdom of fire was led
> To its repose...

In 1868, Longfellow sailed to England, his first trip away from home in twenty-six years. A whirlwind itinerary included stops at Oxford and Cambridge universities to receive honorary degrees, a two-day stay at the home of Alfred, Lord Tennyson, and another evening with Dickens. There was time, too, for breakfast with the prime minister, William Gladstone, and afternoon tea at Windsor Castle with Queen Victoria.

Victoria later confided to her husband's biographer, Theodore Martin, that while she and Longfellow walked down a corridor, "I noticed an unusual interest among the attendants and servants. I could scarcely credit that they so generally understood who he was. When he took leave, they concealed themselves in places from which they could get a good look at him as he passed. I have since inquired among them, and am surprised and pleased to find that many of his poems are familiar to them. No other distinguished person has come here that has excited so peculiar an interest."

After his death on March 24, 1882, at seventy-five, dozens of memorials were erected throughout the United States. A national campaign to fund a bronze statue to be unveiled at Dupont Circle in Washington, D.C., was chaired by Theodore Roosevelt. In England, Longfellow became the first American to be honored with a marble bust in Poet's Corner at Westminster Abbey, his likeness enshrined alongside that of Geoffrey Chaucer. "Never had a poet been so widely loved," Charles Eliot Norton declared in an essay that commemorated the centennial of Longfellow's birth, "never was the death of a poet so widely mourned."

Widely, but not forever. Longfellow seems to have understood the vicissitudes of fame as well as anyone. His first book of consequence, the travelogue *Outre-Mer: A Pilgrimage Beyond the Seas*, published when he was twenty-eight, concluded with a prophetic riff: "Dost thou covet fame?" he asked. "This little book is but a bubble on the stream; and although it may catch the sunshine for a moment, yet it will soon float down the swift-rushing current, and be seen no more!"

Still, Longfellow did what he could to hold the sunshine as long as possible. When he died, he even left behind a collection of pencil stubs wrapped in pieces of paper identifying, in his handwriting, the works that he had composed with each one.

"Above all, Longfellow wrote poems that were meant to be enjoyed," Christoph Irmscher said. "Storytelling, unfortunately, goes against the modernist belief that in order to be any good a poem has to be concise and compressed and difficult to figure out." Perhaps Longfellow provided his own best summary in "A Psalm of Life":

> Lives of great men all remind us
> We can make our lives sublime,
> And, departing, leave behind us
> Footprints on the sands of time.

BREON MITCHELL

"Just the Right Word," Fine Books & Collections, no. 16 (July/August 2005).

I f I were asked to name a private collection assembled on a modest budget that has the potential to become an important resource at a major research institution, I would cite as my prime example Breon Mitchell's two thousand dictionaries of exotic languages.

The idea that Mitchell—an educator, translator, and since 2001, director of the Lilly Library at Indiana University—is a bibliophile of the first rank ought not to surprise anyone. He is custodian of one of the great rare-book and manuscripts collections to be found in North America. But in the case of his dictionaries, gathered over the past decade, his passion transcends professional responsibility and is decidedly personal—a combining, as it were, of intellectual rigor with human nature.

"I've been collecting since I was fourteen years old," Mitchell told me in the first of two conversations we have had for use in my book *Every Book Its Reader: The Power of the Printed Word to Stir the World*. We were talking in those interviews primarily about his work as a mediator of literary texts. Of particular interest to me were his rendering of Franz Kafka's *The Trial* into English and his belief that new translations of timeless works amount essentially to new works of art. But his activity as a determined book hunter kept entering the discourse, as it inevitably does in discussions like this.

Mitchell told me how, in 1965, while studying at Oxford University as a Rhodes scholar, he had come to buy a book of uncommon antiquarian interest. In that instance, a prior owner of a German-language edition of Thomas Carlyle's life of Frederick the Great was chillingly established by a bookplate affixed to the front pastedown featuring a swastika, an eagle in profile, and the engraved name of Adolf Hitler.

What made this a really good collecting story was the fact that the leather-bound history had been gathering dust on a shelf for years in the London shop of Maggs Bros., on Berkeley Square. Snapping it up for £5, Mitchell later determined from a reading of Hugh Trevor-Roper's *The Last Days of Hitler* (1947) that this was a well-worn copy of Hitler's favorite book. Joseph Goebbels also had a copy of this book, and he read aloud from it to his doomed führer as Berlin was about to fall to the Allies, making the Mitchell find an association item of no small consequence.

That, of course, was a story of serendipity, one of those you-gotta-be-kidding-me eureka moments that every collector dreams about having. The activity I found most interesting to discuss, however, was Mitchell's systematic assembly of obscure dictionaries. His interest in lexicons grew out of his interest in linguistics and translation and his work as a professor of Germanic studies and comparative literature at Indiana, a position he still holds in addition to his duties at the Lilly.

"I started out to collect one dictionary for every language in the world, but then it became much more interesting to get the *first* dictionaries published," he explained of his purpose. "Then I decided to limit myself to non-European languages and living languages. A further limitation was that I wasn't going to collect any of the major languages of the world either, regardless of geography, and I would be the one to decide which are the major languages, based on the number of people who are speaking them."

What Mitchell was doing, obviously, was what every deliberate collector must do, which is to establish a focus and define the parameters. By excluding all major languages, moreover, he could do something that just might have relevance down the road as a collection that would complement, not replicate, the holdings of an institution such as the Lilly, which, as it turns out, will receive the books as a gift from Mitchell. "A collection like this needs to be in an institution," he said, pointing out that a number of the dictionaries he has acquired do not appear to be represented in any other research library.

"There are some other collections of dictionaries, but they generally focus on a particular language or two. I know of no institution that is specifically building a dictionary collection at all like this one, so there is a definite utility to it."

Mitchell said that there are more than six thousand active languages in the world, most of which have no dictionary at all. "The number of languages for which a dictionary exists is probably around 1,000, though it could be as many as 1,500." The last relevant compilation—indeed, the only one—was done in 1958 by Wolfram Zaunmüller, a German scholar, whose *Bibliographisches Handbuch der Sprachwörterbücher* is woefully out of date.

"I am making a database of my own collection, and one of the things I want to do is put together a bibliography continuing Zaunmüller to the present," Mitchell said. Most of Mitchell's dictionaries are bilingual and represent languages spoken on all inhabited continents, with English, French, Spanish, German, Italian, Portuguese, or Russian typically being the second language. The vast majority of these, he said, have traditionally been prepared over the years by three distinct groups: missionaries, explorers, and the military. With the rise of linguistics as an academic field, professional linguists are now producing most of the new dictionaries, he added.

"I was interested at first in what we might call the exotic languages or rare languages spoken by very few people. But some of these languages we might think of as rare are in fact spoken by millions," he said, citing the languages of the Indian subcontinent, of native or indigenous populations of the Western hemisphere, and of African regions as examples. "There are more than eight hundred different languages in Papua New Guinea alone, which is the only country in the world, by the way, in which pidgin English is an official language." Thus, Mitchell admits another category to his shelves: pidgin and creole languages.

In New Guinea, pidgin English is known as Tok Pisin, and a dictionary Mitchell has of the dialect was prepared in 1943 for use during the war with Japan. It includes lists of phrases along with admonishments to servicemen not to be "the first to walk across a stream near the coast"—a warning to be wary of crocodiles—followed by the suggestion to "always have a native cross first."

Pasigraphy—a system that "teaches people to communicate with one another in writing by means of numbers, which convey the same ideas in all languages"—is represented by an 1871 book. "Under this system, you would say 'I love you' with the numbers 1605, 1895, and 709," Mitchell said, not needing to add that this unorthodox proposal for a universal language fell by the wayside.

Another example of an artificial language is Bolak, or the "blue language." According to Mitchell, the French preface to the only Bolak dictionary describes the language as a "new international idiom" that takes "only a few minutes to learn" and that is accessible "to any person of moderate intelligence," so long as that person is prepared to apply one rule: "facility."

Mitchell's copy of an 1861 Zulu–English dictionary with ten thousand entries contains numerous annotations and corrections inserted by the book's former owner, A. N. Montgomery, an author of books related to South African history. Mitchell's copy of the 1878 revised edition of the dictionary is annotated and signed by its black African printer.

"I also collect Gypsy languages and Inuit languages," Mitchell said. "I have a very early Eskimo dictionary—a Latin–Greenlandic–Eskimo dictionary, printed in 1804 in Copenhagen." He has Australian aboriginal dictionaries and a dictionary of Tokelauan, the language used by native peoples in New Zealand, American Samoa, and other Pacific islands. Another dictionary, of Rapa Nui, is the "first two-way dictionary of the language of Easter Island." Yet another: a copy of the "first and only dictionary" of Nyoro, a Bantu language spoken by more than five hundred thousand people living east of Lake Albert in Uganda.

Mitchell estimates his holdings of Native American dictionaries at more than 125 languages, including one, of the Otchipwe language, acquired at Sotheby's in the Frank T. Seibert sale in 1999 for $4,312.50, the most he has spent for any book in the collection. "With the help of the Internet, I was able to collect broadly around the world and assemble a really fine collection within about two years for very little money," he said. He also noted that he has used all other conventional methods as well, including the development of good relationships with booksellers and the prowling of junk shops and antique stores.

In one instance, a dealer in South Africa asked a basic question: "Who are you, and why are you suddenly buying books that nobody else in the world seems interested in?" When you think about it, the simple answer to both queries pretty much summarizes the true spirit of book collecting at its most satisfying level.

MINOR MYERS JR.

"Preserving the Creative Wisdom of the Past," Biblio 2, no. 5 (May 1997).

O ne of the cornerstone precepts of book collecting is the need to establish a focus, a thoroughly sensible premise that holds that a person who gathers indiscriminately and without direction is little more than an accumulator.

A focus can be as finely defined as the works of one author, or just the various editions of a single book. One enterprising collector in the Midwest, for instance, has put together the quintessential collection of *Alice's Adventures in Wonderland*, more than a thousand copies in numerous editions and languages of Lewis Carroll's timeless tale of childhood whimsy. This collector, a completist if ever there was one, has even commissioned a translation of the book into Yiddish, since none in the language has appeared thus far in print.

At the opposite extreme is the vast library of children's literature assembled by the California philanthropist Lloyd E. Cotsen that documents the last five centuries of illustrated children's literature, including many pertinent drawings, prints, manuscripts, games, puzzles, hornbooks, and toys along with thousands of books. In 1994, Cotsen presented the collection he began assembling more than thirty-five years ago with his late wife, Jo Anne, to Princeton University, where it will form a rich nucleus of research materials for scholars and students and become a "living library" that also will reach out to primary and secondary school children.

From these two examples alone, there quite obviously is a world of possibilities for collectors to pursue. What matters most in the exercise is a lively imagination and an open mind. Minor Myers Jr., president of Illinois Wesleyan University in Bloomington, Illinois, provides an interesting case study of how a collector's focus can represent a certain attitude, and how it can work in many exciting ways to preserve the creative wisdom of another time.

Myers has many interests, a good deal of them consistent with the activities of a person involved as both teacher and administrator at a liberal arts institution of 1,900 students. Among his personal pastimes—*hobby* is far too tame a word—is being intellectually engaged by eighteenth-century music and culture and finding materials printed during that period to illumine them. An amateur harpsichordist, he has collected what he likes to call an "orchestra with no players," an ensemble of "fourteen violins, three violas, two cellos and a bunch of other stuff," all made before 1820. His dream is to form a group of like-minded musicians who will play the forgotten scores he has rescued, in some cases from the scrap heap, on these instruments and give them new life.

"Antiquarian music is just a part of what I collect," Myers said one snowy night over cocktails and dinner at the University Club in Chicago. Our meeting, it bears noting, was arranged by Chef Louis Szathmáry, a mutual friend and great champion of books and book culture, a few weeks before his death. "The one area I pursue with unbridled enthusiasm is the eighteenth century, and that means the whole of it," Myers said. "Anything I can find. Everything I can find. I am interested in music, and I have a special fascination for early violins, but I am fascinated by material from the eighteenth century just for itself. It doesn't have to mean anything or be anything. My motto boils down to this: Anything I can find eighteenth century and cheap, I will buy. Anything. Anywhere. Japan, China, Europe, it doesn't matter. I want to have it."

But why, the question was asked, the eighteenth century in particular, and not something closer to our time, like the nineteenth, or something more remote, such as the seventeenth? "Why do some people like vanilla and not chocolate?" he answered with a shrug. "I don't know. I suppose, probably, because it's a lot closer than the seventeenth century, which means the likelihood of finding more material is greater. But the larger reality is that as a child I formed a fascination for that whole period of colonial America and the American Revolution, and that grew into a fascination not only for the history, but the music, the art, the architecture, and virtually every aspect of what seems still to be the classic taste."

A native of Akron, Ohio, Myers received a bachelor's degree from Carleton College in Northfield, Minnesota, in 1964. After spending a year at Duke University in Durham, North Carolina, he transferred to Princeton University, where he earned master's and doctorate degrees in politics and political philosophy. Before assuming the presidency of Illinois Wesleyan University, he held a variety of teaching and administrative positions at Connecticut College in New London, Connecticut, and Hobart and William Smith Colleges in Geneva, New York.

The impulse to collect began at an early age. Every place Myers has studied, every place he has worked, and every place he has visited have afforded him an opportunity to seek out material, be they the flea markets of New England, the yard sales and library sales of the Midwest, the secondhand bookstores of the West Coast, or the antiquarian bookstores of New York City. When he was a student at Princeton in the 1960s, he used to go into Manhattan and call on David Kirschenbaum, the founder of Carnegie Book Shop who remained active in the business to his death in 1994 at the age of ninety-nine.

"On a whim, I went in to see him just a few months before he died—I had no idea, in fact, that he was still in business until I found him by chance in the phone book—and bought all kinds of wondrous things. These were obscure items that undoubtedly had been gathering dust for years, an autographed letter by John Stuart Mill, something else by an English admiral, neither one in the best of shape, but for $5 each, I wasn't going to quibble. There was a wonderful ink drawing of Paganini dancing on a violin, $10, and an English copybook of eighteenth-century poems and letters.

It was a memorable day of picking up things I least expected to find, and Dave was clearly interested in parking them someplace where somebody wanted to have them."

Myers takes special pleasure in finding music composed in the eighteenth century by people largely forgotten by historians and in seeing what the pieces sound like when brought to life on his own 1787 harpsichord. Among a stack of miscellaneous pieces he bought in France recently were some concerti composed in the mid-1700s by Richard Mudge, an English clergyman and graduate of Pembroke College, Oxford University.

"Mudge's father was a friend of Samuel Johnson's, and I knew of him slightly as one of the lesser-known British composers, someone who had heard Handel on many occasions. When I called Pembroke College, they knew next to nothing about him; he was lost, in other words, even to people at his own college, and it happens that his work is very interesting. What I'm hoping is that we can put on a performance of some of his music at Illinois Wesleyan. He may have been lost, but now he's been found."

Myers is equally enthusiastic about works by two eighteenth-century composers of African descent, Joseph de Boulogne, a man born in the Caribbean who became known as the Chevalier de Saint-Georges in France, and Ignatius Sancho, a son of slaves who made his way from Jamaica to England, where he wrote a number of minuets and dances that were popular in their time, but are unknown today. "They both have strong links to the Caribbean, where they remain little known. They can offer a whole depth to Caribbean culture as it explores its roots."

Other composers represented in Myers's collection include William Hamilton Bird, a Scottish military officer whose travels to India enabled him to transcribe native music so it could be played on the harpsichord, and Sir William Herschel, a German-born British astronomer who discovered the planet Uranus and spent a good deal of time composing music. Another item in Myers's collection, something, in fact, he hopes the university's music and drama departments will mount as a production, is *Lord of the Manor*, a ballad opera written in 1781 by John Burgoyne, the British Army general who fought at Bunker Hill, took Ticonderoga, and surrendered to General Horatio Gates at Saratoga.

While every collector covets completeness and perfect condition, Myers said the age and scarcity of the material he collects very often precludes the acquisition of pristine copies, and that he is grateful for what he is able to find. He recalled a recent discovery in London of "miscellaneous parts" of some eighteenth-century compositions at a secondhand bookstore. He explained what these are: "Let's say you have an orchestra, and you've got a couple of violins, a couple of violas, cellos, bases, horns, and flutes. What you find may be the music for the flute part, and the rest of the piece is missing. You still buy it anyway. You don't ignore it because it is incomplete. If you look at the catalogs of institutions that collect music, like the British Museum, you sometimes will see how thrilled they are just to have the viola part, for example, or the cello part. They don't have anything else from a particular symphony; yet they're happy to have whatever fragment they've got."

The beauty of collecting like this, Myers said, is that it imposes no restrictions whatsoever on his technique. "That's the most exciting aspect of bringing home a pile of miscellaneous stuff. You don't really know what it is until you've had a chance to sort through it all and see what you've got. I've been very lucky. I get these things, and then I get curious."

By admitting the full scope of the eighteenth century into his domain, Myers has found himself learning about such things as the layout of ornamental gardens, the design of country houses, ornithology, theories of mathematics, and the preparation of food. "Essentially, my cookery collection is an attempt to understand English cookery in the time of Handel and Haydn," he said.

"In the eighteenth century, the basic outline for music and for food was the same: Add such ornaments as you will to make the piece the way you like it. When the eighteenth-century cookery writers produced their books, they told you to add salt, pepper, or nutmeg. They didn't say anything about how much to put in; that was left to the judgment of the artist. Creating early music and creating eighteenth-century cuisine are absolutely parallel in every way. There's a wonderful line from Sherlock Holmes that applies here, I think. Watson says, 'Well Holmes, I was with you the entire time, how did you see all this?' And Holmes says, 'My dear Watson, we saw the same things, I simply observed them differently.' So, the more you see things in a different way, the more observations you are likely to make."

As consuming as the eighteenth century may be for Myers, it has not stopped him from developing other collections. A recent area of interest involves what he calls his music theater in Chicago collection. "We have a program at Illinois Wesleyan in music theater in the School of Art and the School of Drama, and so far, the library hasn't had too much of a collection of music theater material. So one day I'm at a flea market, and I say, 'I wonder how many examples of music theater can I get in piles of sheet music that are real cheap?' I find when I'm there a show from Chicago with music by Gustaf Leuters, and words by Frank Pixley, who it turns out worked with my grandfather in the newspaper business in Akron back in the 1880s. I later learned that on the side he used to write the words for musicals. This led me to get interested in Chicago theater. I just started doing this because I was finding the stuff and nobody else had it. I pay about fifty cents to a dollar for the items I buy; it may well be true that I'm the only person alive who is collecting them."

So far, Myers has gathered the music of about 120 shows that originated in Chicago during the late nineteenth and early twentieth centuries and has researched their performance histories. A few, like *Babes in Toyland* (1903), with music by Victor Herbert and lyrics by Glen MacDonough, have familiar names, but most, like *Fun in a School Room* (1907) and *The Flirting Princess* (1909) have dimmed with the passage of time. "There was a show called *The Winning Mists*, that I think is a very good subset for Chicago musical theater,"

Myers said. "It was great out here, but it kind of missed when it got to New York." Meanwhile, a colleague at the university is making plans to mount student productions of some of these musicals.

What is evident from all this is that Myers sets no rigid limits on where his quixotic spirit might take him, and the philosophy he applies to his collecting has influenced the direction he has charted for Illinois Wesleyan University. At a time when so many colleges and universities are backing away from enlarging conventional libraries in favor of more electronic services, he has put in place a program that will double the institution's holdings of printed books and has established a fund that he hopes will get it done.

"This is a systematic buildup, and the faculty will make proposals for areas they want to strengthen," Myers said. "We're getting things that we might have bought five and ten and fifteen years ago, but for lack of money were unable to acquire. Still, we have consultants who come in and say, 'You don't need any more books, what you need is more computers and a basic collection of *good* books.' My answer to that is, 'Tell me, sir, what is a *bad* book that we should not have?' The standard on some campuses has become: 'You don't need to keep a book that nobody has checked out for five years.' And my response there is that when you deaccession things, you are doing it for centuries, not just for this week's shelf. Once we throw something out, it's gone forever."

NOTE
Minor Myers Jr.—who never smoked a cigarette in his life—died in 2003 at the age of sixty after a long battle with lung cancer. After selecting one thousand volumes from his library for its permanent collections, Illinois Wesleyan University sold the remainder—about eleven thousand volumes—at public auction two years later.

Robert Sabuda

"The Prince of Pop-ups," Fine Books & Collections, no. 19 (January/February 2006)

There is a hilarious scene in the Mel Brooks film *Robin Hood: Men in Tights* in which Richard the Lionheart, played masterfully by Patrick Stewart, exercises his royal prerogative to kiss Maid Marian with a passionate flourish before she is permitted to exchange wedding vows with the dashing Prince of Thieves. "It's good to be the king," the Brooks character, Rabbi Tuckman, deadpans to the camera, a sentiment that few of us can argue with, and one that Robert Sabuda, creator of pop-up books par excellence, accepts with grace and aplomb.

In fewer than fifteen years of creating three-dimensional books of matchless imagination and dexterity, the forty-year-old Pinckney, Michigan, native is master of all he surveys, acclaimed by critics, colleagues, and collectors alike as the outstanding paper engineer of his generation and quite possibly one of the best of all time. When you consider that books with movable elements have been with us for hundreds of years that is quite a claim to make.

"He's the gold standard," Ann Montanaro, founder of the Movable Book Society, told me one night during a book function in Princeton, New Jersey. "Robert Sabuda is in a class completely by himself."

I have quietly assembled a modest pop-up collection over the past twenty-five years, and I share Montanaro's high regard for Sabuda's work. This past October, I jumped at the opportunity to meet with him in New York, an interview occasioned by the simultaneous releases of *Encyclopedia Prehistorica: Dinosaurs* and

Winter's Tale, his latest tours de force. We met in the compact studio he maintains on the Upper West Side of Manhattan with his partner and occasional collaborator, Matthew Reinhart, a former graduate student at the Pratt Institute in Brooklyn and now an accomplished paper engineer in his own right

Though traditionally marketed as children's books, pop-ups enjoy a following among adults that borders on the fanatical and are the focus of many serious collections both private and institutional, with excellent examples to be found at the University of Virginia in Charlottesville and the Lilly Library at Indiana University.

From the appearance of his first professional pop-up book in 1994—a sublime production called *The Christmas Alphabet* that daringly featured twenty-six ingenious paper shapes presented entirely in white—Sabuda has broken new ground with each succeeding effort. Arguably his most impressive achievement is a spread in his *Alice's Adventures in Wonderland* that unleashes a soaring arc of 104 playing cards that snap to life as the pages are opened. Some aficionados will claim as their favorite the swirling tornado that roars through the first fold of Sabuda's visualization of *The Wonderful Wizard of Oz,* while others will point to the magnificent tableaux he fashioned of the Golden Gate Bridge, the Capitol, and a Manhattan skyline for *America the Beautiful* or to Santa's reindeer-drawn sleigh in *The Night Before Christmas.* The fact is, all are architectural marvels.

With more than twenty distinctive creations to his credit, Sabuda is quick to point out that if he is indeed the king of the hill, it is a hill populated by very few practitioners. "There are maybe three dozen of us in the world doing this professionally," he said. Sabuda speculated that the paucity of the talent pool is a reality driven not by a lack of audience—his books have first printings these days of two hundred thousand copies and number more than two million copies in print—but by the exacting nature of what he does. Typically, each project consumes a year of tracing, cutting, folding, fitting, nesting, and gluing together paper figures. "Paper engineering takes a certain temperament, I guess, because so much of your time is spent conceptualizing and solving problems."

Sabuda cited an early fascination with "movement and learning how things are put together" for nudging him toward his calling. Just as consequential was his natural talent for drawing, which caught the eye of a high school teacher who recommended him for admission to the Pratt Institute. He now teaches a course in paper engineering there, grants internships to worthy students, and hires graduates to work in his studio.

Because he learned his craft without the benefit of formal guidance, Sabuda is eager to pass on the skills he has mastered. "I am without mentor," he said, noting that his proficiency was developed through trial and error and that only after he began to publish pop-up books did he begin to meet other paper engineers, most of them unofficial members of what he called an "old boy" network. "Not long after I got started, one of the old boys took me aside and said, 'Don't ever share these secrets with anyone.' Well, my feeling is that you have a responsibility to give back. If someone in this studio can do this better than me, I say, 'Hallelujah, have at it.' We work by committee here, and that's pretty unusual to find in an artistic community."

Most of today's pop-ups are produced in Asia and Latin America at costs that allow them to be sold for less than $30 each. "All of this work is done by hand," Sabuda explained, noting that two hundred thousand copies can require the labor of a thousand people.

Sabuda and Reinhart showed me a number of projects they were working on, each in various stages of development. *Sharks*—a sequel to *Dinosaurs*—was ready to go into production. Still being developed was *Mommy?*, a book inspired by Arthur Yorinks's play *It's Alive!*, with pop-ups based on illustrations by the incomparable Maurice Sendak.

"All my sketches start in 3-D," Sabuda said, and he showed me some rough constructions in white card stock of a few ideas he was working on. "Truth be known, we really work in four dimensions, since we have to account for what happens when the book is opened, which requires us to consider the additional element of time. In that second [or] second and a half, things need clearance, things move, things have to fold exactly the way you want them to. Some people will open the book quickly, others more slowly, and the book will respond differently to the ways it is handled, and it has to open upside down as well as right side up."

Sabuda said he constantly tries to design paper sculptures that require the viewer to intuit what they represent by their shape and form and that he is always thinking about the interplay of light and shadow. "You can see through a three-dimensional space, and sometimes, depending on the narrative, the eye is overwhelmed with color. It can be the space; it can be the paper moving, turning, or twisting. I am fascinated by that process, especially when it's white."

Where Sabuda's creative vision will take him is anybody's guess, but whatever he does in the future will always reflect the person he is at that particular moment. "What remains constant is that I have always been a book person and have always loved books for the stories and the pictures, but even more for the object—the artifact. I want to hear the pages turn. I want to feel them. On my tombstone, I want only the words 'Robert Sabuda, bookmaker.'"

LOUIS SZATHMÁRY

"The Matter of the Books," Biblio 2, no. 2 (February 1997).

The community of bibliophiles lost a legend from its ranks on October 4, 1996, with the passing, after a brief illness, of Louis I. Szathmáry II, seventy-seven, a restaurateur, teacher, writer, philanthropist, and dedicated collector whose passion for life and learning inspired everyone who knew him.

A native of Hungary, Chef Louis earned a master's degree in journalism and a doctorate in psychology at the University of Budapest. Born on a freight train in 1919 while his family was fleeing invading Soviet troops, he spent his childhood in the rural home of his grandfather, a determined bibliophile in his own right, where Chef Louis recalled always being surrounded by books. "I played with books, grew up among books, and lived with books," he wrote in an essay in *Biblio* magazine, barely hinting at the lamentable episodes of history that later made him a displaced person whose home and library were among the countless casualties of the Second World War.

That is because grumbling about what once was and what might have been was not a part of Chef Louis's buoyant temperament, something I learned during my very first conversation with him one September evening in 1990 in a cavernous warehouse in Providence, Rhode Island. Our meeting that night was occasioned by the arrival a few days earlier of an enormous collection of books and artifacts at Johnson & Wales University, the world's largest school devoted to the food and service industry, which had bestowed upon Szathmáry the coveted title of chef laureate. Sixteen tractor-trailer trucks had ferried the objects from Chef Louis's adopted home in Chicago halfway across the country to this historic New England city, where in due course they would become known as the Szathmáry Culinary Arts Collection. "Just the tip of the iceberg," he said with a wink of his hazel eyes, waving at cheese graters, meat grinders, nutcrackers, raisin seeders, chocolate molds, fruit choppers, cherry pitters, coffee mills, ice cream scoops, and other antique culinary devices lying in boxes throughout the building. He had spent forty years gathering these items, some two hundred thousand of them, along with several distinguished book collections that he also was in the process of giving away to various institutions.

"I only look ahead," he said softly when I asked him to describe the books he had lost forty-five years earlier in Europe. "We have this attitude in the old country, which is enforced by history and by nature, that says there are times when we must look in the mirror to make sure there are no eyes in the back of our heads. We feel that if God wants us to keep looking back, He would give us at least one eye for that purpose. But we have both of our eyes, and they are not looking behind us or to the sides, but to the front. That is the message—that we should look forward, not backward. Instead of crying about what we lost, we learn what to do for the future."

When Louis Szathmáry sailed to New York from Bremerhaven, Germany, aboard the USS *General Hersey* in 1951, all he carried with him, he was pleased to recall, was $1.20 in cash in his pocket, plus "one change of underwear, two pairs of socks, one Sunday suit, and fourteen books in my trunk." The books, he told me, included a Bible he had received as a child, three books on Mozart, several volumes of Hungarian poetry, and a couple of titles he had acquired from other emigrants before departing for America. Of the thousands of books he would give away in the ensuing years, those fourteen were the only ones he could not bear to part with during his lifetime. "This is what I wanted with me in America," he said. "My books on Mozart, the greatest Hungarian poets, and my Bible."

Nevertheless, his abiding pleasure remained the constant search for books, an activity he pursued with renewed vigor once settled in the United States. "I spent hours in dingy little bookshops, climbing ladders or standing on stacks of dusty boxes to search high shelves," he recalled. "I rummaged through books in bins, on tables outside the door, and amid the garbage that accumulates in the back of used bookshops. I found treasures—valuable items—because I had the time."

Chef Louis's first eight years in America were occupied with working at a variety of jobs in the Northeast, concentrating on the food business, and cooking in restaurants and corporate dining rooms. He moved to Chicago in 1959 as manager of product development for Armour and Co., coming up with ideas for new foods and ways to prepare them. He is credited with improving the freeze-drying process that is used by many food manufacturers today and for designing a kitchen for military field hospitals that could be dropped by parachute and assembled in combat zones. In 1962, he and his wife, Sadako Tanino, opened a restaurant, called the Bakery, on Chicago's near north side close to Lincoln Park. The unpretentious storefront eatery became famous for its continental menu, particularly the filet of beef Wellington, a dish he had invented while still at Armour. "The food critics make fun of it," he liked to quip, "but the food critics can't tell shiitake from Shinola." Sales figures for the restaurant seemed to back him up; over the twenty-six years of its existence, the Bakery served more than one million beef Wellington dinners.

A lifelong scholar, Chef Louis applied his voracious appetite for knowledge to the study of culinary history and food preparation and used as source material the vast library of books he housed in thirty-one rooms he kept just for that purpose above his restaurant. Books he wrote himself included *The Chef's Secret Cook Book*, *Sears Gourmet Cooking Forum*, *American Gastronomy*, *The Chef's New Secret Cook Book*, and *The Bakery Restaurant Cookbook*. He also was editor of the Cookery America and Antique American Cookbooks series, and he wrote more than five hundred professional articles for a variety of food-service publications. A syndicated "Chef Louis" column appeared in more than one hundred newspapers nationwide.

As he approached his seventieth birthday in 1989, Chef Louis announced that he would close the Bakery, which by then was acclaimed as a local institution, a "gastronomic landmark," according to *Gourmet* magazine. As a tribute to the chef, the Chicago City Council renamed the road behind the building Szathmáry Lane. Closing the restaurant was one thing; however, retirement was quite another. Chef Louis continued to operate Szathmáry Associates, a food system design and management consulting business, and devoted increasing amounts of time to what he described to me as "the matter of the books."

"I can count," he said evenly in his heavily accented English, and by that he meant the fleeting years of his life, not the volumes on his shelves. Among his first acts of "retirement" was the gift of twenty-two thousand rare cookbooks to the University of Iowa, some of them going back many centuries, making the institution, overnight, "a major research center in the culinary arts," according to David Schoonover, the curator of rare books there. Especially exciting, Schoonover pointed out, was the many scholarly applications the new collection made possible for students and researchers. The evolution of food and culture, for instance, applies to anthropology; types of foods and where they grow is agriculture; the importing and exporting of foodstuffs is economic history; how people have perceived food is folklore; how food is dealt with by artists and composers is cultural history; food as remedies is the history of medicine. "The Szathmáry Collection of Culinary Arts provides excellent source material in all of these areas," Schoonover enthused at the time. "And it came to us as a 100 percent gift."

Every collector dreams of seeing the books he or she has gathered with such taste and discrimination over a lifetime go on to productive use in the care of other custodians. It was with great satisfaction, then, that Chef Louis witnessed inauguration of the Iowa Szathmáry Culinary Arts Series of books published by the University of Iowa Press. Each title places into print an unusually interesting rarity from the collection he donated to that institution. Books released so far include *The Khwan Niamut, or Nawab's Domestic Cookery,* a collection of Persian recipes from the household of Qasim Uli Khan, first published in Calcutta in 1839; *Receipts of Pastry & Cookery for the Use of His Scholars,* a facsimile edition of original recipes dictated by the late-seventeenth- and early-eighteenth-century English cooking teacher Edward Kidder; *America Eats,* a collection of Midwestern recipes gathered during the 1930s as a Work Progress Administration project by the noted Chicago writer Nelson Algren and acquired in typescript by Chef Louis in the 1960s; and *To Set Before the King,* some two hundred recipes from a kitchen notebook compiled by Katharina Schratt, which Chef Louis bought at an estate auction in 1970. Schratt was a friend, companion, and confidante of emperor Franz Joseph I, who ruled Austria and Hungary from 1848 until 1916.

And there were other bequests of comparable degree. To the University of Chicago, Chef Louis gave some twelve thousand volumes from what he called his Hungarology collection, and another ten thousand to Indiana University. Several thousand menus went to the University of Nevada at Las Vegas, and a small collection of Franz Liszt's letters went to Boston University. Undoubtedly the donation that gave him the most personal pleasure, though, was the treasure trove of historical miscellanea he gave to create the Culinary Archives and Museum at Johnson & Wales University in Rhode Island, which has been attracting thousands of visitors and rave reviews since opening to the public six years ago. One writer for *Country Collectibles* magazine called it a "dream-come-true for people who are fond of kitchen gadgets, food packaging, pictures, and memorabilia."

Increasing amounts of Chef Louis's time were spent supervising installation of his pride and joy in Rhode Island, lecturing throughout the country, and working on new projects that had engaged his attention. One collection-within-the-collection he was uncommonly proud of was a gathering of letters, invitations, wine lists, and various documents relating to food and hospitality in every American presidency, "from George to George" he used to say during the administration of President Bush. Among several hundred pertinent items is one of three existing menus from Abraham Lincoln's second inauguration dinner. Another, in George Washington's handwriting, is a list of table china our first chief executive inherited from a relative. A penciled note from Ulysses S. Grant to his wife, Julia, asks that two bottles of champagne be sent to the Oval Office.

Chef Louis spent so much time in Rhode Island in recent years that the Johnson & Wales officials offered him the use of a house near campus. He declined the offer, choosing instead to stay in dormitories with students whenever he visited and eating with them in school dining halls. Barbara Kuck, one of the sixty-eight foster children he put through prep school and college over the years, is now director of the Culinary Archives & Museum in Providence. Kuck was at Chef Louis's bedside during his final illness, reading favorite books to him and talking about upcoming projects.

When word of his death was announced, John A. Yena, president of Johnson & Wales University, said, "Chef Louis was our teacher, our benefactor, our chef. But above all, he was a friend to all of us and especially a friend to every student."

A few weeks before his death, Chef Louis called to inquire about the progress I was making on my new book. After listening to what I was doing, he offered some sage suggestions and invited me to visit with him in Chicago to conduct some interviews that he would arrange. When I told him about my plans to visit a number of historic libraries in Europe, he added a few that I had failed to mention. "Make me one promise," he said. "When you go to these sacred places, make sure you take your wife with you. This is an experience that must be shared with someone you love."

I recalled then—as I have recalled many times since my first meeting with this delightful, compassionate, brilliant man with the big white mustache—what he said when I asked how it feels to give away books that were such an indelible part of his generous soul.

"The books I give away now, they stay in my heart, just like all the others," he explained with customary simplicity. "I don't have to see them to love them."

SUSAN JAFFE TANE

"Shuddering at Incompleteness," Fine Books & Collections, no. 25 (January/February 2007).

Consider the following story of how a woman bought her first rare book, and tell me with a straight face that it doesn't have a familiar ring to it. You can change the time, place, and circumstances of the acquisition, you can adjust the price that was paid, but the emotional process that drove the transaction should resonate with anyone who has ever crossed the line from appreciative reader to serious collector.

"I live in New York, and I was at the big antiques show they have every fall at the Seventh Regiment Armory on Park Avenue," Susan Jaffe Tane told me in a recent conversation about her initiation into the world of the gently mad, recalling the experience with such clarity it could have happened a week earlier, not in 1987.

"I was wandering around, just window-shopping, enjoying myself. As a girl growing up on Long Island, I had always collected all sorts of things—seashells, matchbooks, swizzle sticks, postcards, you name it—but never books. I have always read, and books have always been an important part of my life, but until that moment, everything I bought was for use and for reading, and I had no qualms about giving books away once I was finished with them."

But when she walked by the booth of the 19th Century Shop, a rare-book dealer from Baltimore, she spotted a "magnificent" first-issue copy of Edgar Allan Poe's *The Raven and Other Stories*. "There was just something about it that caught my eye. I was drawn to it like a magnet, but at first I kept my distance. I was walking back and forth, stealing glances—the truth is that I was lurking—and finally the young saleswoman encouraged me to take the book down and handle it, which I promptly did. She told me, 'It's in wrappers, too,' which of course meant absolutely nothing to me at the time, but it sure sounded impressive."

The $10,000 price tag persuaded Tane to put the volume back, but she couldn't get it out of her mind. "Before the day was done, it was mine, and I had brought it home," she said. "To this day, I don't know what it was that told me to buy that book. All I knew was that I had to have it. It just reached out to me. It said, 'Touch me; make me part of you.'"

Once the prize had been installed in the library of her Upper East Side apartment, Tane quickly came to another realization. "My first time at bat in the big leagues, and I had hit a home run, no doubt about it," she said, noting that the acquisition to this day remains one of the core holdings in her library. "But instead of admiring my triumph and leaving it at that, I also knew that this little guy needed some friends. He looked pretty lonely on that shelf all by himself. It is not inaccurate to say that I had uncorked the magic bottle and that the genie had jumped out. I was absolutely hooked, and everything that followed began at that moment."

What followed took place pretty much in a whirlwind. Within twenty years, Susan Tane had built what is arguably the finest Poe collection in private hands, a collection of such consequence that it is the focus of an exhibition on view now through February in the Hirshland Gallery of the Carl A. Kroch Library at Cornell University. The collection is the subject of a splendidly illustrated catalog published by Cornell to celebrate it, *Nevermore: The Edgar Allan Poe Collection of Susan Jaffe Tane*, with text and bibliographical descriptions by the collector.

An introduction to the catalog by Sarah Thomas, the Cornell University librarian, makes an especially pertinent point: "In an era when much is ephemeral, collections anchor what is known. Catalogs, such as this one, serve as enduring records of what has been so carefully united. They enable the collector to share both representations and descriptions of the artifacts themselves, and they permit readers to glimpse flashes of the excitement and brilliance that characterize the well-constituted collection."

From the very beginning of her activity, Tane determined that she would build a collection of distinction. "I was in my forties, I was successful—I've worked at the corporate level for a company that manufactures process equipment for the chemical and pharmaceutical industries, I have operated a couple businesses of my own, and I'm involved in some marketing—so yes, I had the means to proceed aggressively," she said. "Once I decided that I would collect Poe—and my fascination extends to nineteenth-century American literature in general—I decided to build a collection that would be second to none. Then I gave myself twenty years to do it, and because I am an overachiever, I did it in nineteen."

Having set that daunting goal for herself, Tane began the way so many of us have begun, she started prowling antiquarian bookstores, checking out flea markets, attending auctions, picking up information here and there, making a few mistakes along the way to be sure, but all the while studying and learning her subject. It wasn't long before she determined that she needed professional help. "I found myself a mentor," she told me, and that guide turned out to be the bookseller who had sold her the exquisite copy of *The Raven* at the Park Avenue antiques show, Stephan Loewentheil, owner of the 19th Century Shop and a renowned authority on the life and works of Edgar Allan Poe.

"I was pretty lucky," she said. "Stephan had a fabulous collection of his own that he allowed me to choose from. And we discussed directions I should take, what I needed to do to make something that was good outstanding. It was pretty clear that what I needed was not just wonderful books, but manuscripts, meaningful letters, photographs, ephemera, playbills, broadsides, a full range of relevant material. The result is a collection that is huge, very much in-depth, and of great interest to scholars."

With Loewentheil's counsel, Tane began buying more judiciously, and in some cases boldly. Four years after she took home her first book, she attended the sale at Sotheby's in New York of the Richard Manney library, determined to add the "black tulip" of American literature to her collection, Poe's first published book, *Tamerlane and Other Poems*, one of only twelve copies known. "I sat next to Stephan at the sale, and kept poking him in the ribs," she told me. The price, with buyer's premium, was $143,000, a lot of money by any yardstick, but $55,000 less than what Manney had paid for it just three years earlier in the same gallery, and an unqualified bargain for such an elusive rarity. (For more on Richard Manney and his sale, see the concluding chapter of my book *A Gentle Madness*.)

Tane's collection includes Poe's other published works in numerous forms, key periodical, newspaper, and journal appearances among them (a line Poe wrote in *Graham's* magazine in 1848 comes to mind: "The true genius shudders at incompleteness"). There are several fabulous autographed copies, most notably a copy of Poe's 1831 *Poems*, presented to critic John Neal and later the property of the great New York collector H. Bradley Martin.

Other high spots include an autograph manuscript of "The Spirits of the Dead" (1828), the earliest known manuscript of a Poe poem in private hands; the only surviving manuscript copy of the tale "Epimanes" (1833); a fourteen-line sonnet, "To Zante," dated 1840 and signed by Poe; "Eulalie—A Song," undated but circa 1843, a variant version of a poem written in tribute to Poe's wife, Virginia. Among the correspondence is a lengthy two-page letter written by Poe to Washington Irving, seeking some favorable words about one of his books, *Tales of the Grotesque and Arabesque*, which Poe hoped would help him secure "that public attention which would carry me on to fortune thereafter."

Loewentheil told me he regards Susan Tane as a "very savvy, very bright, very tough collector who knows exactly what she wants and what she needs." He also said she knows when to back off and to "not overpay for the lesser items that she is often quoted by dealers who do not know her well. It has long been my belief that a highly educated collector is a book dealer's best friend. Take a look at her catalog—how many collectors get to write their own catalog, by the way?—and you will instantly see what I mean."

Tane told me she has made no decision about the future of the collection, other than her commitment to keep everything together. She has already presented a wonderful collection of Herman Melville material to Cornell, but she is still having too much fun with Poe to call an end to her quest. "I love doing this. I love putting all the pieces together, and there's still so much more to learn."

Sarah Thomas of Cornell took note of Tane's zeal for the hunt and concluded her preface to the catalog with these inspiring words: "Long live the collector!"

KIRBY VEITCH

"My Beamish Boy," Fine Books & Collections, no. 21 (May/June 2006).

There was a time not so long ago when a youngster like Kirby Veitch would have been described as bookish, and nobody would have given a second thought to such a studious characterization. These days, however, teenagers who prefer reading to watching mindless reality shows on television or joysticking their way through some vapid computer game are considered nerds or eggheads, yet another quaint term from the recent past.

"The joke around school is that I sleep with books, and the truth is that sometimes I do exactly that," Kirby told me during a telephone conversation a few weeks before his seventeenth birthday, just a year after a devastating illness had come within a whisker of taking his life. "I love having books all around me—on the bed, on the floor, over in the corner. I don't collect them, but I am a reader and I have my favorites. I've always got my nose in a book."

Kirby is a particular fan of fantasy and science fiction. His father, the cartoonist Rick Veitch, is the author of several illustrated novels with futurist themes, most recently *Can't Get No*. Kirby included among his favorite authors George R. R. Martin and Orson Scott Card, writers whose work I had to admit was unfamiliar to me, though both, I quickly learned, have enthusiastic followings. "I'll read pretty much anything," Kirby quickly added. "Right now I'm really enjoying Joseph Campbell's *Hero with a Thousand Faces*, and I've got a shelf with Norman Mailer standing right alongside Mark Twain. And I like a lot of trash fiction, too"

As heartening as this conversation was—it always thrills me to come in contact with young people who profess a genuine passion for books—it was not occasioned by any desire on my part to probe this young man's eclectic reading habits or to find an uplifting example of print emerging triumphant in an increasingly digital environment. Instead, it was to follow up on a telephone call that his mother, Cindy Leszczak, had made a few weeks earlier to the *Diane Rehm Show*. Rehm's talk show is broadcast live from Washington, D.C., to more than a hundred National Public Radio stations, and on the morning of Leszczak's call, I was appearing as a guest. I had spent the first half hour talking with Rehm about *Every Book Its Reader: The Power of the Printed Word to Stir the World*, my fifth book, which had been published the previous month by HarperCollins. At one point, she asked me to discuss a segment where I write about the uncanny power that books have to affect people's lives at times of great peril, and I cited several telling examples, each about someone who had found peace and comfort from the written word in the face of a serious, debilitating illness. One of these people, the late Milwaukee bookseller David Schwartz, said, upon learning that he had terminal lung cancer, that Leo Tolstoy's *War and Peace* would be "a good book to die with."

When it came time to take questions from listeners, Rehm said hello to "Cindy in West Townshend, Vermont," an engaging woman who proceeded to describe her son's experience the previous year with a form of pleurisy that had compressed his lungs and made it almost impossible for him to breathe. It was "one of those diseases," she said, "that we all thought had been eradicated." Just fifteen years old at the time, Kirby had undergone surgery at the Dartmouth-Hitchcock Medical Center, near Hanover, New Hampshire, to drain his lungs of fluid, an agonizing experience that he was reluctant to repeat a second time, even though his doctors were insisting it was essential to keep him alive.

"My son looked at me and didn't quite know what to do," Leszczak said. And then the boy started reciting aloud some lines he had memorized from Lewis Carroll's "Jabberwocky," the nonsense poem in seven stanzas that appears in *Through the Looking-Glass and What Alice Found There* and is celebrated for its many invented words. "Come to my arms my beamish boy," he mumbled. "O frabjous day! Callooh! Callay!" Leszczak recalled the doctor looking at her son quizzically for an explanation. "I haven't read all the books I want to read," the boy said simply, and he was upset, too, that he couldn't remember all the words to the poem.

The doctor had an idea and went off to find a computer. Leszczak, meanwhile, wheeled her son down to the hospital bookstore, where they spent a few minutes looking at various volumes. "I just want to touch a few of them," he told her. When they returned to the medical wing, the doctor had found "Jabberwocky" on the Internet and had a copy for Kirby to read. Then they prepared him for the surgery that would save his life.

Leszczak spoke of this experience for four minutes without interruption in what I have come to think of as my *Sleepless in Seattle* moment. It is my firm belief that the most basic vital sign of the writing business is what you hear from your readers, and this was one of the most poignant responses to anything I had written in my professional life.

"What a wonderful, moving affirmation of what it means to read, to hold a book, to enjoy, to love," Rehm said when Leszczak had finished. "I'm speechless" is the best that I could muster, and then we went to a break. When we came back on the air, I asked Leszczak, if she were still listening, to please contact me, and I gave out my e-mail address.

Leszczak got in touch within a few days, as did several dozen other listeners from around the country, including two writers eager to pick up on her story and a noted Ohio collector of everything pertaining to *Alice in Wonderland*, who was interested in getting a transcript of her comments for publication in a Lewis Carroll Society journal. "It's really funny—I sew for a living, I do slipcovers and drapes, and I very often sew with Diane Rehm playing in the background," Leszczak told me in the first of several conversations we had over the next couple of weeks. "I love books, my husband loves books, Kirby loves books—we don't have a television in the house—and when you were talking about your passion for books, I could sense a personal connection there, and I called on impulse. All I really wanted to say was that books have done so much in my life, in my son's life, and that there are a lot of people out here who are still turning the pages."

To suggest that a favorite poem had helped save his life is something of a stretch, Kirby said when I had a chance to talk with him, but he allowed that it did perform an essential function all the same. "I think what reading did, it took my mind off the thought that I might die," he told me matter-of-factly. "It acted as a distraction, as a way to get out of the four corners of the hospital room."

"Jabberwocky" came to mind in the hospital, he said, "because it is a very whimsical poem, and I felt like I needed a little whimsy in my life. I do love Lewis Carroll, and it just came to mind. It kept my thoughts off being sick, and my mom's thoughts off my being sick."

Now a high school senior (this bookish lad's superior grades enabled him to skip a year), Kirby is thinking about a career as an artist and a writer, more or less following in his father's footsteps, and he was waiting to hear from a number of New England colleges when we spoke in February. "I'm still reading all the time," he said toward the end of our conversation. "But that's probably because I haven't discovered girls yet."

ERIC WASCHKE

"The Known Book World," Fine Books & Collections, no. 14 (March/April 2005).

One of the most compelling books about books published last year was Owen Gingerich's spirited account of the thirty years he spent traveling the globe in search of every first- and second-edition copy of Nicolaus Copernicus's *De revolutionibus orbium coelestium* (*On the Revolutions of Heavenly Spheres*), persuasive proof that book passion comes in many shapes and sizes and that personal ownership of the artifact is not always the dynamo that drives the engine.

His thorough census and documentation of some six hundred copies of the seminal work that suggested that the Earth went around the sun is solid scholarship. But only the most naive among us would suggest that Dr. Gingerich, a senior astronomer emeritus at the Smithsonian Astrophysical Observatory in Cambridge, Massachusetts, wasn't having a heck of a good time while he was at it. The tales he shares in *The Book Nobody Read*—a book whose title is an ironic reference to a belief put forth in 1959 by Arthur Koestler that Copernicus had negligible influence on his earliest readers—showcase the adventures of a determined bibliophile in action.

Another recent memoir—Aaron Lansky's *Outwitting History*—takes a somewhat different tack, though once again, it is the thrill of the chase that comes through so memorably. In this case, it is the story of a young man fresh out of graduate school who, in 1980, embarked on a mission to save a language that was in peril of disappearing, and succeeded spectacularly through a combination of dedication, chutzpah, and good luck.

Lansky's guiding approach was straightforward enough: to gather as many forgotten books in Yiddish as he and his volunteers could find. To date, they have rescued well over a million volumes, many of them from Dumpsters and dank basements. They put them in the hands of academic institutions willing to teach the language, thereby providing a lifeline between the past and the future. The National Yiddish Book Center that Lansky established on the campus of Hampshire College in Amherst, Massachusetts, is a legacy for the ages and worth visiting for anyone passing through the area.

I love stories like these because they bring richness to what "civilians" not afflicted by the compulsion for books might otherwise regard as a pointless pursuit accented with a touch of eccentricity. And it isn't necessary to have the same degree of intellectual rigor as Gingerich or the deep moral purpose of Lansky, either, to join in the fun.

A person I would regard as something of a kindred spirit to these two is a bookseller I've had occasion to meet several times over the past few years. He has embarked on a decidedly quixotic campaign to explore what he calls the "known book world," his way of saying that he visits as many bookstores as he can on all inhabited continents. This is quite an enterprise considering that the Internet is making the purchase of books a faceless procedure devoid almost entirely of human contact, not to mention adventure.

At last count, Eric Waschke had traveled to fifty-three countries and called on some three thousand bookstores. Ostensibly he is acquiring fresh stock for the business he operates in Vancouver, British Columbia, the aptly named Wayfarer's Bookshop. But something else is afoot here, if not an entry in the *Guinness Book of World Records*, then certainly a valid claim to having visited more colleagues in more places than anyone else now plying the trade.

Waschke, born in 1968 in Montreal, and his family lived successively in England, the Philippines, and Germany, following the peregrinations of his entrepreneur-engineer father. While still in his teens, Waschke began working part-time as a book scout for Antiquariat Kiepert in Berlin. The search for maps, topographical prints, and publications of local, regional, and general history brought him in contact with dealers throughout Europe and whetted his appetite for exploration. When he graduated from the University of British Columbia in 1992, he decided to become a bookseller specializing in the field.

He opened his own shop in 1996 and soon hit on the idea of an around-the-world odyssey with bookstore visits at every stop. "My core business is the Western contact with exotic places, and because I deal in exploration, this in a sense is my own expedition through the world," he told me. "I am also interested in books published in different languages, so there's that, too. But I don't think anybody else has really gone around visiting bookshops on a systematic basis like this, and I thought it would be fun to give it a shot."

The locales he has visited are a jumble of seductive names. Liechtenstein, Hungary, Portugal, Brazil, Thailand, Nepal, Hong Kong, Korea, Russia, India, Greece, Australia, Tahiti, Namibia, Vietnam, Latvia, Cuba, and South Africa are a few that jump out. He usually stops in at ten bookstores or so in each major city. "It has pretty much paid for itself," he assured me. "I find books that I never see in the United States or Canada, and I have people who are interested in owning them."

By far the most unlikely treasure trove he encountered was at a guesthouse outside Fort Portal, Uganda, in the foothills of the Ruwenzori Mountains, between tea plantations and the Kibale Forest National Park. "I found a collection of books there on African exploration that included an odd volume of Sir Richard Burton's *Zanzibar* (one of his rarest books), Ludwig von Höhnel's *Discovery of Lakes Rudolf and Stefanie*, and about a hundred other important books of African exploration."

Waschke said he travels, on average, about 130 days a year. He made seven trips in 2004, a modest undertaking compared to the previous year, when he spent eight consecutive weeks traveling in Asia,

Africa, Europe, and the two Americas, twenty-three flights all told, with thirteen stops. His professional memberships include the Royal Geographical Society, the Antiquarian Booksellers' Association of Canada, and the International Map Collectors' Society.

"My purpose as a bookseller is to constantly learn," he said. "Wherever you go, you see a different mix of books, and I have a good memory, so I store things away in my head. When I started out, I probably passed up on a lot of good things simply because I didn't know what I was looking at. I basically buy the things I know are good, though sometimes you take a chance. But as I go along, it's less and less of a chance." And what, pray tell, has Waschke learned most of all from his experiences? "What I have learned most of all," he said, "is that you can find a good book anywhere."

TOM WOLFE

"Lone Wolfe," Biblio 4, no. 2 (February 1999).

W hen Tom Wolfe's sweeping new novel of America at the dawn of a new millennium was nominated for a National Book Award, the feeling in some circles was that peace was at hand for the flamboyant author—known worldwide for his razzmatazz vocabulary and natty white suits—and the literary establishment he has been lampooning so mercilessly for more than a quarter of a century.

Just being short-listed for America's most prestigious honor for fiction, of course, is a moment of no small consequence for *A Man in Full*, Wolfe's eleventh book. The nomination was even more noteworthy for the fact that it was announced three weeks before the 742-page opus was scheduled to arrive in bookstores, a curious paradox that made it the odds-on favorite to take the prize.

But book awards are anything but predictable, and when the winners were announced in New York on November 18, 1998, the nod went to Washington, D.C., author Alice McDermott and her widely admired novel *Charming Billy*, a quiet reflection about Irish Americans and the way a lost love can continue to haunt a person's life. McDermott was the surprise choice (Robert Stone's *Damascus Gate* was also a leading contender), so much so, in fact, that she had not prepared any acceptance remarks in advance.

When the chair of the five-judge jury, Thomas Mallon, disclosed her selection, he noted that he and his colleagues preferred "stealth" over "horsepower" in their fiction, an obvious reference to the subtle style of McDermott on the one hand and a poke at what many readers believe is the most bizarre scene in *A Man in Full* on the other, the mating of a champion stallion and a brood mare in a Georgia stable.

When the awards were announced, Wolfe was in the middle of a three-day publicity tour to Atlanta, where most of *A Man in Full* is set and where people stood in line for hours to get autographed copies of the book. "Congratulations to Alice McDermott," Wolfe told the *Atlanta Journal-Constitution*. "I love awards when I get them, but I don't sit around wringing my hands when I don't." Four days later, the novel made its debut appearance on the *New York Times* bestseller list in the No. 1 position, and on November 22, Wolfe was interviewed at length by Morley Safer on *60 Minutes*.

Wolfe pretty much defined the parameters of his ongoing feud with the literary establishment in 1973, when he was in his early forties and already well known for four books. As one of the most vocal practitioners of a new style of writing that claimed to produce a form of literary expression that was the successor to traditional fiction, Wolfe had brazenly thrown down the gauntlet in *The New Journalism*. The anthology, which he edited, featured selections from two of his own books, along with choice excerpts from some other writers who were attracting acclaim for their work with the form, Hunter S. Thompson, Norman Mailer, Joe McGinniss, George Plimpton, Joan Didion, Gay Talese, Rex Reed, Truman Capote, and Barbara Goldsmith among them. Wolfe addressed the issue directly—some might even say arrogantly—in the form of a question: "Namely, what is it precisely—in terms of technique—that has made the New Journalism as 'absorbing' and 'gripping' as the novel and the short story, and often more so?"

He offered several precise answers, each one involving a traditional fictional device, which, he lamented, had been abandoned by most contemporary novelists in the years following the Second World War. "Realism is not merely another literary approach or attitude," he said. "The introduction of detailed realism into English literature in the eighteenth century was like the introduction of electricity into machine technology. It raised the state of the art to an entirely new level. And for anyone, in fiction or nonfiction, to try to improve literary technique by abandoning social realism would be like an engineer trying to improve upon machine technology by abandoning electricity."

Because mainstream novelists had veered toward more experimental and interior forms, he continued, new opportunities had opened up for writers who could offer readers works that were just as exciting, instructive, meaningful, and artfully constructed as fiction but different in that they were based entirely on fact. The new movement, which began in the early 1960s, came in the form of a discovery "that it just might be possible to write journalism" that would "read like a novel," he wrote. The journalists who pioneered this notion thought at first that they were merely "dressing up" like novelists, waiting for the day when "they would work up their nerve" and take a whack at writing fictional works of their own. "They never dreamed of the approaching irony. They never guessed for a minute that the work they would do over the next ten years, as journalists, would wipe out the novel as literature's main event."

In the fall of 1979, Wolfe made a superb show of practicing exactly what he had preached with publication of *The Right Stuff*, a gripping study of the American space program in its infancy. A few weeks after the book had been released, I interviewed him at the Copley Plaza Hotel in Boston. Wolfe had worked seven years on the book—about five years more than he originally thought it would take—and one of the reasons for the delay was his growing concern over the cocky challenge he had issued to the literary community in *The New Journalism*.

"I suffered from a very serious, very complicated form of writer's block," he told me. "I'd already been through all the normal kinds." What had slowed him down most of all was anxiety that he "couldn't accomplish the task I had set for myself," and there were times when he had even considered "chucking" the project all together. "But seven years isn't such a long time when you figure it took me three years to get my junior lifesaving badge, so I just stuck it out."

In the end, Wolfe altered the scope of the work drastically. Instead of tracking the space program through the Gemini and Apollo programs as he had first intended, he focused instead on the lives and experiences of the seven Mercury astronauts. And he still needed a nudge from his wife, Sheila, to get the manuscript off to Farrar, Straus, and Giroux, his publisher since 1965. "She came into my office one morning and announced that I was done. 'But I haven't gotten these guys to the moon yet,' I told her. 'Not in this house, you don't,' she said, and that was it. I was finished."

The Right Stuff seemed to validate every claim Wolfe had made in *The New Journalism* six years earlier. It recorded blockbuster sales, won the National Book Award for nonfiction, and became the basis of a wonderful 1983 film starring Sam Shepard as the daredevil pilot Chuck Yeager. The very title itself entered the English language in much the same way that Joseph Heller's *Catch-22* had become an idiomatic expression to describe frustrating situations characterized by contradictory conditions eighteen years earlier. As a phrase, "the right stuff" suggests a larger-than-life persona, a can-do attitude that combines superior skill, unparalleled courage, cool élan, and devil-may-care chutzpah to accomplish the kind of tasks that only a few people on earth are capable of taking on. Wolfe likened the Mercury astronauts to the "single combat warriors" of ancient times whose one-on-one, give-no-quarter duels to the death determined which army would win a war. David had the right stuff, in other words, when he declared his readiness to take on Goliath *mano a mano* in the battlefield and then wasted no time leveling the Philistine champion with a well-aimed stone to the forehead from his slingshot.

This was not the first time Wolfe had coined a phrase that would become familiar to millions of people, and it wouldn't be the last, but it certainly became his best known contribution to the language. His 1976 book of essays, *Mauve Gloves and Madmen, Clutter and Vine*, is most notable for the piece that gave the world a perfect catch phrase—the Me Decade—to describe one of the most self-indulgent periods in American history.

His other books include *The Electric Kool-Aid Acid Test* (1968), a penetrating depiction of the West Coast drug culture as practiced by the novelist Ken Kesey and his band of acolytes known as the Merry Pranksters; *Radical Chic and Mau-Mauing the Flak Catchers* (1970), an acerbic take on the course of American liberalism, with an almost surreal party at the Manhattan home of the late conductor Leonard Bernstein for the Black Panther Party as the principal case in point; *The Painted Word* (1975), a jaundiced appraisal of modern art; *In Our Time* (1980), a compact collection of sketches he had drawn for *Harper's* magazine; and *From Bauhaus to Our House* (1981), an influential evaluation of American architecture.

A lifelong writer, Wolfe received a bachelor's degree from Washington and Lee University in Virginia, where he was a star pitcher on the baseball team, good enough to earn a tryout with the old New York Giants. Five years of graduate study at Yale earned him a Ph.D. in American studies in 1957.

Toward the end of my first interview with Wolfe twenty years ago, I asked what he planned for his next book. The 1980s were just about to begin, and my assumption was that this most celebrated of contemporary social critics would be taking an acute look at the coming decade with the same degree of zeal and acumen that had energized his earlier commentaries. "Well, the fact is that I'm planning to write a novel," he said. "It will be about 'the city' in a generic sense, but most likely New York City," where the courtly native of Richmond, Virginia, had lived since going to work for the old *Herald Tribune* as a feature writer in 1962. "I want to do something in the tradition of Thackeray's *Vanity Fair*, where deep down the real subject—the principal character—was London itself. Today, there are so many important events taking place in cities, and the fiction writers aren't doing anything with them."

When we met in 1987 for our next interview, nine years had passed, and Wolfe's long-awaited first novel, *The Bonfire of the Vanities*, was just beginning to arrive in bookstores. Once again, we met in a fancy hotel, this time in the Ritz-Carlton overlooking the Boston

Public Garden, and again there was a discernible sense of relief that a book so long in the making had finally been seen through the press. True to his word, Wolfe had written a huge book that got all of its force from the vicissitudes of a huge American metropolis. In the process, he had managed to define, with precise insight, nuance, and detail, the essence of a frenetic decade, the white-hot 1980s, when Wall Street bond traders perceived themselves as indestructible "masters of the universe." An unqualified triumph, it went on to record sales of seven hundred and fifty thousand copies in hardcover, and many millions more in paperback.

Though unquestionably fiction, what dazzled readers most of all about *Bonfire of the Vanities* was the unwavering grain of authenticity that ran so seamlessly through it. In the novel, Sherman McCoy— a high stakes bond trader who considers a million dollars a year one step above welfare— suddenly finds himself caught in a social nightmare. One night, while driving his $120,000 black Mercedes from Kennedy Airport into Manhattan with his gorgeous mistress Maria Ruskin at his side, he misses a turn on the Triborough Bridge and gets hopelessly lost in the Bronx. A sequence of events worthy of Franz Kafka brings the car to an uneasy stop on a darkened ramp; when two young black men approach from the shadows to help, the couple panics and screeches away, striking one of them, and leaving him helpless on the street. The injured youngster—an honors student, it turns out, not the mugger Sherman and Maria had feared—lapses into a coma after providing meaningful leads to the hit-and-run car and ultimately dies from his injuries. McCoy is arrested, and before long, the city is gripped with an incident that crosses all racial, ethnic, social, and political lines.

A key "character" in the novel is the South Bronx criminal courthouse. It was there, Wolfe told me, that he went often while researching the book. "The courthouse is one place where high and low at times are involuntarily going to come together. So I said, 'All right, I'll just start poking around the criminal courts, and I'll look for my characters there.' I just started with raw reporting."

In the true serial tradition of William Makepeace Thackeray and Charles Dickens, *The Bonfire of the Vanities* first appeared as installments in *Rolling Stone* magazine, though in the earlier version, Sherman McCoy was a writer, not the broker he became in the book. Wolfe said he made the change because it allowed him to explore a world he knew nothing about, the wheeling and dealing of Wall Street. He spent considerable time in brokerage houses and among the big-money players. The same kind of anxiety that had gripped him while writing *The Right Stuff* returned again, he admitted, and he readily agreed that he was taking an enormous risk by attempting a work of fiction at this point in his career. "I was forever mindful of the fact that I had spattered off quite a bit about how superior nonfiction was to the novel," he said.

"What I was really saying was how untalented—or not so much that as obtuse—contemporary novelists were. And that's really asking for trouble. It seemed to me that the people with the greatest natural talent as writers were turning away from the richest material and were writing these very private novels. And what I was saying was that they were all wrong, that they should be looking at society on a large scale rather than private lives. Well that's another way to be asking for trouble. So when I started writing my novel, I was petrified."

Once again, I asked Wolfe what he planned next. Another novel? This time he didn't commit himself to anything specific. "I hope at the very least I can now speak with greater authority when I get the urge to speak on fiction and nonfiction," he said. "I put down the challenge to myself, and if I've been successful, then that's very gratifying. What I'd like is to be thought of as somebody who can deal with prose in any direction."

That might have ended the friction with the literati right there, but two years later he wrote a cover article for the November 1989 issue *Harper's* magazine titled "Stalking the Billion-Footed Beast"—another way of suggesting how many million stories there are in the Naked City—more pointedly subtitled "A Literary Manifesto for the New Social Novel." In it, Wolfe wrote that if the American novel was to survive, then it had to return to "a highly detailed realism based on reporting," and the model for what he was talking about was none other than *The Bonfire of the Vanities.*

He used such phrases as *puppet masters, neofabulists,* and *minimalists* to criticize contemporaries who "were in love with the theory that the novel was, first and foremost, a literary game, words on a page being manipulated by an author." The places they wrote about, he continued, were unidentifiable. "You couldn't even tell what hemisphere it was. It was some nameless, elemental terrain—the desert, the woods, the open sea, the, snowy wastes. The characters had no backgrounds. They came from nowhere. They didn't use realistic speech. Nothing they said, did, or possessed indicated any class or ethnic origin."

Wolfe returned to the central theme articulated in *The New Journalism* and stated it anew: "If fiction writers do not start facing the obvious, the literary history of the second half of the twentieth century will record that journalism not only took over the richness of American life as their domain but also seized the high ground of literature itself. Any literary person who is willing to look back over the American literary terrain of the past twenty-five years—look back candidly, in the solitude of the study—will admit that in at least four years out of five the best nonfiction books have been *better literature* than the most highly praised books of fiction."

Not long after publication of that piece came word that Wolfe was working on another novel, and once again the anticipation began to build. The publication of *A Man in Full* in November became a "literary event" of major proportions, and the announcement of a National Book Award nomination several weeks before people could even buy it only heightened the excitement. Farrar, Straus, and Giroux responded by ordering a first printing of 1.2 million volumes for the novel. In London, all the major dailies ran major weekend profiles of Wolfe a week before publication, and on November 2, *Time* magazine featured the sixty-eight-year-old author on its cover.

Reviews written by America's leading critics, meanwhile, began appearing in a rush all over the United States. Most of them were generally positive, but some were decidedly mixed. Writing in the *New Yorker*, John Updike spoke for a number of the cognoscenti by dismissing *A Man in Full* as "entertainment, not literature, even literature in a modest aspirant form." Over at the *New York Observer*, fellow National Book Award finalist Harold Bloom (for *Shakespeare: The Invention of the Human*), praised Wolfe for daring to make the moral teachings of the Stoic philosopher Epictetus a central element in the novel. "Let us amiably rejoice in Wolfe," Bloom concluded, "who entertains all those of whom he rightly disapproves."

For my third conversation in three decades with Tom Wolfe, I drove to New York City one Monday morning early in November, where a day of pretour interviews had been scheduled by his publisher. He had set up shop in a tenth-floor suite of the Carlyle Hotel at Madison Avenue and Seventy-sixth Street, a few blocks from his elegant home on the Upper East Side. Celebrated for his impeccable Southern manners, Wolfe once again was resplendent in his trademark white outfit, this one a three-piece double-breasted suit with a blue-striped shirt, polka-dot tie, off-white socks, and brown-white spats.

With commercial success and critical approbation already assured, Wolfe agreed that he was feeling pretty good about himself. "But my overwhelming feeling is tremendous relief," he said. "This took so long to finish it's almost criminal. It just shouldn't take that long."

A Man in Full is a sweeping novel about class, race, new wealth, urban culture, moral conviction, and sexual politics, with no fewer than five plotlines developing simultaneously, each one the product of intensive fieldwork. Most of the novel is set in Atlanta, where a less-than-flattering portrait of the dynamic Southern city "too busy to hate" caused ripples of protest but didn't stop thousands of people from turning up for Wolfe's readings, signings, and public appearances.

Wolfe spent much of the 1990s learning about such experiences as prison life in California, quail hunting on massive South Georgia plantations, Atlanta politics, and the emerging black middle class. What is undeniably the most extraordinary scene in the novel—it is, in fact, the only sex scene in the book—involves several thousand pounds of horseflesh brought together in a breeding stable on a twenty-nine-thousand-acre plantation Wolfe calls Turpmtine. "I was witness to such a coupling, and I knew instantly when I saw it that I had to use it in my novel," he said. "This was at the plantation of a real estate developer. He had a lot of guests and he really wanted to give everybody a good time one day when they weren't shooting quail, and there it was. I was shocked. You actually could feel the earth move." While many readers might be tempted to pair *The Bonfire of the Vanities* and *A Man in Full* as companion volumes, one a biting commentary of Wall Street culture during the white-hot 1980s, the other a satire on freewheeling real estate barons and the emerging black middle class in the South during the decade that followed, Wolfe said that he never harbored any such intentions himself. Although he spent uncounted hours in Georgia gathering material, the first draft was set primarily in New York City, with only occasional forays down south. "I had the basic story for several years, but I had made a colossal blunder," he said. "I knew I wanted to include plantations in South Georgia, because I had seen them for the first time, and I had never seen anything like it. Such unbelievable forms of conspicuous consumption." In the novel, Turpmtine is owned by the flamboyant real estate developer Charlie Croker, whose half-billion-dollar debt becomes the catalyst for much of the action. "I made the mistake of saying, 'OK, I'm going to have a man on this plantation that exists just for shooting quail thirteen weeks every year, but he's going to be an Atlanta developer who made it big and lives in New York," Wolfe said.

After "struggling with this concept for years," he finally decided that if the plantations were so intriguing, then the book had to be set in Atlanta. So in January 1996, Wolfe essentially chucked eight hundred pages of manuscript and started from scratch with Atlanta as the primary setting. "The whole thing fell beautifully into place from that point. But then in August of that year I had a heart attack, and a huge quintuple bypass operation," which put everything on hold. By November, Wolfe was writing again, and a manuscript was finished within a year. "I've always said that all books are written in six months, and the rest is dancing around the subject. Well, this one took me a year to write."

Wolfe readily admits that his personal hero is Émile Zola, the nineteenth-century French author who took special pains to make sure that he always had his facts straight. "I know that in certain ways I'm not much like Zola," he said. "He writes very funny scenes, but he doesn't play them for laughs. They become dead serious. But he used to call his technique 'documenting.' He'd go out to the mines, go down in the mineshafts, to get material, or he'd go to the French slums and the washhouses, where poor people did their laundry, just to get the detail exactly right. I feel the same way."

The word *anachronism* never came up during our interview, but everything about Tom Wolfe's view of fiction writing does suggest another time and place. His new novel is not only a "traditional" novel, but also a "traditional *nineteenth-century* novel," he maintains.

It gives very little away to report that Charlie Croker becomes exposed to the tenets of Stoicism after making unlikely contact with the most sympathetic character Tom Wolfe has ever created, a thoroughly decent young man named Conrad Hensley who hits rock bottom after suffering through one nightmarish humiliation after another.

"I felt that a man like Charlie Croker might be receptive to this if he's in a sufficiently weakened state, and he has nothing else to hang on to. I mean he doesn't even have his beautiful second wife to hang on to, because she's not in this for better of for worse, she's just in it for the better."

Wolfe has unsheathed his scalpel to dissect the foibles of American society, yet what he does, he insists, is not satire. "I've always hated the word satire, even for *Bonfire of the Vanities*. Satire is the truth taken to an extreme for the sake of mockery. The dictionary just says that satire is a piece of writing that dwells on the foibles of mankind. I would hope that all novels would meet that test. To me, satire is a limiting thing, and certainly the religious part of this book, in my mind, is not at all satirical. There's a real soul-searching that goes on here by Conrad and Charlie."

Wolfe said he plans to write another novel, this one vaguely concerned with education, and he hopes to have it finished within three years. "The message I try to keep sending out into the literary world, which is never listened to, is that reporting is the heart of the modern novel. In all successful writing, content, the material, the milieu, is about 70 percent of a book, and talent is about 30 percent. When you're young, you think that talent is 95 percent, because that's all you've got, and material is 5 percent."

And while he would not say directly whether he has mellowed in recent years, he does have a sense of passing time. "The interesting thing about realizing your mortality, really feeling it, is that when you're young, it is an abstraction to know that we all have a finite time on this earth," he said.

"We are, as Epictetus says, a bowl of clay with a quart of blood, and eventually you have to give it back. I think that just sets the soul at ease."

With two novels now under his belt, Wolfe said that writing fiction "still has a novelty about it" for him, which is why he is so keen on writing another. "But I still think that nonfiction is the most important literary movement since the Second World War, particularly since the novel has become more and more precious," he said.

"There's a novelist who recently wrote a book called *Thumbsucker* about a man who sucks his thumb until the age of twenty-one, and it seems that this author himself sucked his thumb until the age of nineteen. Well, I kind of regard what is being done generally in fiction today as thumb-sucking novels, in which having cannibalized the first twenty-odd years of your life, you begin finally to suck on your thumb with the desperate hope that something is left on your bones that you might turn into meaningful fiction."

That people are responding enthusiastically to his novels by the millions is further validation, Wolfe feels, that realism still matters in the waning days of the twentieth century. "You cannot give up realism without giving up the power of the novel," he concluded. "Unfortunately—or fortunately for me—I'm the only person who seems to understand this very basic, simple fact. I used to worry about handing the keys to the kingdom over to other writers by saying that. But I see now there's nothing to worry about. They're all wed to thumb sucking."

NOTE

Not long after this piece appeared in print, the *New York Post* suggested in a gossip column that, in his interview with me, Tom Wolfe had taken potshots at the novel *Thumbsucker*—which at that time had still not been published—as a way of settling scores with the author, Walter Kirn, who had written a decidedly unflattering review of *A Man in Full* in *New York* magazine. In an interview with MSNBC, Kirn denounced Wolfe's "attack" on him as "overkill" and added: "If Wolfe has a flaw, it's that he doesn't get enough of himself into his books. I think a little introversion and self-analysis might be in order for him." A few months later, however, in an almost surreal about-face, Kirn wrote this in the literary journal *Tin House*: "Initially, I laughed off Wolfe's remarks as self-serving and uninformed, but after rereading my novel I agree with him," though he offered little else by way of conciliation and made no effort to hide his obvious contempt for Wolfe. For his part, Wolfe offered no further public comment on the matter; his third novel, *I Am Charlotte Simmons*, a take on American higher education, was published in 2004.

MICHAEL ZINMAN

"Finding Value Where There Seems to Be None," Biblio 2, no. 4 (April 1997).

We talk all the time about the importance of establishing close working relationships with booksellers, and for very good reason. The joy of the hunt is by far the most satisfying part of the drill, with serendipitous discoveries always providing the most joyful of moments. But every collector needs a little help along the way.

An appropriate reminder of this axiom comes with the release of a bibliography, *Canvassing Books, Sample Books, and Subscription Publishers' Ephemera, 1833–1951, in the Collection of Michael Zinman,* compiled and edited by Keith Arbour. Its publication represents the culmination of every bibliophile's dream—the creation of a collection that not only breaks new ground but also becomes the basis of a scholarly work. Printed on the dedication page are three words: "for Robert Seymour."

Robert Seymour is the second-generation owner of Colebrook Book Barn in Colebrook, Connecticut. Forty years ago, he began taking note of some unusual books that kept cropping up in his travels to find new stock for the business established by his father, Seth Seymour. The items, known familiarly in the trade as "sample books," were incomplete dummies put together by publishers for their agents to use as sales tools with prospective clients.

Dismissed for years as worthless ephemera, some scholars have been persuaded recently to take a second look at these volumes, especially since many of them are now known to contain the first states of some pages in various important works, while others contain samples of bindings totally unknown to bibliographers. Almost all of them, moreover, include promotional material that provides commentary on texts, authors, illustrations, publishers, agents, and readers that is not available anywhere else and thus constitutes a provocative resource for cultural historians.

But this newfound respect has been a long time developing. As Michael Zinman points out in his preface to *Canvassing Books*, for many years this material "occupied a position on the collectors' feeding chain slightly lower than nineteenth-century American Bibles, a topic I am familiar with."

As a collector, Zinman is best known for the vast gathering of early American imprints he has assembled over the past twenty-five years and for the collection of Bibles printed in North America he has built in a variety of "first" states—first German, first Greek, first Jewish, first Catholic, first illustrated, first Braille, and so on. He was the focus of a lengthy segment in my book *A Gentle Madness* and is well known among the community of bibliophiles for his "critical mess" approach to collecting. He states it again in his preface to *Canvassing Books*, which is worth quoting here: "If you accumulate enough of anything, at some point the accumulation takes on a life of its own, and one of importance, too."

I once asked Zinman why he bought, sight unseen, 268 cartons of pornography covering the years 1950 to 1975, which turned his stomach when they were delivered to the Ardsley, New York, offices of his business, Earthworm Inc., which buys and sells heavy construction machinery. "The quantity and the dollars were reasonable at the time," he said unhesitatingly. "They were practically giving it to me." Yet when he saw what he had bought, the content was so repugnant to his sensibility that he was reluctant even to send it off to the dump for fear of being misidentified by his neighbors as a person to avoid. So he shipped the material instead to a bookseller in Texas with the hope of anonymously giving it away. The upshot came a few years later when the University of Texas Law School at Austin took the collection, overjoyed at the opportunity to have some specific examples of the material examined by Lyndon Johnson's Commission on Pornography and Obscenity, whose records were on deposit at the university. The fact that the university chose to call the archive the Zinman Collection of Pornography in honor of the donor caused some amusement, but at least scholarship was served.

While he certainly has the means to collect at the highest levels, Zinman has chosen instead to seek out and gather material that is not on the edge of current fashion and that as a consequence can be acquired at very low cost. "None of the stuff I collect is expensive," Zinman said in his gritty New York accent. "More often than not, the booksellers are thrilled at the opportunity to unload all this material that has been collecting dust in their cellars. There was a time when I put out the word that I would pay one dollar for any almanac printed in the nineteenth century, and I got swamped in almanacs. My approach to collecting is that you immerse yourself in the stuff, and that you let it expand from there into something worthwhile."

Similarly, Zinman is now collecting all sorts of nongovernmental constitutions—codes of structure and conduct for such groups as bridge clubs, labor unions, debating societies, parent-teacher associations, fraternal organizations, church auxiliaries, and everything in between. "Where it is headed, nobody can say," Zinman said. "But at some point the collection will acquire a certain intellectual weight, and something useful just might come out of it."

For years, Zinman has been intrigued by the occasional "sample book" he noticed in his bibliophilic wanderings and quietly built a collection of about six hundred items, a formidable assemblage, to be sure, but modest when compared to the one formed by Robert Seymour in western Connecticut. Unusual in this instance is that Seymour had not been acquiring the material for customer stock; he was getting it for his own enjoyment.

"I used to go book hunting all over the place with my Dad, and I would just pick them up when I saw them," Seymour recalled in an interview. "They weren't highly regarded at all, and the fact is that a lot of dealers had thrown them out. Nobody wanted them. I could get these things for $1 to $3 each, and if they were marked more than $5, I didn't buy them, figuring they were probably overpriced. I've had some dealers sell them to me for 50¢ apiece."

There came a point, however, where Seymour recognized the importance of what he had. "It became obvious to me that these books represented a major chapter in American publishing history. It spanned more than one hundred years, and it demonstrated how books were marketed and sold in remote areas of the country through most of the nineteenth century. I had always planned on compiling a bibliography of what I had put together, and I would even take the books out every now and then as an inducement to getting myself started, but I never got very far with it. So when Michael came along with his offer, I felt it was time. Something else that came into play was the fact that I wasn't finding enough new material to keep my interest going. When that happens, you're ready to move along."

Many months passed between the time Zinman and Seymour made their verbal agreement, however, and the time the sample books finally changed hands. As fate would have it, they arrived unannounced one fall day in 1995, just as Keith Arbour was setting up shop in Ardsely to work on a project commissioned by the Haydn Foundation for the Cultural Arts, a nonprofit organization established by Zinman.

"My fellowship was to prepare a detailed bibliography of the thirteen thousand items in Michael's collection of American imprints," Arbour recalled in a telephone interview from his home in Mobile, Alabama, where he teaches early American history at the University of South Alabama. "The very week I started that project, Bob Seymour drove up in a truck filled with this huge collection of sample books, and I was just bowled over by what I saw in those boxes. It was immediately apparent to me that what we had here was a wholly untapped research source. So little work had been done on subscription publishing, and the little amount that had been done was confined to a very narrow range of the canvassing books available in research libraries. This collection suggested a sense of the whole context. I saw this as the opportunity of a lifetime."

The descriptive bibliography that emerged from this opportunity is a thorough compilation of 1,784 books, along with a complete list of seven hundred publishing houses and titles, a detailed index, and twenty pages of illustrations to go along with Arbour's fourteen-page introduction. Altogether, this is an impressive performance that is sure to secure stature as an essential reference. At first glance, the sample books look like any other nineteenth and early-twentieth-century books. Many of them sport covers with gold embossed titles or gaily decorated designs known as pictorial cloth. If a volume was to be issued with several bindings, examples of the variants would be attached inside; if wood engravings or photographs were to be included, examples would be enclosed as well. Various leaflets, handbills, and sales advice pamphlets might also be tipped in. Especially interesting are the sales pitches publishers recommended for their agents. A typical example is found in the prospectus for a book titled *The Happy Home*: "The object of this volume is to put in the hands of every parent and child the means of making home the delightful, instructive, love-inspiring, friend-making place it ought to be." Appearing in the rear of the books were lined blank pages where the names of customers, or subscribers, could be written in.

"What I found fascinating is that a very high percentage of these traveling sales people were women, and given this specific time in American history, that alone is extraordinary," Arbour said. "Here they are, traveling through the countryside by themselves, unescorted, going door to door to gather subscriptions for these books. Equally remarkable is that at the local level—and they usually operated in rural areas not served by bookstores or libraries—these women are essentially running the book subscription business, while the men are back in Philadelphia and Hartford or wherever running the presses. It is women who are running things at the grassroots level."

Subjects and genres included in *Canvassing Books* include African Americana, women's health and etiquette, juvenile books, the Civil War, biographies, exploration, travel, and religion, though Zinman and Arbour both agree that it is merely the beginning of what will be a wider bibliographical effort.

One early admirer of the accomplishment is Thomas V. Lange, curator of early printed books and bindings at the Huntington Library in San Marino, California, and also a collector of sample books. "I've been collecting them for twenty-five years, and I have about five hundred right now, which makes my collection the second largest in existence," Lange said. "I must say that I am in total awe of what Bob Seymour accomplished. It includes some things that I knew nothing about."

Lange said that the publication of *Canvassing Books* has prompted him to abandon work on a similar effort he intended with his collection. "I confess I am a bit jealous, because it's exactly what I had been working towards. I would have done some things a bit differently, but it's a strong beginning step toward a full catalog of subscription books. The indexing I did on my collection includes such details as which geographical areas the agents visited, because in the back of the canvassing books, where people listed their names, you see where the customers lived. But that's a very minor quibble. Overall, I am very pleased by what they have done, and my book is no longer going to happen."

The beauty of these sample books, Lange stressed, is the insight they have to offer historians. "This is a fascinating subject that impacts on other areas of book and cultural studies. In parts of America where there were no libraries, the impact of door-to-door book sales is greater than anyone realizes. In many ways these men and women determined which books were made available to a particular readership. In a very significant way, they helped create the intellectual agenda by the kinds of books they were selling."

Zinman sums up how all this was made possible by Robert Seymour. "To better understand and grasp the magnificence of his effort, consider that his holdings alone were more than *seven times* greater than any other institutional or private collection," he writes in his preface to *Canvassing Books*. "It is most uncommon for a single person to create a new pathway in book collecting, but this is what Robert Seymour did."

MICHAEL ZINMAN II

"Anything Can Be Anywhere," Fine Books & Collections, no. 13 (January/February 2005).

One of my very favorite observations on the "disposition to possess books" was put forth a century and a half ago by the Scottish historian and bibliophile John Hill Burton, who offered that "the general ambition of the class" is "to find value where there seems to be none, and this develops a certain skill and subtlety, enabling the operator, in the midst of a heap of rubbish, to put his finger on those things which have in them the latent capacity to become valuable and curious."

I offer this quaint maxim not to discourage the gathering of certified winners, nor to denigrate in any way the high-spot collectors and the connoisseurs of fine first editions that leave so many of us weak in the knees with their beauty. But there is a certain charm to the image of the maverick who pokes about the hinterlands for targets of opportunity, the free spirit who defies the accepted rules of engagement and still emerges victorious. Some of these people actually make their living as book scouts, each and every one abiding by the credo, attributed to the fictitious bottle scout Zack Jenks in Larry McMurtry's *Cadillac Jack*, that "anything can be anywhere."

Whenever I hear about people quite literally plucking the most unlikely of prizes from the trash—items that have been discarded as worthless, unattractive, undesirable, or irrelevant—I think of Michael Zinman, the architect of what he describes as the "critical mess" philosophy of acquisition, a technique to collecting on a massive scale that he has made uniquely his own and with stunning success.

I first met Zinman in the 1980s, when I was beginning research for my book *A Gentle Madness*. He came widely recommended to me as someone I just had to interview, not only for the outstanding collection of early American imprints he had been assembling over the previous decade but also for what we might delicately call an "antic temperament" that combined a wicked sense of humor with a killer instinct, someone with a hands-on, hard-nosed attitude who lived by the carpe diem credo, seize the day, and all that implies.

Central to Zinman's approach was the casting of a wide net; so many of the items he found came his way because he was willing to buy in bulk, the idea being that if the price was right—and with Michael Zinman the price always has to be right—there were bound to be nuggets of gold nestled among the pebbles. This works for the most part with material that is largely unknown to the vast majority of people, which in Zinman's case was old pamphlets, broadsides, almanacs, writs, contracts, journals, tracts, and assorted bits of ephemera from the seventeenth and eighteenth centuries that are often tattered and unsightly and require extensive research to document.

When his collection of eleven thousand pieces went, en bloc, to the Library Company of Philadelphia in 2000 as part of an $8 million gift-sale package, that venerable institution, founded in 1731 by Benjamin Franklin, became one of the most consequential repositories in the world of this material, second only to the American Antiquarian Society in Worcester, Massachusetts, and, in a heartbeat, positioned ahead of Harvard, Yale, the Library of Congress, and the John Carter Brown Library in Providence, Rhode Island.

Zinman has found rarities at flea markets, secondhand bookstores, antique shops, and even among the detritus of discards from major libraries that had been sold as scrap paper. Such finds included the first American sporting book, which was a sermon on the pleasures of fishing, published in 1743; the first American sex manual, printed in 1766; the first drug and pharmacy catalog, from 1771; the first American city directory, for New York in 1786;

a 1794 *Hamlet*, which is the first American edition of any play by Shakespeare; and the first American *Cinderella*, dated 1800. There also is the only known copy of a broadside of a poem by the African American poet Phillis Wheatley and the only known broadsheet printing of George Washington's 1792 State of the Union speech.

Now sixty-seven, Zinman, head of an international energy company, hasn't slowed down a bit and still finds great satisfaction in "handling the goods," as he puts it. In the five years since his imprints went to Philadelphia in 231 cardboard boxes, he has added another eight hundred items to the collection and is working on another endeavor: constitutions.

He rattled off a couple of examples of the seven hundred or so documents that he has come across thus far: the Constitution of the Association of Automatic Piano Players of the District of Columbia, the Constitution of the Ohio Colored Teachers Association, Constitution of the Pen and Pocket Knife Grinders and Finishers, the Constitution of the Sixth Avenue Railroad Company, the Constitution of the American Turf Club. "I paid maybe ten bucks each for these, maybe less, because nobody wants them, nobody knows what they are. Why do I want them? This is how the social organizations that form the fabric of this nation were put together. They all followed the American Constitution; some of them take direct paragraphs out of the Constitution itself."

And what got him started along this track? "I was at a book fair in Boston, there was a bunch of pamphlets at a booth, one of these fell down on the floor, and I got a look at it. I think what happens after a while is that things begin to click. I saw several constitutions of really odd organizations over a period of time, and I got interested. It's a whole continuum. The idea is, you're always looking. You're looking for something."

Ultimately, these documents will go to the Library Company of Philadelphia as well, the perfect repository, given its proximity to the National Constitution Center just a few blocks away on Independence Mall.

Anything else Zinman's been up to? "Oh yeah," he said. "I have a collection now of books published for the blind in raised letters before the development of Braille, about 1830 to 1890. I have maybe eighty examples of this stuff. It is so uncommon, you never see it." Unless, of course, you keep an alert eye, in which case the Zack Jenks truism applies: "Anything can be anywhere."

NOTE
There are a few people in the book world, bless them all, who are never-ending sources of great copy. Michael Zinman is one of them.

PLACES

SWEDEN

"A Swedish Library Tour," Biblio 3, no. 1 (January 1998).

The most effective way to grasp the essence of a country's book culture is to call on its libraries, a strategy that proved especially useful for me during a recent research trip I made to central and northern Europe.

My purpose in undertaking this bibliographic expedition went well beyond visiting historic book sites—informative talks with dealers, curators, preservationists, computer experts, collectors, educators, and scholars also were on the agenda—but libraries are always a good starting point for determining national book attitudes, and for being pointed in other useful directions.

Never has this strategy proved more fruitful for me than in Sweden, a Scandinavian nation of only six million people, but a country with a rich history that goes back many centuries. In Stockholm, my first stop was at the Royal Palace, where I was treated to a guided tour of the Bernadotte Library, one of the most beautiful book rooms to be seen anywhere and home to a decidedly eclectic collection of titles acquired by seven members of the Bernadotte dynasty, a family with French roots that has ruled Sweden without interruption since 1818.

The Bernadotte Library is very much a private collection, but one with a paradoxical twist to its composition. The current Swedish monarch, King Carl XVI Gustaf, has no books of his own shelved in what is, in effect, his ancestral library. "The king has some wonderful books in his residence, but they do not enter this room until we have a new king or a new queen in the palace," Carola Sjögren de Hauke, the head librarian, pointed out while identifying volumes contributed by previous rulers. What she was saying, in the gentlest of ways, is that only the books of deceased monarchs are admitted into the Bernadotte Library, and only then after the monarch's heirs have had an opportunity to pick through whatever titles they want for themselves.

Sjögren de Hauke said that researchers are allowed access to the materials, but their scholarly value is difficult to gauge, given the less-than-systematic approach that was applied to their gathering and the lack of focus. "A good many of the books were formal gifts," she said, although at least one of the Bernadottes, King Oskar II, who reigned from 1872 to 1907, was a genuine bibliophile. Of the one hundred thousand volumes in the library, he is by far the most generously represented on the shelves, with fully seven sections of the north wall in the 122-foot-long library reserved for his books.

"He was the third son of Oskar I, and he never expected to be king," Sjögren de Hauke said. "His oldest brother, Karl XV, died after thirteen years as king, and his other brother died of tuberculosis. Fifteen years before he became king, Oskar anonymously won a second-place medal from the Swedish Academy for his poetry, an achievement that inspired him to be a writer. Literature was his life, and most of the good books in here came from him."

Originally known as the great drawing room, the rectangular library was the last wing built in the palace, which started going up in the 1720s and took seventy years to complete. The library room opened in 1796. First-time visitors are immediately struck by the total absence of lavish adornment. The floorboards are plain pine, the shelves are stained Swedish oak, the ceiling a basic white, set off by four tasteful chandeliers. An upper balcony, also lined with books, is similarly modest. "Rococo decorations were part of the original scheme," Sjögren de Hauke said, "but there was very little money available at the time. Sweden had just emerged from some very expensive wars, and they couldn't afford the gold paint they had wanted. I am delighted they left it just the way it is."

For the first ninety-one years of its existence, the Bernadotte Library also served as an unofficial national library and was the legal depository for all books published in Sweden. In 1877, the Royal Library, also known as the National Library of Sweden, was established as a separate entity and moved to new quarters, taking with it thousands of books from the palace library.

In addition to caring for the books of kings and queens, Sjögren de Hauke maintains an archive of five hundred thousand official photographs taken over the years of Bernadotte activities. A colleague, Antoinette Ramsay, supervises an extensive library of art books.

Although some wonderful titles stand out in the Bernadotte Library—an exquisite decorated volume of Jean Blaeu's 1664 world atlas that entered the library upon the death in 1972 of King Gustav VI comes immediately to mind—the room is most impressive for the visual statement it makes on the inspirational power of books. "I have worked here for eighteen years," Sjögren de Hauke said, "and every time I walk in this room, it is like entering a cathedral."

About forty-five miles northwest of Stockholm, on the Sko peninsula, in stark contrast to the Bernadotte Library, is a magical time capsule of a palace containing a library that very few people know about, and it appears today much the way it did when a colorful succession of regal owners began stocking it generations ago with books acquired through a variety of means, many of them purchased, some received as gifts, others seized from conquered foreign neighbors as war booty.

Skokloster *slott*, or castle, was built in the mid-1600s on land overlooking Lake Mälaren, a scenic site previously owned by a thirteenth-century Cistercian nunnery. When Sweden converted to Lutheranism in the sixteenth century, the property was seized by the Crown. In 1611, King Karl IX granted the estate to Herman Wrangel, a twenty-four-year-old Estonian nobleman who had helped Sweden foster close ties with the Baltic states. Wrangel continued to prosper, rising from governor of the district to the rank of field marshal.

Wrangel's son and heir, Carl Gustav Wrangel, distinguished himself as a victorious commander of both field and naval forces in numerous foreign adventures, earning great wealth and honors, and serving at one point as governor-general of Swedish Pomerania. An amateur architect, he closely supervised construction of the castle, which began in 1654. Three and a half centuries later, it endures almost exactly as it was conceived and built, complete with original artworks, fixtures, "gilded leather" wall coverings, furnishings, kitchenware, domestic implements, tools, even the seventeenth-century privies and chamber stools, and yes, more than twenty thousand books and thirty thousand prints brought in by successive generations of affluent occupants.

Skokloster castle remained privately owned and occupied well into the twentieth century and was acquired by the Swedish government in the 1970s. Wisely, no effort has been made at creative restoration. Walls have been cleaned and touched up lightly where necessary, with everything remaining largely the way it always has been. The eighty-room building is open to visitors from May to September, with guided tours offered five times daily.

Among the highlights to be seen are the various armories owned by successive owners, most prominent among them a tower room featuring pinewood paneling installed in 1669 and displaying dozens of seventeenth-century handguns and rifles. Equally fascinating is an unfinished banquet hall, left exactly the way it was when Carl Gustav Wrangel died unexpectedly in 1676, prompting uncertain workers to walk off the job. Uncovered ceiling beams and untiled floorboards remain fully exposed; ladders still climb up the walls, old lathes, hammers, and saws lie nearby where they were left more than three hundred years ago.

Not on the formal tour are seven rooms on the top floor, each one facing the water, each one named for a European city (Stockholm, Cologne, Rome, etc.), and each one containing the books gathered by the castle's various occupants and augmented by collections from other family estates in Sweden that were acquired and brought to the library.

My guide for this visit was Elisabeth Westin Berg, for the past twenty years curator of this extraordinary collection. It was a gray morning in October, crisp, cool, and drizzly, making sweaters and coats necessary apparel. There is no central heating in the building, and no electricity in the library. The only light inside these seven rooms comes from the windows, which have an eastern exposure. "The combination of cold air and good circulation throughout the castle has been surprisingly healthy for the books," Westin Berg said pleasantly, as she pulled out volume after volume for me to examine. The most revered item in the library is Saint Bridget's *Epigramma libri presentis,* commonly known as *Revelationes,* one of only five known copies printed on vellum.

The collections include books published between 1466 and 1840, most of them dating from 1550 to 1750. The oldest book in the library is a copy of Cicero's *Officiis,* printed in 1466 on vellum in Mainz by Johann Fust, a financial backer of Johannes Gutenberg and one of his successors. On the back pastedown, the Skokloster resident who acquired this book, Carl Gustav Bielke, has written that the precious incunable was a gift and that he had authorized a new binding. Bielke was a dedicated bibliophile who bought actively at auctions in Stockholm and Uppsala and who took deliberate steps to maintain the integrity of the collection.

Determining the provenance of the books in the library is Westin Berg's primary concern these days, and she is hopeful that in time a catalog will be accessible on the World Wide Web. Subject areas range from theology, history, constitutional law, topography, and technology to architecture, astronomy, exploration, and philosophy.

"The intellectual landscape of Sweden over a particular period of time is represented here in this library," she said, noting that unlike the books of professors and educators, which often were dispersed when the owners died, books owned by the nobility generally were passed on from generation to generation. In the case of Skokloster, the continuum extended well into the twentieth century.

"We can determine to a great extent the ideas and the thoughts that were available to these people and what kinds of things interested them by studying the books in this library. That is why the provenance is so important. By knowing which family brought in which books, we can speculate on the reading interests of different people at different periods of time."

A number of marvelous maps, globes, and atlases are included in the rooms, each one an obvious rarity in its own right. Books are shelved in cases that are latticed with wooden grids. The walls are decorated with delicate paintings of various plants and animals. Ceiling beams are painted gaily with ribbons, flowers, and ornaments in a variety of colors, and the pinewood floors date from the construction of the castle in the 1600s. One of Wrangel's seventeenth-century books, *Architectura recreationis*, by Joseph Furttenbach, a German, stipulates an eastern aspect as best for storing books—precisely the arrangement incorporated in the design of Skokloster.

A totally unexpected surprise was the presence at Skokloster of a painting known to book lovers the world over, a wacky construction of a librarian fashioned out of books in the sixteenth century by Giuseppe Arcimboldo, an Italian artist whose bizarre compositions of human forms include portraits arranged out of fruits, flowers, and vegetables. (A G. P. Harsdörfer wood engraving based on this painting appears on the back dust jacket of my book *A Gentle Madness*.)

And how did the original of this famous painting enter the castle's collections, and where did it come from? Westin Berg shrugged. "We don't know; possibly it was war booty."

My trip to Sweden also included a visit to the Nobel Library, located near the Royal Palace in the same building that houses the Swedish Academy. Its function is to gather books from around the world that will be used by the judges to determine who will win the Nobel Prize for literature each year. My visit, by pure coincidence, came the day after the Italian theater personality Dario Fo was named the recipient for 1997.

Especially distinctive about the Nobel Library's collecting policy is that it focuses exclusively on books written by living authors. Since the library was established in 1901, its considerable holdings have become a window into the development of twentieth-century world literature and offer insight into such delicate concepts as literary merit.

Also on my Swedish itinerary was a tour of Kungliga Biblioteket, the Royal Library (the National Library of Sweden), newly expanded with the addition of ten underground *bokmagasins*, or storage chambers, that were blasted out of granite and packed with enough compact shelving to store books acquired through the year 2050. Some 144,000 cubic yards of pulverized rock—enough rubble to fill thirty-three thousand trucks—was hauled away from the site between 1992 and 1997 and is being used in the construction of some new railroad beds outside of Stockholm. My visit to this boldly conceived repository—a tangible commitment by one nation to the preservation of books that extends well into the next millennium— made for a perfect coda to an eye-opening trip.

GERMANY

"Dispatches from Deutschland," Biblio 3, no. 2 (February 1998).

If there is a finer showplace in the world devoted exclusively to the history of writing, bookmaking, and printing than the Gutenberg Museum in Mainz, Germany, I would very much like to hear about it.

Just a forty-minute train ride from Frankfurt, the museum houses four floors of exhibition space that is open to the public and that offers, in a sweeping panorama, an inspired look at the myriad ways humans have found to record and pass on to future generations their history, literature, and culture.

The centerpiece exhibits in the museum, as one might expect, celebrate the landmark accomplishment of Johannes Gutenberg, the patrician's son and former goldsmith who developed an ingenious way of printing words on paper and vellum that has endured for five-and-a-half centuries. Precisely where in this medieval city on the Rhine River Gutenberg set up the Western world's first modern printing shop remains uncertain, but it could not have been very far from where today the museum pays tribute to his achievement with impeccable taste. It is that reality, in fact, that makes a visit such a memorable expedition and, for bibliophiles, almost a sacred pilgrimage.

Founded in 1900 as a living memorial to Gutenberg, the museum moved its collection of four thousand exhibition items into its current quarters in 1962 and has been visited over the years by more than three million people. A fanciful bust of the inventor created by Finnish sculptor Wäinö Aaltonen stands outside the main entrance at Liebfrauenplatz 5, near Dom Cathedral in the center of the old city. The gateway, a construction of bronze plaques, shows printing blocks from six centuries in relief. The main building features a striking rococo facade. Known as Zum Römischen Kaiser—the Roman Emperor—this structure was built in 1664; it houses administrative offices for museum staff and a seventy-thousand-volume library that, not surprisingly, is particularly strong in the history of typography and bookmaking.

Visitors expecting to see little more than a respectful tribute to a native son are in for a pleasant surprise. Gutenberg's accomplishment takes center stage, but only as part of a much larger scheme devoted to documenting the entire continuum of written and printed words. A working replica of what Gutenberg's press may have looked like has been installed in a small shop on the basement level. Live demonstrations allow visitors to see how molten metal alloys are molded and punched into letters of the alphabet, how words and sentences are assembled line by line into "sticks" of type, and how they, in turn, are used to make impressions on paper with oil-based inks, another Gutenberg innovation.

"We do not know precisely what Gutenberg's press looked like," said Dr. Eva Hanebutt-Benz, director of the museum, during my visit there. "None of his type has survived, either, and none of his business records. We can only make educated guesses about how many presses he had operating in his shop." She paused and summarized with quiet understatement the full extent of Gutenberg's legacy: "What survives is the book."

The *book* of which she speaks, of course, is a treasure known variously as the Mazarin Bible, after the French bibliophile Cardinal Jules Mazarin, whose opulent library in Paris included the first copy to attract scholarly attention; the Gutenberg Bible, after the printer himself; and, in recent times, the Forty-two-line Bible, for the number of lines in each printed column of most copies (a few of the first leaves have forty lines of type, and a later Bible printed by Gutenberg had thirty-six). Some 180 copies of the two-volume book are believed to have been printed in Gutenberg's shop starting around 1450, and forty-eight are known to survive today. Two of these can be seen in a mezzanine vault at the Gutenberg Museum. They are joined by a number of other magnificent items, including the 1459 Mainz Psalter, a book printed with Gutenberg type by Johann Fust and Peter Schöffer, his successors.

Displays on the first floor feature prints produced in Mainz from the sixteenth to the twentieth centuries, with detailed information on the graphic techniques. An impressive array of vintage printing presses occupies a good portion of the space, among them old iron handpresses, cylinder presses, an 1824 Columbia press, and two Dingler toggle presses. Nearby, other tools and devices show how engravings, etchings, lithographs, copperplates, mezzotints, and intaglio prints are made, and another area is devoted to bookbinding.

Although printing is the core theme of the Gutenberg Museum, attention is also devoted to the production of medieval manuscripts and, on the second floor, to milestones in the book traditions of Islam and Asia. Visitors can find examples of clay tablets from Mesopotamia, hieroglyphic carvings on stone, and books written on palm leaves and in Japanese script. One rarity featured is a dharani—a Buddhist prayer—printed from a woodblock in A.D. 760. The world's earliest known forms of printing—Korean stamps carved from wooden blocks—are represented here, too, as well as fragments from papyrus scrolls.

An exceptional collection of books printed by William Morris at the Kelmscott Press—the largest such collection in Germany— is displayed in an art nouveau area on the second floor. Samples from other presses include items produced by Aubrey Beardsley, Thomas Cobden-Sanderson, Max Klinger, and Heinrich Vogler. Additional cases house displays of miniature graphic arts, posters, bookplates, collages, and paper theaters (early pop-ups). Yet another section deals with the history of papermaking, and an entire area is devoted to the book arts of the twentieth century, with an emphasis on impressionism and expressionism in book illustration.

My afternoon in Mainz came after a day spent in Frankfurt am Main at the Deutsche Bibliothek, a gleaming national library complex that opened last spring. Since the reunification of East Germany and West Germany into the Federal Republic of Germany in 1990, three separate libraries have been consolidated into one national system known collectively as the Deutsche Bibliothek. The other facilities include one in Berlin known as Deutsche Musikarchiv, devoted to music. The third, in Leipzig, formerly served as the state library of the German Democratic Republic and is called the Deutsche Bücherei. In addition to maintaining its original collections, this unit now serves as headquarters for a national program of book deacidification and preservation.

An essential goal of my recent foreign travel has been to determine national priorities in collecting and preserving books. Germany presents an unusually interesting question: Do the recent history and politics of the various German governments influence in any way what kinds of materials are gathered and collected under what is now, essentially, one roof?

"We deal with that issue in a most straightforward way," Professor Klaus-Dieter Lehmann, director general of the Deutsche Bibliothek, told me. "We collect everything about Germany and the German people, and in particular everything printed in the German language, which cuts across all lines. And our policy is to keep everything we acquire. So deciding which books are worthy of preservation is a very simple matter. We choose to preserve them all."

Frankfurt is one of the world's great book cities, in a league historically with Venice, Leiden, and other notable centers. Aptly, my meeting with Professor Lehmann and his staff came a week before two hundred thousand people inundated Frankfurt for a venerable rite of publishing known as the Frankfurt Book Fair, a huge trade event held every October that traces its lineage back to the fifteenth century and that remains, by far, the largest such event to be mounted anywhere.

Leipzig, home of the Deutsche Bücherei, has a book heritage of comparable significance. A three-hour train ride from Frankfurt, the beautiful city enjoys a rich history and has been booming since reunification, with massive construction projects everywhere. The Deutsche Bücherei was established in 1912 by a consortium of Leipzig publishing houses to serve as a repository for their books, journals, and newspapers. The boardroom walls display portraits of the library's "founding fathers"—a Who's Who gallery of prominent Leipzig publishers.

Since reunification, the library's mission has been modified to include the preservation and conservation of the national collections. My visit to Leipzig included an introduction to the mass deacidification processes that have been developed here. Unlike older rag papers, industrially produced materials from the mid-nineteenth century contain acids that decompose the cellulose fibers in the paper, producing what are now known as "brittle books."

Three main deacidification technologies use a variety of sophisticated machines. One, a procedure called leaf casting, actually splits pages for treatment, then reassembles them with a center layer of support paper. Currently, about twenty-two thousand sheets a year are being preserved in this manner. Another process can deacidify at one time up to 350 pounds of books in what amounts to a water-free bath. All told, about two hundred thousand books a year are being treated in this manner.

Bookish visitors to Leipzig should include on their itineraries a couple of hours at an extraordinary museum now housed in the Deutsche Bücherei, the Deutsche Buch- und Schriftmuseum. A private collection established in 1884 by Heinrich Klem, it is devoted to book writing, bookmaking, book design, book distribution, and book appreciation in all its guises, with special emphasis on Leipzig. The museum works in a visually eloquent way as the perfect accompaniment to, not a replication of, the Gutenberg Museum several hundred miles away in Mainz.

On the fifth floor of the Deutsche Bücherei is an entirely different kind of collection, one that recalls a far less noble side of German history. Here, in a steel vault, is what is now known as the Anne-Frank-Shoah-Bibliothek, an international research library for the documentation of the persecution and annihilation of six million Jews during the Second World War. Of special interest are nine thousand *exil* books banned by Nazi Propaganda Minister Joseph Goebbels.

Like Frankfurt, Leipzig is famous for an annual book fair, an event started in the twelfth century to promote commerce but that, with the advent of printing, also began to attract publishers from all over Germany as exhibitors. By 1500, just fifty years after Gutenberg's development of movable type, Leipzig accounted for eleven printing shops, the most of any German city. As the Leipzig fair attracted more and more outsiders, the city grew as a storage center for unsold inventory.

The only major interruption in the Leipzig fair came during the Nazi years. The first post–Second World War fair was held in 1947, and since reunification it has attracted exhibitors from around the world. Unlike the Frankfurt fair, which strictly showcases newly published books, the Leipzig book fair includes a fully integrated antiquarian book fair. Sixty-two dealers of rare and antiquarian books were represented last year, each of them members of the German Antiquarian Book Trade Society.

So, if you're on your way to Germany, you can work into your itinerary some marvelous side trips to museums devoted exclusively to the history of books and bookmaking, you can drop by a couple of libraries, and you can do a little book hunting on the side.

NEW YORK CITY

"Fit for a Czar," Biblio 3, no. 3 (March 1998).

Three-quarters of a century after they were sold for hard currency by a financially strapped Soviet Union, some of the spectacular books that once graced the shelves of Romanov palaces in imperial Russia went on view last fall in the New York Public Library (NYPL) to rave reviews.

"I had been wanting to do an exhibition of the Romanov material from the time I came to the library thirteen years ago," Edward Kasinec, chief librarian of the NYPL's Slavic and Baltic Division, said with evident pleasure a few hours before *The Romanovs: Their Empire, Their Books* was opened to the general public. "But the truth is that this would have been very difficult to mount while the Soviet Union was still in place, and I would have done it with great reluctance."

With the dissolution of the Soviet Union in 1990, however, the climate has been far more agreeable for the library to showcase its trophy collection of Romanov material. That, and the fact that its Slavic and Baltic Division—the oldest organized department of its kind in the United States—observes its one hundredth anniversary in 1998, made a persuasive argument for displaying the items now.

The libraries of twenty-six members of the Romanov dynasty, as well as volumes bearing the markings of nine imperial palaces, are represented in the NYPL collections, but the majority of books, manuscripts, watercolors, and original photographs selected for the exhibition were the property of five family members: Alexander II, Alexander III, Nicholas II, Grand Duke Vladimir Aleksandrovich

(the son of Alexander II), and Grand Duke Konstantin Konstanti-
novich (the cousin of Alexander III).

Installed in the Edna Barnes Salomon Room at the library's
Center for the Humanities at Fifth Avenue and Forty-second Street,
the exhibition was majestic by any measurement. A dozen sturdy
exhibition cases, with items placed on each side, were arranged
according to themes that suggested the scope and influence of the
Romanov dynasty, which ruled Russia from 1613 to 1917. The logo
of the exhibition featured the bookplate of Russia's last emperor,
Nicholas II, designed by Baron Armin de Fölkersam, with a legend,
translated from the Russian, that reads, "His Majesty's Own Library,
Winter Palace."

"Nicholas II had about thirty thousand volumes in his personal
library at Winter Palace," Kasinec said. "He was the administrator
of a vast, very complex, multinational empire. He used books as
reference material and also for his own enjoyment. In the Alexander
Palace, which was the residence of the imperial family, it was the
tradition to read for pleasure in the evening."

While a good many of the titles were intended to amuse Romanov family members, there is very little to suggest that these are
ordinary books. Included among the items on display (the exhibition
ran from November 4, 1997, to February 29, 1998) were sumptuous
coronation albums, presentation copies of regimental histories, hand-
tooled bindings, various maps and reports pertaining to military
campaigns and territorial expansion, pamphlets, lithographs, books
printed on silk, and an album of watercolors produced in the 1830s
that depict Ottoman costumes.

Uncommonly interesting are items that celebrate the tercen-
tenary of the Romanov dynasty in 1913. These objects, according to
Marc Raeff, Bakhmeteff Professor of Russian Studies emeritus at
Columbia University and the author of a detailed essay written for
the exhibition catalog, "were meant to consolidate the image and role
of the dynasty and heighten the population's fervor, and to reaffirm
the union between church and state." Just four years later, whatever

"fervor" the general population may have had was for anything but the Romanovs; the dynasty was gone, and the Russian Orthodox Church was marginalized by the new Soviet government.

"An important factor to keep in mind is that while many of these books are beautiful and rare, they also are books that tell us something about the way these individuals viewed their historic role and their obligation to administer an empire that, at its height, occupied one-sixth of the world's surface, from America to the Elba, and all the way down to the Hawaiian Islands and California," Kasinec said.

The NYPL exhibition appeared at the same time that an animated film about the Romanovs, *Anastasia*, began making the rounds of movie theaters, and followed hard on the heels of a 1996 extravaganza at the Metropolitan Museum of Art that featured a fabulous selection of Fabergé items, and which broke all attendance records for a decorative arts show. Just three weeks after the official opening of the Romanovs exhibit, the NYPL bookstore reported that all the exhibition catalogs had been sold, further evidence that interest in the pre-Soviet period remains as strong as ever.

One of the cocurators of the NYPL show, Robert H. Davis Jr., of the Slavic and Baltic Division staff, noted that the exhibition "stands the traditional idea of Romanov 'riches' on its head, making *books* the focus of attention, and demonstrating that, in many respects, a finely bound tome or photo album is, in its own way, every bit as spectacular and revealing as the art and jewelry that we traditionally associate with the Imperial House, and perhaps even more so."

Sprinkled among the books, watercolors, manuscripts, and maps were a few glimmering artifacts, including some swords, pieces of jewelry, elaborate dinner menus, and colorful uniforms, but they were there strictly for color, Kasinec said, and as "background" to the books. "We happened to have these things in the collection, and we decided what better time to use them than now."

As interesting as the Romanov books are, they are hardly sufficient to sustain a sophisticated research library. Thus, in addition
to dramatizing the major themes of the exhibition, the NYPL emphasized that its three thousand Romanov items are just one small
segment of a much larger collection of related materials.

"These pieces that you see here are dispersed throughout various departments in the library," Kasinec said. And the Slavic and
Baltic Division that he directs includes more than four hundred
thousand items, making it, in essence, a library within a library.

"Why do you suppose the Soviets approached us to buy the
Romanov material in the 1920s?" he asked. "We were already in place,
and we had been in place since 1898. Once they decided to sell the
books, this was the logical place for them to go." Indeed, research
materials in the Slavic and Baltic Division are so rich they have
been consulted over the years by many thousands of readers, many
of them prominent Russians—Leon Trotsky, Vladimir Nabokov,
and Alexander Kerensky among them.

One section of the exhibition was devoted to matters of "sellers,
salesmen, and buyers," and to how these materials once considered
so dear to Russian rulers were later seized by the Soviets and sold
on the open market to foreigners. Nothing was sacred, not even the
crown jewels, which also were put up for sale. A 1925 photograph
displayed at the show pictures the gems laid out on a cloth like so
much black-market contraband. Another photo shows Romanov
family books tightly tied in bundles and being readied for shipment
abroad.

"In the two decades after the Revolution," Raeff writes, "various Soviet ministries and agencies first confiscated much of this
wealth, and then sold portions of it abroad to Western collections
and collectors at auction and, more surreptitiously, through an assortment of art dealers, antiquarians, businessmen, and librarians.
The beautiful icons, furniture, decorative arts, books, manuscripts,
and photographs found receptive buyers among both Western European and American museum and library collections."

At a time when nations around the world are becoming increasingly protective of cultural material they consider part of their national patrimony, it is worth remembering that some nations through history have willingly parted with the cornerstones of their heritage for cold cash.

"I think part of it simply is that the Soviet leadership was eager to expunge a part of their history," Kasinec said. "Why would they want to keep the relics of the ancien régime? Think of what happened after the French Revolution. They began to expunge, to sell, to nationalize, to remove as well. But the Soviets knew where these materials were going. In his memoirs, Trotsky says the first place he visited when he was in New York was the public library. So they knew this library, and they respected it."

The story of how three thousand Romanov books made their way to Manhattan begins with a simple letter dated October 13, 1923, written by Anatoly Vasilievich Lunacharsky, a Bolshevik intellectual who served as commissar of enlightenment from 1918 to 1929, to Edwin Hatfield Anderson, then the director of the New York Public Library, inviting representatives from the Slavic and Baltic Division to visit Russia. The NYPL's book-buying trips to the Baltic states, Russia, and the Ukraine quickly followed.

Another photograph pictures the late Armand Hammer, one of the major figures in twentieth-century Russian American relations, who, with his brother, Victor, operated Hammer Galleries in New York and dominated the sales market for Russian paintings, objets d'art, and precious books during the 1920s and early 1930s. Purchase of many association copies now in the NYPL collections were arranged through them.

Other documentary items in the exhibition make clear that other dealers and institutions were actively involved in acquiring books from Romanov collections. Noted booksellers Israel Perlstein, Alexander Schaffer, and Hans P. Kraus arranged numerous transactions in the United States; William H. Robinson Ltd. was similarly involved in the United Kingdom. Perlstein, in particular, dealt in Slavic antiquarian books for more than half a century and arranged for the purchase of Russian imperial association copies by the Library of Congress and the law library of Harvard University, in addition to the NYPL.

Clearly, the NYPL was by no means alone in seeking out Russian imperial books. In Cambridge, Massachusetts, Archibald Cary Coolidge, a legendary director of the Harvard College Library earlier this century, was the prime mover in building a major research collection of Slavic and Eastern European collections. He traveled extensively through Eastern Europe seeking out books, committed funds for their purchase, and laid the foundation for what is generally regarded as the world's finest Eastern European collection outside of Russia. He and his colleagues acquired thousands of books with an imperial provenance, many of which are housed today in the International Legal Studies Library and the Houghton Library at Harvard.

The migration of Romanov books to New York is somewhat different in that they were not being acquired for an educational institution but for a library established and funded by private individuals to serve the general public. That the NYPL continues to build and maintain major research-level collections is a testament to its continuing mandate of service to all. At a time when people debate the changing role of libraries, it is enlightening to take note of an institution that still believes books, not computers, are its primary resource.

Toronto

"Canada's Book Stronghold," Biblio 3, no. 5 (May 1998).

For many of the sixty thousand students enrolled at the University of Toronto in Ontario, the two concrete towers on St. George Street that dominate the downtown campus are known as Fort Book, an apt name for a mighty bastion of knowledge that is the central repository for ten million volumes.

More formally known as the John Robarts Research Library and the Thomas Fisher Rare Book Library, the concrete buildings, opened twenty-five years ago, make an impressive statement, inside and out, on the primacy of books in the life of a modern university. At a time when many institutions are uneasily groping through what is sometimes called a paradigm shift away from a printed-books mentality to greater reliance on electronic sources of information, it is comforting to see an arrangement where both worlds seem assured of continued financial support.

Part of that confidence comes from the security of having a "protected budget" at the University of Toronto for buying books, meaning that however adventurous the mandate may be to bring in expensive new computer equipment, the latest software, and sophisticated research services, cuts will not be imposed on the money that is needed to obtain printed materials, and the allowances are adjusted annually for inflation. The current budget for book acquisitions is $18 million.

"Our experience so far is that anything we have done electronically—and we have tried to stay at the leading edge in those fields—seems to result in people using more things in print," Carole

Moore, chief librarian at the university, said during an interview in her office on the second floor of Robarts Library.

"I think the better job we do in making more things accessible, the greater support there is for this protected acquisition system we have," Moore continued. "The scientists want database access, and so do the humanities scholars, for that matter, but what we also are seeing here is a revival of interest in some types of books. We circulate nearly seven million items a year, and from my perspective, that's all you need to know. Instead of worrying about what direction libraries are going to take, it seems to me that the future simply could be more of everything."

Richard Landon, director of the Fisher Library and my host during a recent trip to the campus, totally agrees. "The people who do the research, the scholars, they say they want more manuscripts, more books. That is very clear to me now more than ever, and I've been here since 1967."

The University of Toronto enjoys unusual stature in Canada. Not only does it have the largest single concentration of books in the country, but also it serves as a kind of national library, providing some of the function for the nation's twenty-six million citizens that the Library of Congress does in the United States. There is a formal national library located three hundred miles away in Ottawa, the federal capital, that serves as the legal depository for all books published in the country, but it has only been in existence since 1952, and its collections are strictly limited to Canadiana.

As one might expect of a large university with many academic disciplines to support, the scope of the University of Toronto's holdings extends well beyond the history, literature, and culture of Canada. "Fully 90 percent of the books we have were published outside our borders," Landon pointed out, and the rich manuscript collections he maintains embrace a wide variety of interests as well.

The Thomas Fisher Rare Book Library, named for a prominent nineteenth-century Toronto mill owner whose descendants have provided generous support to the university, is a structure of uncommon beauty comprising six levels, or "mezzanines," of books coiled around an open atrium. Close to six hundred thousand volumes reside here, all but forty thousand of them acquired during Landon's time at the university. Some five thousand linear feet of manuscripts are there as well. "My greatest goal in life," he said in the laid-back drawl of British Columbia, where he grew up, "is to fill this building up by the time I retire."

A guided tour of the Fisher Library in Landon's company is an unqualified treat, a rare opportunity to spend time with a bookman whose primary pleasure is to comb the world for thrilling new acquisitions. He is joined on these scouting trips by his wife, Marie E. Korey, formerly head of the rare-book department at the Free Library of Philadelphia and, since 1990, the librarian of Massey College in the University of Toronto. She also is custodian of a collection in the history of printing that includes five working nineteenth-century iron handpresses. With the late Edwin Wolf 2nd, Korey was curator of the landmark *Legacies of Genius* exhibition mounted jointly by the Library Company of Philadelphia and the Historical Society of Pennsylvania in 1988.

The Fisher Library does not have a Gutenberg Bible, but it does have on long-term deposit from a German collection a Catholicon, printed at Mainz in 1460 on Gutenberg's press and with his type. "What makes this copy a lot of fun," Landon said while deftly balancing the volume on a guardrail in the second mezzanine, "is that it's not in a fancy binding, and researchers can examine the physical evidence without having their hands slapped. We'll let you look at the cancels and the watermarks, whatever you need to see; we had one scholar here from Wolfenbüttel a while back who spent a week just with this book."

Shelved a few feet from the Catholicon is a 1425 Book of Hours decorated throughout with illuminations so exquisite that some scholars believe they were painted by the Bedford Master, an anonymous fifteenth-century artist of exceptional talent. "This copy is so

All monetary references in this essay are to Canadian dollars, unless otherwise indicated.

fresh and crisp because it was in a private collection in Germany for three hundred years and never opened. Most Books of Hours are pretty well thumbed through, but it's pretty obvious nobody ever read this one very much."

Landon is understandably proud of these rarities and the many other choice illuminated books and incunables he has acquired, just as he is pleased to note that the Fisher Library has the only First Folio of Shakespeare (1623) in Canada, as well as nice copies of the Second (1632), Third (1664) and Fourth (1685) Folios as well. But he is equally delighted to point out some of the lesser-known items that make the Fisher Library particularly attractive to researchers.

"We have some extraordinary collections here. In 1968, for instance, we bought from Richard Freeman his Charles Darwin collection. Freeman did the bibliographical handlist of Darwin, and we used his collection as the basis to build on, so that we now have the best collection of printed matter on Darwin in the world. The books I want most of all are the books that nobody else has, because that means scholars have to come to Toronto to use them."

Landon likes to quote the late Robert Rosenthal, a noted rare-book librarian at the University of Chicago, "who used to say he couldn't care less whether he had a first edition of *Paradise Lost* or not, because you can find that anywhere, and I agree with him to some extent. The fact is that we have to have a *Paradise Lost* here because we are the most important library in Canada; but the reputation of a research library is based to some extent on what you have that people can't see anywhere else."

Wherever in the world he travels in search of books, Landon said he keeps his desiderata "up here," in his head. "You like to think that you can specialize and build on strength, and it's always a good idea to support the curriculum, but I don't always have to do that. I've been trying to build up an Australian collection with the expectation that, at some point, the university will be setting up something in South Pacific studies. It's part of my job to define areas of the collection to be built, and I have not been interfered with in that function."

One factor that never influences his decision to acquire an item, however, is whether it will be of immediate use to anyone. "The notion that you have some kind of time frame in which something has to be read is at odds with the definition of what constitutes a research library. The definition of a research collection is one word—*potential*. When I buy a book for the university, I don't care if it goes unread for a hundred and fifty years."

Landon also said that great collections take time to build, and that nothing worthwhile happens overnight. "It took me twenty-five years to find *Anne of Green Gables*, and I had to pay $5,000 Canadian for it. But if you're going to have what you think is the greatest collection of Canadian literature in Canada, then you've got to have *Anne of Green Gables*."

And of course every "great" book in a collection by no means has to be a first edition. To emphasize that point, Landon retrieved a copy of the ninth edition copy of Thomas Gray's *Elegy Written in a Country Churchyard*, dated 1754, which he acquired in 1988 as the university's seven millionth book. "The Friends of the Library asked me to get something nice, and I guess they thought I'd find a nice incunable for $25,000 or so, but I happened to know of the existence of this in Philadelphia." Landon described the complicated genealogy of the book, and how he acquired it for the Fisher Library for $325,000, in U.S. dollars. Of particular moment is the fact that this copy of Gray's *Elegy* was once the property of General James Wolfe, commander of British troops in 1759 in the climactic battle in which French soldiers under the command of the Marquis de Montcalm were driven from Quebec. Although Wolfe died at the hour of victory, legend holds that on the eve of the battle he repeated from memory Gray's *Elegy*. The university's copy, heavily underlined and full of marginal notations in Wolfe's hand, was sent to England with the general's remains and followed a circuitous route back to North America in 1916 through Dr. A. S. W. Rosenbach, finally returning to Canada ten years ago.

From that high spot, Landon indicated the eight millionth book he acquired for the university, a first edition copy of Sir Hans Sloane's masterwork in two volumes, *Natural History of Jamaica* (published in 1707 and 1725). "For me, the great item in this whole sequence was the eight million and first book, a Cologne Chronicle, 1499, a nice copy and much rarer than the Nuremberg Chronicle, of which we have two. The eight million and second book was the only Jane Austen title we didn't have, *Mansfield Park* in three volumes, 1814. The eight million and third was a five-page holograph letter of Galileo, one of only four Galileo letters in North America."

Founded in 1827 as Kings College, the University of Toronto, like virtually every institution of higher learning in Canada, is publicly funded and supported. A catastrophic fire on February 14, 1890, destroyed the library, and all books except for those out on loan were lost, including a full set of Audubon's *Birds of America*. With the help of universities in Europe and the United States, a new collection was built that within ten years was stronger than the one it replaced, but the push to achieve international status began in the mid-1960s, when Claude Bissell, university president, committed the institution to building graduate research programs of international renown. Money was allocated to hire faculty and strengthen the collections.

"The decision was made to go after all kinds of things in a big way, history of science, medicine, every manner of Canadian material, French eighteenth-century material—we have wonderful collections in Voltaire and Rousseau," Landon said. "And it was a good time to buy. I just ran across an old invoice for eight books we bought from Jake Zeitlin in 1972. There was a 1470 Aristotle in there, a 1665 copy of Robert Hooke's *Micrographia*, things like that, and the total price was $10,650 American. You could find those books now, I suppose, but they would cost you forty or fifty times what they cost us twenty-five years ago. So we've had some pretty good luck along the way."

NOTE
By 2005, the University of Toronto was ranked third by the Association of Research Libraries for total holdings in North America with 10,342,574 volumes, up from fourth position the previous year, and topped only by Harvard and Yale universities, giving it the largest library collection among publicly funded institutions on the continent.

NEW YORK CITY II

I wrote this piece to run in the February 1999 issue of Biblio, *but an opportunity to interview Tom Wolfe at the Carlyle Hotel in Manhattan—along with an assurance that my profile of him would be featured on the cover of the magazine—persuaded me to delay publication of what I had already submitted. A month or so later, however—and with no prior warning to anyone—*Biblio *announced that it was ceasing operations, leaving this article—which I rather liked, because I truly love New York—an orphan. I am pleased to see it finally find a home in this collection.*

O
nly in New York, it seems, could you have book exhibitions of international consequence showing simultaneously at two nearby libraries, each one an unqualified triumph, and each one the subject of a splendid catalog.

In the instance of both shows—*The Wormsley Library: A Personal Selection by Sir Paul Getty, K.B.E.*, at the Pierpont Morgan Library, and *A Treasure House of Books: The Library of Duke August of Brunswick-Wolfenbüttel*, at the Grolier Club—the items on display were borrowed from important collections in Europe to celebrate noteworthy milestones in the United States and represented significant coups for their sponsors.

The Morgan Library event marked the first time that Sir Paul Getty, son of the late American oil billionaire John Paul Getty, has allowed any material from the library he has been assembling with exceptional taste and tenor over the past thirty years to be displayed publicly. The exhibition opened on January 27, 1999, as part of a yearlong series of events organized to commemorate the Morgan Library's seventy-fifth anniversary as an independent institution.

The Grolier Club exhibition, meanwhile, brought a choice selection of items from a remarkable library established in Germany more than 350 years ago by Duke August the Younger of Brunswick-Wolfenbüttel, and represented the first time any materials from that repository had crossed the Atlantic; the show was put on in honor of the 115th anniversary of the founding of the Grolier Club, the nation's oldest and most renowned bibliophilic society.

A sixty-six-year-old native of the United States, John Paul Getty II moved to England from Italy thirty years ago. Described by journalist Dominic Lawson in the London *Sunday Telegraph* last year as "probably the greatest philanthropist ever to have lived in this country," he was given an honorary knighthood by Queen Elizabeth II in 1986 and became a British citizen last year, a formality that allowed him the right to be called Sir Paul. His charitable gifts to English causes have been estimated at well over $200 million and have benefited a variety of interests, including vital support for the National Gallery and the British Film Institute. One of his bequests provided for the design and construction of an award-winning building to house the famous collection of chained books at Hereford Cathedral and to enable the cathedral to retain ownership of the Mappa Mundi, a unique thirteenth-century map of the world executed on a single sheet of parchment which came within a whisker of being sold at auction a few years ago.

An ardent Anglophile, Sir Paul lives on a thousand-acre estate west of London in the Chiltern Hills along the Oxfordshire-Buckinghamshire border known as Wormsley. A worthy building to house what is uniformly acknowledged to be the finest private library assembled by anyone in the latter quarter of the twentieth-century was designed by the architect Nicholas Johnston; his scale model of the structure is a centerpiece of the Morgan Library exhibition.

But most impressive of all, needless to say, are the 110 printed books, *livres d'artistes*, manuscripts, engravings, and elegant bindings that serve as a sampling from the library, estimated by Robert J. D. Harding of Maggs Bros. Ltd., of Berkeley Square in London, Sir Paul's agents for all book purchases and the publisher of the exhibition catalog, to number about eight thousand volumes. If there is a connecting theme in the exhibition, it is the art and craftsmanship of the book in all its facets and all its glory, with particular emphasis on English works and traditions over the past nine centuries, but with stunning examples from a wide variety of traditions.

"Essentially, we've tried to show a little bit of everything here," Harding said as he pointed out some of his favorite pieces. "It's bindings, it's illuminations, it's calligraphy, it's typography, it's paper; we've tried to give some sense of the whole art of the book, from the Middle Ages right through to the modern." And that, essentially, is the scheme of the larger collection at Wormsley, he added, "although I'm not so sure it's anything more sophisticated than wonderful books being bought as they become available." Having the means and the conviction to seize the moment are essential in building any great library, but equally important—and Sir Paul takes special pains to make the point in the short foreword he wrote for the catalog—is the determined collector's willingness to accept excellent professional advice. Bryan D. Maggs, a principal in a firm of booksellers that has been operated by members of the Maggs family for six generations, has represented Sir Paul exclusively at various auctions around the world, and serves as the Wormsley librarian. "Bryan knows the books backwards and forwards," Harding said. "He's been there from the beginning. I've known the library myself for about twenty years." Given a display case by itself in the lobby outside the main gallery at the Morgan Library is the copy of Geoffrey Chaucer's *Canterbury Tales* edited and ushered through the press in 1477 by England's first printer, William Caxton, and purchased last July at Christie's in London for $7.5 million, the highest price ever paid at auction for a printed book. With fears expressed in some quarters that the Caxton, one of a dozen surviving copies, might be bought by a foreign collector or institution, Sir Paul's declaration that the treasure would never leave the United Kingdom except on temporary loan was greeted with enormous relief. This is the only Caxton in the Wormsley Library—there are, by contrast, sixty-three books printed by him in the Morgan collection—"but if you are to have only one, this is not a bad one to have," Harding said with evident satisfaction. "You could wait a lifetime and never get a chance to buy that Caxton; you have to grasp the opportunity when it's presented." To buttress the point, Harding walked me over to a display case containing three of his personal favorites, not because they are necessarily the dearest items in the library, although they are quite extraordinary, but because they confirm his contention that great material is still out there, somewhere, available to be acquired by intrepid collectors, sometimes from the unlikeliest of sources.

"This section here represents discards from American institutional libraries," he said simply by way of introduction. The items lying open under glass before us included the following: a twelfth-century folio manuscript on vellum identified as the Zacharias Chrysopolitanus, featuring four large historiated initials set against burnished gold backgrounds, acquired in the 1987 to 1989 sales at Christie's of the Edward Laurence Doheny Memorial Library in Camarillo, California, known more familiarly as the Estelle Doheny Library for the legendary "countess" who assembled it so assiduously in the name of her late husband.

The Ottobeuren Gradual, a quarto manuscript on vellum consisting of 264 leaves and dating from 1164, with text in a Germanic Romanesque minuscule, including three full-page and two half-page miniatures, fourteen historiated initials, and many elaborated initials, formerly the property of the John Carter Brown Library in Providence, Rhode Island, was acquired in 1981 at a Sotheby's sale.

Listed as No. 1 in the catalog is a fragment of text on vellum from the mid-seventh century containing parts of four chapters from a history of the early Christian church by the historian Eusebius, written in Latin, possibly of Celtic heritage, and arguably the oldest surviving portion of a book produced in England. The manuscript survives because it was used in the sixteenth century as a wrapper inside the bindings of two medical texts now owned by the Folger Shakespeare Library in Washington, D.C., where it was discovered in 1984 when work was being done on the volumes; Sir Paul acquired the item in 1989.

William M. Voelkle, curator of medieval and Renaissance manuscripts at the Morgan and one of the organizers of the Getty exhibition, pointed out that transactions of this nature are not uncommon when the materials in question fall outside the scope of an institution's collecting policy. Most of the "great items in the world" are now in private collections or in institutions, he pointed out, and thus off the market. "So the only way you are going to get major pieces like these is if a library has a major shift in focus and decides to sell." The John Carter Brown Library concentrates on Americana, so it was not surprising that officials there would sell what Voelkle described as a "German luxury manuscript" they had received as a gift; similarly, the seventh-century fragment discovered at the Folger fell well outside the area of Elizabethan and Jacobean drama. The Zacharias Chrysopolitanus was bought by Maggs for Sir Paul in the landmark sale of the Doheny Library, which had been consigned in its entirety to Christie's by the Archdiocese of Los Angeles and sold for $37.4 million, then the most ever realized at auction for a library.

"Nobody discards these books because they think they're worthless," Voelkle said with obvious understatement. "They sell them because they realize they are quite valuable, and that they can use them to further their own interests." In fact, it was a good-natured discussion along these very lines that set in motion the decision to allow some Wormsley treasures to be shown in New York. "I had met Sir Paul through a mutual friend a couple years ago, and when I met him, he asked me how the Morgan was doing," Charles E. Pierce Jr., director of the Morgan Library, told me in an interview. "I told him we were doing just fine, and he said he was sorry to hear that because he was rather hoping he could buy a few of our things. He was really very sweet and funny about it, so I said, 'Well, that's not the situation, but would you ever consider allowing the library to host an exhibition of some of your favorite books relating to the art of books?' One thing led to another, and eventually it came to pass."

Given the background and preoccupations of John Pierpont Morgan, the prime force in creating the unique library on Madison Avenue that bears his name, and the passion and interests reflected in the development of the Wormsley Library, the arrangement seems to have been a natural. "One of the wonders of the Getty collection is that it mirrors in many ways the kind of collecting that Pierpont Morgan was doing, and in showing these things, we are showing the kinds of things that have served as the basis for this institution," said Anna Lou Ashby, the Andrew W. Mellon Curator of Printed Books for the Morgan.

Picking a first among equals in the exhibition is impossible, although the 1482 edition of Ptolemy's *Cosmographia*, with its hand-colored world map printed from woodblocks sent more than one chill running up and down my spine. From this exquisite highlight, Robert Harding led me to a display case featuring six exquisite bindings created in the sixteenth century for the collector Sir Thomas Wotton, known as the English counterpart to Jean Grolier for his love of lavishly bound books. One of the titles—a 1516 edition of Sir Thomas More's *Utopia*—may have been presented to Wotton's father, Sir Edward Wotton, one of Henry VIII's executors, by the author.

Voelkle expressed particular affection for the copy of John Keats's *Some Poems* bound by Sangorski and Sutcliffe in 1912 in purple goatskin inlaid with 4,500 pieces of colored leather and studded with 1,027 jewels. "Begun nearly two months before the *Titanic* disaster, it took about two years to complete," the catalog explains; "it is awash in moonstones, garnets, pearls, topazes, amethysts, opals, turquoises, chalcedonies, and a tourmaline." One of Voelkle's tasks in preparing for the exhibition was to count every jewel, and he did it twice. "But I took them at their word on the strips of leather," he said.

For Roger S. Wieck, another curator of medieval and Renaissance manuscripts at the Morgan who worked on the exhibition, a personal favorite is the Psalter written and illuminated on vellum by a French artist known as the Master of the Ango Hours for Anne Boleyn sometime between 1529 and 1532, just before she became the second wife of King Henry VIII. Another favorite is a sequence of thirteenth-century illustrations picturing scenes from the life of St. Thomas à Becket, considered to the earliest known portraits of the archbishop who was executed by four knights in Canterbury Cathedral on the orders of King Henry II

A thorough summary of the exhibition is presented in the fully illustrated catalog, which was edited by H. George Fletcher, formerly the curator of printed books and bindings at the Morgan and, since September, the director of special collections at the New York Public Library.

Twenty-three blocks uptown at the Grolier Club, *A Treasure House of Books* enjoyed a spirited run of its own, drawing appreciative notices from those fortunate enough to view the fifty-eight items on display. They were selected from a private library mindfully formed in the seventeenth century by Duke August the Younger of Brunswick-Wolfenbüttel to be an enduring resource for succeeding generations of scholars. At his death, the 135,000 titles he had gathered made it the largest European library north of the Alps. It formed the nucleus of a collection that today totals about 800,000 volumes, 450,000 of them published before 1850. There also are twelve thousand manuscripts, a thousand of them dating from Medieval times. The core collection of 150,000 books published in the seventeenth century serves as the German national collection for that period, which may well be a unique accomplishment for a private collector.

Duke August was wealthy and well educated, and he demonstrated a hunger for books at an early age. When he was thirteen, he had his own binding stamp; by the time he was thirty, he had agents scouring Europe for books he could add to his ever-growing library, and every item that entered the collection passed through his hands first. Employing a cataloging system distinctly his own, Duke August ordered all of human knowledge into twenty categories and assigned codes to books that anticipated in some respects the formulation of the Dewey decimal system. He designed a "book wheel" made of oak that held the six hefty volumes of his catalog and revolved at the turn of a crank to simplify access.

"His library in its time was one of the greatest collections of modern Europe, and he conceived of it from the start as a public institution," Dr. Werner Arnold, curator and cataloger of the Wolfenbüttel Library said in an interview at the Grolier Club. "He referred to his library in his will as 'one of the inestimable treasures of our land.' What is very important is that he collected the books of his time, which was the period of the Thirty Years War [1618–1648]. The leading discipline of the library was theology, but he was very strong on history, philosophy, and music." A man of peace, Duke August the Younger had specific religious and philosophical views, and many of the books he acquired supported his convictions. "But he took care to find books from the other side," Arnold said. "And you can see that he held every book in the library in his hands; he signed off on everything, and he paid the invoices himself." In his will, the duke directed that his library "should as one entity forever be, remain, and be kept in this our residence as long as our princely dynasty shall continue and survive," and he made provisions for the hiring of "qualified and learned" people to run it. His requests were carried out faithfully in the years to come. Librarians included the philosopher Gottfried Wilhelm Leibniz and the critic and dramatist Gotthold Ephraim Lessing.

The fifty-eight items selected from the duke's library for the Grolier exhibition included some exceptional books. A copy of Martin Luther's 1522 translation of the New Testament, known as the September Testament, illustrated with colored woodblocks from the workshop of Lucas Cranach, was opened to an image of a personification of Babylon, or evil, in the form of a regal woman in a crown and red dress riding a seven-headed dragon. The catalog for *A Treasure House of Books* is fully illustrated in color and includes thirteen superb essays.

Brought over from Germany with the books, and displayed in the first floor gallery on the far wall for the duration of the show, was a wooden plaque in a carved frame crafted in 1636 stating, in Latin, the three golden rules of Duke August's library. They are summarized in the catalog as follows: "The visitor should not upset the order of the books, he should not steal any of them, and he should show respect for their contents." Good advice that, in any century.

NOTE
J. Paul Getty Jr. died on April 17, 2003, in London, at the age of seventy. An obituary published in the *Independent* estimated his charitable giving at "well over £200m in the last 20 years."

IRAQ

"Booking in Balad," Fine Books & Collections, no. 22 (July/August 2006).

I have said on numerous occasions that I will go pretty much anywhere in pursuit of a compelling book story, though I must confess that an invitation I received from a total stranger gave me pause to reconsider such a bold declaration of purpose, if only for a short while.

This past February, Lieutenant Colonel Brian C. McNerney, public affairs officer for the Third Corps Support Command, asked if I would consider speaking at the dedication of a new library. The catch was that the library he had just established was in a recreation building at Camp Anaconda, a sprawling supply complex and air base forty-two miles north of Baghdad, at Balad.

Prior to its opening, there were no organized reading facilities available to the twenty-five thousand service and civilian personnel assigned to the base. There were first-run Hollywood films, an impressively equipped gymnasium, two swimming pools, a plethora of computer terminals with high-speed access to the Internet, and even Burger King and Pizza Hut restaurants, but up until March 16, 2006, no libraries and no formal place set aside for reading.

McNerney would later cite the priorities young people have today for their leisure activities as the most likely reason for that omission, but he said uncertainty over the time American forces would remain in Iraq had likely been a factor as well. "Nobody knows how long this base is supposed to exist, so there were infrastructure issues to consider," he told me. "It would not be inaccurate to say that when this massive operation was being pulled together, provisions for a library were not part of the original scheme of things."

All that changed when McNerney traveled to Germany last year to take part in a memorial function to commemorate the ending of the Second World War. While there, he met a number of army veterans who had served with the Sixty-fifth and Seventy-first Infantry Divisions, and he learned how they had set up public libraries in Germany in the immediate aftermath of the war. One project in particular, the Europa-Bücherei, continues to function today as the municipal library for the city of Passau in lower Bavaria. That operation lends out three hundred thousand books a year.

During his trip to Germany, McNerney wondered aloud if any of these veterans, most of whom are now in their eighties, would be interested in replicating their triumph of sixty years earlier on a modest scale in Iraq. To his delighted surprise, the answer was a resounding yes. Assuming responsibility for the project in the United States was Robert Patton, an eighty-four-year-old resident of Chapel Hill, North Carolina, who was among the first American soldiers to liberate the Mauthausen concentration camp in Austria in 1945. He is a retired computer executive whose specialty in civilian life was problem solving.

As immediate past president of the Sixty-fifth Infantry Division Association, Patton initiated a spirited effort that quickly won the backing of residents in the Piedmont region of North Carolina, home to Duke University, the University of North Carolina, and North Carolina State University. "My imagination went out of control," Patton told me. "Colonel McNerney said he needed books. I asked what kind he wanted. He said he had basically nothing, so he needed the gamut. He told me he how much space he had, and I took it from there."

Patton said it helped that he lives in an academic community that has a thriving book culture. "I also felt that regardless of whatever political views anyone has about the war in Iraq, books give us a kind of common ground where we can all agree on something. And the response was just remarkable. Everyone wanted to contribute."

Patton mobilized dozens of volunteers, including staffers at the Chapel Hill Public Library and Boy Scouts from Troop 39, one of the nation's oldest continuously chartered troops, who boxed books and loaded them onto trucks for transfer to Pope Air Force Base, where they were sent to Balad in two shipments. The ten thousand volumes gathered included fiction and nonfiction, literary titles and thrillers, biography, history, and commentary, altogether "a pretty solid critical mass of material to get us started," McNerney said.

McNerney said his ultimate goal is to turn the library over to the people of Balad. Indeed, phase two of the project will focus on books with particular local appeal: richly visual children's books, for instance, or titles that bridge language barriers, or professional monographs such as medical texts.

While I was in Balad, a project undertaken by Captain Yancy Caruthers, a nurse in civilian life at Ozarks Medical Center in West Plains, Missouri, had just presented one thousand medical books and journals published since 2000 to staff members at Balad General Hospital, all of them donated by his friends and colleagues back home.

In his first e-mail to me, McNerney introduced himself as "another lover of books, an inveterate collector and believer that— more than anything else—inside them we can find the wisdom to make the future a little less war-ridden than the present and the past." A career army officer with a master's degree in English from Michigan State University, McNerney is a former literature instructor at West Point who wrote a thesis on the Vietnam War writings of novelist Tim O'Brien.

In accepting his proposal, I asked McNerney if it would be possible to see Ur, the Sumerian city in lower Mesopotamia where the Old Testament tells us the prophet Abraham was born, where writing as we know it began to take shape some five thousand years ago, where humanity's first literary text, *The Epic of Gilgamesh*, is believed by some scholars to have been composed, and where the world's first libraries may well have been located.

He not only arranged for me to visit that legendary city—which I judge to be one of the highlights of my professional life—but said he would try to squeeze in a trip to Mosul, where Sir Austin Henry Layard uncovered the ruins of Nineveh in the 1840s and found the fabled library of Ashurbanipal, containing some twenty-five thousand cuneiform tablets that are now a prized holding of the British Museum in London. Unfortunately, a major air offensive up north precluded our getting there.

McNerney laughed when I described him as a modern-day Don Quixote embarked on a fanciful mission to bring books to the desert. He did agree, though, with the observation I made at the dedication of the Halbert and Red Circle Library—the name is a reference to the shoulder insignia of the Sixty-fifth and Seventy-first divisions—that where there are books, there is always hope.